The Guardian

Chronicles of Dover's Amalgam

Elizabetta Holcomb

The Guardian
Copyright c 2016 Elizabetta Holcomb
All rights reserved.

No part of this publication may be reproduced, distributed, or transmitted an any form or by any means including electronic, mechanical, photocopying, recording, or otherwise without the prior written consent of the author.

This book is a work of fiction. Names, characters, places, and incidents either are products of the author's imagination or are used fictitiously. Any resemblance to actual events or locales or persons, living or dead, is entirely coincidental and beyond the intent of the author or publisher.

The author acknowledges the trademarked status and trademark owners of various products, bands, and/or restaurants referenced in this work of fiction, which have been used without permission. The publication/use of these trademarks is not authorized, associated with, or sponsored by the trademark owners.

Editor:
Brenda Letendre, Write Girl Editing
www.facebook.com/writegirlediting

Interior Design and Formatting:
Christine Borgford, Perfectly Publishable
www.perfectlypublishable.com

Cover Design:
Daniela Conde Padron, DCP Designs
www.dcpdesigns.net
www.facebook.com/dcpdesigns

Acknowledgements

FOR MY DAD WHO TAUGHT me to never give up. I finally did it!

For my children and husband who have encouraged and dreamed with me all these years. I could not have done this without you.

For Bessie and Tanya. I do not need to say why. You know.

For Alaina who tells me when my plots are stupid. Yes, Harry Styles is the character sketch for Benjamin. After all of your hounding, I can't see him as anyone else—thanks.

For Thomasina. My first fan. A girl could not ask for a better childhood friend. Thanks for reading all of my stuff even when it sucked. A big thank you for naming your first born a kicking Cajun name. Your little girl, Beau Angelle, is the character sketch for her namesake in this series. It's my way to honor our lifelong friendship and take you with me in this new journey. You always said I could do it!

For Brenda and Jaimee who patiently led me through the publishing process. I made it to the other side and you guys are still my friends . . . yay me!

For my beta and proofreaders: Jillian Malloy, Bessie Whipp, Carole Smith Turner, Tanya DuBois, and Alaina Hebert.

Dedication

To my mom who gave me the genes of creativity and introduced me to the library at an early age. We spent our summers lost in the worlds books opened up to us. I wish Heaven had an email address so I could forward you a copy of my book. I will love and miss you forever.

Chapter 1

White Cliffs of Dover, Year 1316 of King Edward II reign

JARETH TREMAINE, THE FIRST DUKE of Dover, was bleeding to death. Not only had death found him, but it asserted a lingering alliance of pain and torture rather than steal his life and depart.

No one desired to claim credit for this war—neither Hun nor Englishman. Although the Hun Empire was extinct, somehow they managed to return and lay siege on the English Channel. Confusion abounded among the duke's men as they fought valiantly, yet it was nasty and bloody. Death was everywhere. It hid behind craggy rocks used by the archers for protection. It was under the apple tree in the manor's orchard. The Huns, known for their archery skills, were taking no prisoners. They wanted lives, and they took them in droves.

This war brought senseless death—in many cases, accidentally. A knight, overtaken by a swarm of warriors, turned quickly only to fall and perish upon his own sword. An archer ready with bow poised to fly his lethal arrow was taken out from behind by a single shot to the head. His stance did not change as he fell to the ground dead, still drawing back the bow, the arrow lame beside his body.

The smell of decaying flesh hung in the darkness. Gabriel squatted on his heels beside the Bastard Duke and surveyed the battlefield. Cannon fire from the east rang out, and simultaneously a shower of fire flakes rained down around them.

Minh, his fellow guardian, yanked on the duke's tunic. "Bizarre," he commented. "Cannons? Really?" Once a general in the Ming Dynasty, the Asian warrior had been in charge of the Ministry of War. Gabriel crinkled his brow as he patted out the embers burning holes in the hose on the duke's thighs.

"Yep," Gabriel growled without as much a glance at his cohort. He ducked down as he worked, and didn't bother to assess what was going on around him. The noise was loud enough for his vivid imagination to flourish. He set his face into a grim mask as he tore open the duke's gambeson. "Twenty-first century shrapnel." He inspected the large piece of metal protruding from the duke's chest, and then pulled it out. It was buried shallow enough not to cause alarm, but somewhere lay a bigger problem.

Minh turned away. "I say cannon fire in thirteenth century England and you say yep. That is unacceptable to me." He reached into the quiver slung over his back and pulled out a fresh arrow. "I'm so bloody confused. *Huns?* How did those devils come back from the grave?"

"They're exterminators," Gabriel retorted, and leaned back on his haunches. "Someone, somewhere has breached time." He frowned at the piece of cannon shrapnel he held, and turned it in his hand for better inspection. "Quite frankly, we've been robbed." He tossed the offending metal to the side. The vile thing stuck in the sludge as he rubbed a bloodied hand over his sweaty brow. "We need to get Jareth to a safe place."

A loud boom sounded and shook the ground under them.

"Let's take him straight to the duchess. Screw the rules. I don't see why we should wait like idiots," Minh said. "History decrees it will be her anyway. What are we waiting for? A religious sign or something?"

"She'll be scared," Gabriel said. His brow wrinkled as he contemplated Minh's suggestion. It was tempting. He shook his wrist and counted the time bands there. Five—as it should be. "Besides, I've been instructed not to involve her." He bent forward again and lifted the chain mail away from the wound. There was another gash above Jareth's navel that traveled left across his abdomen.

"She'll be terrified," he rectified. He let the mail fall back and looked up with a scowl. "I say we take him to Harrow. That would be another way of flipping off the rules. That should make you happy." Blood seeped onto the ground from the wound he'd irritated. "I didn't expect to see him blasted to shreds like this."

"*That should make you happy,*" Minh mimicked under his breath. He shook his head and looked away, his ear cocked to the sounds of battle caging them. "What would make me happy is knowing how all of this pans out. Look at him, Gabriel." He motioned unseeingly to the duke as his eyes scanned the nearby copse. "He'll die if we don't break the bloody rules. Better sooner than later, I say. That's my vote."

Gabriel felt a pang of sentiment as he looked down at the duke who was still a boy, newly twenty. There were some who wanted a piece of credit for this day. This eve the duke was miraculously saved from death. Dr. Harrow Mills would be no different. That was why this mission was important and secretive. The more people involved, the more likely things could go wrong. Saving Jareth was not a popularity contest; it was essential to the future of the Amalgam.

His sentiment died when an arrow whizzed past his ear. He bowed his body over the duke's prone form and glared at Minh. Jareth was not safe as of yet. He still lay dying, and his fellow guardians were all that stood between his death and a place of refuge. Things were progressing and he had little time to think. His mind raced with probabilities and scenarios that would, in all likelihood, never happen. The arrow was a stray. They were far enough from the thick of things. He was sure his anger toward Minh held no ground. One had to watch or die taking care of business.

And Minh was vigilant. He had to give him that.

The noise level, the dying man before him, the saving of the world was all coming to a head. Gabriel wanted nothing more than to march off this battlefield and into his home where his wife and family awaited his return. It was Christmastime there and they would have eggnog. They always had eggnog on cold December nights. He wanted family time, not the growing burden of babysitting a trouble-prone duke.

Minh wouldn't agree. To him, families were for other people—those whose lives did not involve killing and jumping through time portals as though they were the New York City transit. This was where they were different. Gabriel was devoted to his wife—Minh's sister—and the brood who resembled a combination of his long-limbed body and fair features and her dark, petite form. Minh did not have a family, nor did he want one.

"The dilemma is how we gonna get him to the castle without

leaving a trail of blood? They'll find us. They're like animals. Fierce trackers. It's obvious this is a blood mission. They've been sent to terminate Jareth." Gabriel was thinking out loud. "If we get him to the castle, I'm sure she'll be there. It's what Jareth remembers. We just have to get him there."

"I say we take him back with us—through the portal. Take care of him ourselves." Minh glanced in the direction the arrow had come. "It should have been us. We owe him our lives, so let's save his."

Gabriel let his impatience show and folded his arms over his chest. "You say the duchess and now this? He left specific instructions. We can't, under any circumstance, take him back for treatment. Time is a privilege we cannot waste."

"He didn't mention we'd be facing *this*." Minh took a moment to indicate the wound. "You suggested Harrow," he pointed out. "Grab his feet."

Minh took hold of Jareth's arms and crossed them over his chest. "Hurry, we must act now before the battle shifts. We're not prepared for gunfire of this caliber."

"We're not prepared for gunfire in any form," Gabriel rejoined. "This is medieval England, after all."

Doubling through the chain mail, Minh immobilized Jareth's arms so they would not drag. "We haven't got all day. I'm not planning to sit here like two pansies. Let's move. Maybe fate will intervene."

Gabriel's eyes narrowed because he did not believe in fate, but providence. Knowing Minh though, he understood that the comment was made to fill space, not to be taken literally. They were both edgy and confused by the turn of events. Gunfire in the thirteenth century, the severity of the wound the duke sustained . . . and just where in the heck was the duchess? They were groping in the dark. Besides, he knew the fate Minh spoke of. It was the knowing that kept him calm while things went crazy. He had five captured wormholes around his wrist that he could use if he had cause to doubt, but they had been instructed not to mess with the sands of time unless commanded.

He took note of Minh's swift, cautious movements. He was a superb archer with the heart of a lion, yet his gentle care indicated the fondness they both shared for this fallen man, and that alone softened

Gabriel. It took the bitter sting out of being shot at and being sent out on a mission no one could guarantee. But still, he said nothing. Words spoken too soon had a way of coming back to haunt, the same way jumping time could come back and bite. Fate needed to show up now, preferably before Jareth bled to death.

They worked quietly together to carry Jareth's body across the moor along the outskirts of the battlefield, stopping only once to kill six Huns. Gabriel was a bit sluggish, still pining over an arrow that missed its mark. He flat out told Minh he was slow and gave no excuse for him. Just like that, they were at it again.

"Bastard!" Minh said as he stomped over to the fallen body of a Hun. Roughly, he seized hold of the arrow protruding from his chest, used his heel against the carcass to stabilize it, and yanked. "Sometimes I question Jareth's judgment." He pointed—using the bloody arrow—to Gabriel's chest. "It's not my fault you were shot at. It's called war, man. Deal with your issues on your own time—not here. Not now. I'm moving as fast as I can whilst carrying our commander in chief basically on my back."

Gabriel hunched down a notch and took a defensive stance as Minh advanced with murder in his eye. He reached for the sword slung over his back. Although a spear was his weapon of choice, he did not have time to be choosy; there was an Asian assassin stalking him. "It felt like I was carrying more of the load, you bastard."

"What a vile word." The words that drifted up from their patient were weak, but deep and audible. The pure English dialect was refined and proud. Their heads jerked to the fallen man they had just dragged half a mile.

Gabriel's mouth snapped closed on his war shout, while Minh slowed his brisk wiping of guts from the arrow against his pant leg, as well as his pace. The blood and matter would undoubtedly ruin the leather of his favorite pair of pants. It took a fraction of time to absorb that Jareth was actually speaking—to them. Calling them out for uttering a word he despised.

"I am quite sure that I am the only bastard present," Jareth said as he attempted a seated position and failed. He cradled his abdomen and grimaced. "And either I am dying or covered in ketchup." His lips twisted wryly as he got a good look at what was exposed of his abdomen. "Dying. Let us not overlook that I am dying for the sake of your arguing."

"Your Excellence," Gabriel's lips lifted in a wry smile. He sheathed his sword as if a dead man was not speaking and he wasn't a moment away from gutting his friend. That Jareth mentioned ketchup would be comical if not for the circumstances—the duke refused any food that so much as touched the stuff. He narrowed his eyes on Minh. "We were just discussing your shrewdness."

Minh was already rushing to the duke's side. He uncapped a flask of water. "Try not to speak, your grace. You need strength. We have far yet to carry you."

The water gushed the same way Minh's words did—fast and unbridled, and sloshed over Jareth's parched lips.

"Maybe he can walk," Gabriel said.

Minh looked horrified.

Jareth turned his head from the flowing water as he brought his hand before his eyes. Blood trailed down his fingertips and onto his palm like a scarlet glove. He winced as he looked between Gabriel and Minh. "You request that I walk, Spartan? You were trained to be heartless in battle, but are you daft as well?"

"I vote daft," a female voice offered from the copse they had just departed.

Gabriel grabbed his sword and pivoted for attack. Again, Minh had failed to keep them safe. A growl rose in his throat. "Where is that razor sharp hearing, Mr. Minister of War?" he asked Minh, who was already beside him with a bow drawn and aimed at the two cloaked figures emerging from the dense area of trees.

"I was busy," Minh hissed.

The warriors stood side by side, ready as the two approached. One of the strangers was short, and wore a red cloak of no marking. The other was stout and medium height, dressed in a traditional black cloak worn by the royal archers. Both of their faces were hidden by the darkness of their hoods. The only thing for certain was one was female.

"Let them pass," Jareth said, his voice low. Gabriel used his body as a protective barricade while Jareth struggled to keep his head elevated and eyed those who approached.

"You're wounded, your grace," Minh said over his shoulder. His eyes never left the cloaked duo. "And delusional," he added under his breath. He tightened his grip on the bow as he aimed at the shorter, leaner prospect that was quickly approaching. "You don't know what you're saying. They could be assassins."

The short one uncovered her head to reveal pale, multi-colored hair, and narrowed her eyes on Minh as if daring him to fire the arrow he pointed at her breast.

"At least one of you is sensible," she said. Her jaw was set in stone so it was a miracle her words were audible. "Funny, it's the one dying." She waved a hand toward the duke. Her dialect was familiar to them. The way her tongue dragged her words lazily in a distinct southern drawl was singular. And that hair. They would recognize it anywhere.

"Your grace?" Minh's face went from fierce to undefined confusion in a second flat. His hooded eyes tapered further as he looked from the girl to Gabriel.

Gabriel lowered his sword. "You were supposed to meet us at the castle."

Minh cleared his throat as he bowed to the small lady who shoved between them, shouldering her way to the one they were protecting. The duke was supposed to be dying, but instead he spoke quickly, explaining his injuries in broken Norman French and Modern English as the girl approached. Her face was a mask of concern as she crouched down and raked her gaze over his bloodied torso.

"My name is Elizabet," she said as she untied her cloak and let it fall. She placed her fingers over his lips; her eyes paused on the stained and ripped gambeson. "You've got to speak slower. I don't understand French. Slow down. English—please."

Jareth shook his head to rid her fingers from his mouth. "The wound is deep." He articulated each syllable, and spoke slowly by her command. "I can tell you how to treat it if you can tell me what is severed. What do you know of anatomy? Are you a physician?"

She worked quickly over him; assessed the wound and removed the mail that was heavy over his ripped clothing. Jareth's face went from wonderment and confusion to a mask of pain as she seemingly ignored his words to probe the wound. Finally, his head fell back onto the soft ground with a dull thud and his eyes squeezed shut.

Gabriel caught Minh's gaze in the moonlight. "Elizabet," he said. "Her name is Elizabet. And he's going to tell her what to do." He rolled his shoulders. "Looks like it's going to happen here. On the battlefield. Here's the fate you were begging for. Just a change in scenery."

"I heard her," Minh said, and his brow wrinkled. He lowered the bow that was still raised, and pointed it nowhere in particular. "Them." He waved the arm holding the bow toward the duo he spoke of. "And yet, my eyes do not believe my ears. Why do things like this still take me by surprise? Who would bring her to a battlefield? It isn't safe. Now we have another person to drag to safety." He jerked his head toward the yet unidentified cloaked person. "What the hell?"

"Shut thy mouths," the stout, forgotten one said as she barreled between them on the same path Elizabet had taken. The fat one spoke in French—the king's language. "Make that three. You have to get us all from here safely." Her hands clenched as she shook her head. "What are you waiting for? His grace will bleed to death while you stand about all agog. We should move him to the castle. Now."

"All agog?" Gabriel asked, using his fingers as quote signs. One eyebrow arched as he gazed at Minh. He placed his hand on the pommel of his sword, turned to watch the ladies worry over Jareth, and with the other hand, waved toward them. "Here's your answer to what the hell. Bloody Mrs. Wheatley comes to save the day and as always, she hasn't thought anything through. Of course it would be Jareth's *baby*sitter who thwarts the plan of the Amalgam. . Do you ever do as you're told?"

Mrs. Wheatley bristled and her large backside swayed as she aided the girl, going to her knees beside the wounded duke. She ignored Gabriel. Obviously, some things stayed the same no matter what year it was.

"I dare say this is a breach of trust." Minh came out of the fog of confusion he had managed to create for himself. Quickly, he clothed himself with the same righteous indignation Gabriel wore. "And of safety. Of confidentiality." He stood a bit straighter. "It's a battlefield, woman. What were you thinking?"

The hood on the elderly lady's cloak trembled as she shook her head and worked to rid the duke of his chain mail. The vigorous efforts had the cloak spill off and reveal the white hair beneath. "I did what I had to do. And I'm not his babysitter." The words hissed from her mouth in distaste. "I'm the closest thing to a mother he's got."

"And doing what goes against code is in whose best interest?" Gabriel asked in smooth Norman French. "You've risked the life of the duchess by bringing her here." He felt a twinge of guilt for badgering the woman. She was more than a nursemaid to Jareth, but she had no right to play guardian in this arena. "As Leader of the Amalgam, I have to ask what you were thinking."

"I was thinking he would die unless I fetched her," Mrs. Wheatley said. She used the hem of her cloak to press the wound. "We all know this is how they meet. I had to get her. It's the way of things."

"There's the crux of the problem." Minh switched languages, which was more discreet. "We know how this ends. Why not bring her to the castle and wait for us?"

"It's obviously the best choice—isn't it? Considering *how* it may end." Mrs. Wheatley gave them both a view of her aged face as she defied ideations. "Do I need to remind the two of you imbeciles that he *is* the Amalgam? Did you stop to consider that this is how it's supposed to happen? That it was I all along who brought her here?" Her face became sheepish suddenly; her movements slowed. "Besides," she said as she motioned to where they had come from, "I brought a portable gurney so we could carry him."

Minh smiled a true, full on grin. "Bless you. I shall never doubt you again. My back thanks you."

Gabriel frowned. Minh was so easy. "This does not excuse the danger you have brought upon the Tremaine household. If anything happens to the—"

"His wound is fatal," Elizabet cut in. Everyone had disconnected her from the picture until she spoke. Never mind that her presence was like ice water poured down a shirt on a winter morning. Elizabet was the future, not the past. Her blunt accent and loud volume brought her to the now with them. But his wound was not fatal. Gabriel had eaten breakfast with a twenty-eight-year-old Jareth that morning. "I can't help him," she said, and closed the exposed wound with quivering, bloodied fingers. She worked quickly, as if she wanted to flee.

Gabriel and Minh blinked in disbelief, tried to translate and process what she had just proclaimed. They stared at one another blindly. A lone holler of agony drifted from the battlefield and jarred Gabriel back to the present. He looked down on the man whom he called his best friend.

There was not an ounce of disbelief that this was Jareth's finest hour—not his death hour. Mrs. Wheatley was not misled when she said the girl was his only hope. What was done was done. Gabriel would make her the future and the past. This was the way it was written to be.

"You're mistaken," Gabriel said gently. He placed his hand reassuringly on her shoulder.

The girl's body trembled as she fumbled to reclothe the bloody man before her. She yanked at the chain mail while she attempted to disengage Gabriel's hand from her shoulder. Her smallest finger snagged on a broken link of metal and it sliced a neat, deep gash along the side of her digit. It bled onto the duke's torso, adding her blood to mingle with his.

"I understand you are distraught . . ." Gabriel went on.

"My daddy takes care of animals," Elizabet stated baldly. She flexed her shoulder until his hand fell away, and she pulled the chain mail closed as best as she was able. She then went to work on what was left of Jareth's tunic, as if hiding the wound would make it go away. "He's a vet. As in veterinarian. I thought that I could do this, but I just can't." She shook her head and her hands stilled. Everyone heard the audible swallow of bile as her body shuddered once. "I can't."

"Please," Jareth said, his eyelids fluttering. His hands trembled as he reached out to her. "I can teach you . . ." The blue of his eyes were hidden behind closed eyelids as he slipped into unconsciousness.

Elizabet brought her bloodied hand to cover her mouth as if she wanted to scream. Her gaze traveled over the young duke. His black hair was matted with sweat and blood, squashed from his previously discarded helmet. The face that was hailed as handsome was dirty and caked with dried blood. Unrecognizable. There was a gash under his left eye. His dark, bushy eyebrows were in a relaxed pose as his body shut down from pain.

She turned her head and vomited all over Jareth's fallen sword and shield.

Gabriel shared his shocked reaction with Minh. Minh rolled his shoulders after a split second, gave him the impression he was done trying to sort this mess out.

The gravity of the situation hit Gabriel. Elizabet had no idea who Jareth was. This Elizabet was a younger version who had been dragged here by a bossy servant. It would take time for her to thaw to the situation at hand. They would have to be careful how much they revealed and when. She would flip out if they told her she was looking at the father of her children, the love of her life. He guessed she was around seventeen given the youthful plumpness of her face.

"Fetch the gurney, Minh," Gabriel directed. He couldn't allow any more time to slip away. He reached down and squeezed Elizabet's shoulder as she wiped her mouth. Tears dripped from her eyes. "Let's get him to the castle posthaste. We've no more time to lose."

Chapter 2

JARETH THOUGHT THEY WERE GHOSTS when they first appeared years ago. He had been seven years old and a new resident of Dover Castle. He had also been young and foolish. That was how he categorized his life: the time before and after he was enlightened. Wisdom and foolishness.

Gabriel and Minh came to him in the east tower where he was locked away, translating documents for the king. It was unnatural how they appeared from behind the locked door and spoke of future things he had difficulty understanding—thus the conclusion of thinking them lost souls or ghouls. But they wore his color blue and each had his coat of arms tattooed on their right arm—a Catherine Wheel with a white Talbot dog in the center. They revealed them to him to garner his trust and prove they were allies.

Jareth was responsible for their lives. He had traveled through time, saved them from certain death, and gave them new lives. He taught them to fight for justice and mankind. To save the future from turning on itself and destroying life by way of fear and lack of knowledge. In turn, they came to him when he was young, before he was a time traveler, and taught him the way of the future so he would be prepared for what was to come.

They came as apparitions and then in complete forms as they merged into time through a portal of light. They would die to save him. Jareth's life was gravely important to the threads of time, and these men had sworn an oath to protect him. He was destined to lead a group whose DNA had been altered by nature. They had come to him to train him. To prepare him for the meeting of his first host, which would occur soon after his twentieth birthday.

But this was the first time they brought someone along—a new person with specific healing skills. Elizabet had saved his life even though he had to tell her what to do. Her skills lay primarily with animals; she had to be forgiven that. A possible fatal wound that required healing by third intention was out of her scope of practice. Not out of his, however. The pity lay in that he was indeed the patient. They had brought her here and left her *alone* with him. And neither Gabriel nor Minh had decided to show their face to explain.

Elizabet had thrown up so many times that he believed she may fall ill and render her services useless. That was over the first three days. It had now been a month since he was wounded, and still she turned colors when it was uncovered.

"Here's the book you ordered." Elizabet tossed the leather-bound tome precariously close to the bandage on his abdomen and his body tensed. She smirked as the book flopped onto the bed beside him, missing the wound by a fraction of an inch. "Happy reading."

Jareth narrowed his eyes. "Are you not staying?" It both disturbed and intrigued him that he cared.

It was a recent event that they could converse—speak and hold a conversation. Earlier, their relationship had been merely that of patient and nurse. Jareth would tell her how to treat and she would perform. In the first days, not being able to get a venous line had almost been the death of him. She finally managed it, though. He thought her magnificent after that, able-handed and well spoken, with an air of superiority. He was quite sure that she was faking the confidence, but that made it all the more interesting.

Normally, he detested conversation, but she made it entertaining, and now that they were at leisure to speak, he planned to ferret an advantage and find out why she was chosen. How did she play a part in his future life of the Amalgam? He knew Gabriel and Minh well enough to understand they did nothing without purpose. Somehow, this girl was tied to him. She was crucial to him; he only had to figure her out without scaring her to death. He did not know how much she was told—very little if he discerned correctly. They had practically thrown her together with him. She did not even know his name. Not well done at all.

"Do I have a choice?" she asked. Her face turned pink as she glanced away. "Besides, I need to change your bandage." She waved her hand in the general direction of his abdomen without looking at it.

He had no family, so to speak. No one, really, to guide him how to act in the company of a lady. What he did value was the mind. The way it wrapped around a concept and understood that a simple idea or task was not singularly one opinion. Everything had multifaceted properties begging to be solved or unscrambled.

Therefore, she made him uncomfortable, because she did not fit into any one category. She had no properties or categories. Elizabet just *was*. He was not accustomed to the confusion this invited. Good character rarely acknowledged confusion. It was an oxymoron to strength and dignity. The way she spoke of his injury was hindsight to her. The trouble was that no one, even if they felt it, claimed to be annoyed with him since he was bestowed the title of Duke. Elizabet's every fiber reeked of discontent.

But still, he liked her and he suspected she liked him, as well. It was evident in the way she cared for him. In the way she spoke even though she did not think he understood. The fevered way she attempted nursing care when she lacked skill or knowledge. Elizabet trusted him to guide her through his own healing, yet he knew she studied when she was away. How else would she come to know words such as 'debridement of a wound'?

Jareth toyed with the edging on the book and watched her fix the covers over the bed. It was something she did even though she was aware he could not stand having his feet bound. She used exaggerated strokes as if she was deflecting his curiosity, tucking the heavy bed cover under and around his heels. She was angry—again.

He let a smile curve on half his lips. He would do something for her, after she had done so much for him. "You are relieved of your duties." There. He had said it, even though he really did not mean it. He was, of course, willing to let her go. She was not a vassal or a servant. If she stayed, he wanted it to be because she wished to stay.

Elizabet's motions stiffened yet another fraction. "I wasn't aware that I had duties. I thought I was doing a favor. Or maybe just plain kidnapped . . ." Her voice trailed off as she turned away.

Perhaps her discontent of caring for him came from the fact she had been forced to do so. It was not her choice to be here with him. Jareth surmised that she was not someone who liked to be dictated to. He hoped if she felt free, then she would perform her 'duties' with a fraction of joy. Using reverse psychology was risky, but he prayed it worked.

"I am familiar with the term," Jareth said as he wiggled his feet until the covers loosened from the tuck. "Kidnapped. It means to be taken. Stolen. Is that how you feel? As if you were stolen?"

"Stolen," Elizabet repeated. She clasped her hands behind her back and leaned forward against the foot of the bed, her thighs against the thick post. "I was lied to. Mrs. Wheatley told me this would be an adventure, not a nightmare. I thought you would have a small flesh wound."

Jareth tilted his head; he tapered his eyes slightly. "I have offended you."

Her eyes rounded. "Offended? No. Not offended. I wouldn't call it that." She shrugged with one shoulder. "I'm not sure when you'll let me go home. I can't be here for days. My grandma will send out a search party. Again. I can't pretend that I ran away. Again." Each time she said 'again,' her voice raised an octave. It bordered hysteria.

"I apologize that you had to lie."

It had been necessary that she remain during the first days of his care. It was not until a venous line had been established and he no longer needed nursing around the clock that Mrs. Wheatley had been allowed to fetch her.

He sensed Elizabet was not afraid of him, but maybe she did not yet trust him, either. It was not wrong of her to feel kidnapped, but it had been many days since she had been forced to stay. Kidnapped sounded criminal and without honor. Jareth had honor in droves. The fact she could not see that made him a touch angry. He was right, though. She needed to feel free; he would liberate her even though he did not desire it.

"You have told me that your grandmother accepted the excuse you presented." Jareth rubbed the book cover with his fingertips, but watched her. "And I fail to be convinced that you are afraid. You seem at ease with me and where you are. I cannot see any evidence of discomfort."

A puff of air passed Elizabet's lips. "Apathy. Blame movies for that." She shrugged. "I've seen every time travel, science fiction picture known. It's nothing new. In theory."

"And motion pictures are to blame for this apathy you claim?" He adjusted his back against the pillows. The slight movement caused him to wince with the pain. Purposely, he used modern terms to remind her he was not naïve to her world. She threw things—ideas—around as if to intimidate him. She had no idea . . .

In fact, his world was a mixture of old and new. Jareth liked what the future entailed and he had incorporated many modern aspects into his time. Elizabet did not know the extent of his dealings with the future. She had been confined to one room—his private chamber. The girl would be hysterical if she knew what lay beyond the walls and in the tunnels under the castle. She would faint if she knew he was a capable surgeon and physician. She would run screaming if she were to see the fully functioning surgery suite beneath the castle exterior.

"You shouldn't move around." Elizabet leaned forward and reached out to stop him. "You'll start bleeding again." She stopped before she actually touched him, and glanced at where the bed sheet covered his torso. Her hands hovering—she seemed terrified the blood would start again. It was uncanny how she was fearful of a little blood, yet accepting of where and how she was transported, all for the sake of adventure.

Jareth smirked despite the hot poker digging into his wound. "Some movement is good. It prevents unwanted clot formation." He tried a disarming smile once again. "Have a care. You may have to do something nice for me."

"I resent that." She snatched her hands away and tucked them in her armpits. She gave herself a fierce hug. "I've done everything that was asked of me."

"And yet you feel kidnapped. Stolen." He looked Elizabet straight in the eye, his half smile becoming a slight sneer despite his attempt to appear docile. For a while, he thought he saw a twinge of remorse or guilt, but then blatant irritation crossed her face and she did not try to hide it. He shook his head methodically and looked away. "The ever petulant Elizabet."

Elizabet snorted.

Jareth allowed a smile, this time real—which was altogether unusual. Smiling was not a habit of his, but this one was easy and unplanned. And caused by that particular noise she made when she was put out. It was a little huff that sounded positively swinish.

"All right. Let us try this. We know so little of one another, perhaps you can tell me a bit about yourself," he suggested.

"You want to know about me, when I know so very little about you?" Elizabet's face contorted into a mask of anger. "Your friends are nothing but a pair of bullies. All their rules." She blew a piece of her multi-colored hair from her eyes when it fell over her face. Her hair was held back today, but her bangs were uneven from the rest and kept creeping into her vision. The way she wore it reminded him of a horse's tail. "Don't ask questions," she went on in an imitation of a man's voice. "Don't talk about what goes on. Lie if asked." She gave him a sharp look. "I'm supposed to never freak out, and go along with everything you tell me to do. Like I'm some sort of servant or something. You want to know about me; well, I want to know about you. Starting with your name." Her eyes widened. "And who reads in Latin? "She flipped her hand toward the book lying next to him. It seemed she was attempting to get everything in while she had the chance. The girl gave the term 'flight of ideas' a whole new meaning. "Do you even understand that they don't make books in that language anymore? I had to order it on eBay. Do you know how much that cost me?"

She was fishing too, but Jareth would not offer more information than she yanked from his battered body. He was the one doing the prying, not the other way around. And he read in Latin. It mattered not that in the future it was considered a dead language. In fact, even his thoughts were in Latin. He got the sudden urge to strangle Gabriel and Minh for not debriefing him. It was not like them to leave him in the dark concerning someone. It would help if he knew who she was and how much information he could leak to her without breaching some sort of rule or code.

"Goes without saying that you heal at an astronomical rate." Her hands found their way out from their confinement to flail in the air. "Now, *that* is something I don't get—for sure! How does one find Zithromax in this time period? And IV antibiotics, no less."

"One does not find Zithromax in medieval England," Jareth said loud enough to silence her for a moment. If he did not jump in, she would never give him the chance to speak. He had learned that about her early. Once she started talking, she never stopped. "Nor Vancomycin." Then, quietly, "It was smuggled in."

So much for not allowing her to fish, he thought with self-loathing. He might as well supply the pole and bait.

"Of course it was smuggled in. Unless I missed the antibiotic factory lesson in my history of the middle ages." Elizabet wound her arms back around her torso in a tight hug. She used her hands like exclamation marks, commas, and italics. If she ever lost a limb, she may be silent forever.

His eyes traveled to where his sword was mounted near the hearth. It was on the tip of his tongue to reveal the antibiotics had merely been smuggled up the castle steps from his private stock, just to see if she would combust on the spot. That way he wouldn't have to lift his sword to frighten her into silence.

Instead, he asked, "Why do you vex me so?" His voice was weary as he realized he had slipped—again. She now knew an approximate time and place. The clues could lead her to endless possibilities if she cared to search the small details.

What he wanted was to invite her to sit next to him and read for him, preposterous as that was. For some perverse reason, he liked her simple accent that had not refinement. He must be going mad. Perhaps his wound was infected and death would find him after all. "Why do you not rest and sit with me?"

Elizabet blinked. Her fingers twitched where she hugged herself. "You want me to sit? With you?"

"Aye," he said, then smiled ruefully at his choice of words. "Yes." He motioned to the place next to him. "I would like you to read to me." He tapped the book with his index finger. "I think it would be beneficial if we studied this together. Perhaps we will stop bickering and go back to being companionable."

She glanced at the small wind up clock at the bedside. Her lips slid sideways as she shook her head. "I can't. Mrs. Wheatley will be here any minute." She looked at him. "Shucks," she added with heavy sarcasm.

"Have it your way," he murmured, and glanced at the clock, as well. He sighed. "Listen, it is within my power to put this away from you. If being beneficial to the good of future mankind *upsets* you, then by all that is holy, let me release you."

"You think I want to leave and never come back?" Her face puckered as she asked.

The immediate denial in her tone startled him, but he did not let on. "I have heard your complaints and I am willing to release you." Jareth waved a hand toward her. "Do not seem so confused. You have gravely mentioned that you have had to lie and that you have been kidnapped. I am quite the villain." He smirked and let his hand touch upon the bandage over his abdomen. Surely, a more worthy villain would be one who got around better. "This is what you want—is it not?"

She snapped her wrist in his general direction. "You go on and on about releasing me from my duties, yet you have a list of things you send with me each day." She reached into the pocket of her jeans, produced a crumpled scrap of parchment paper and tossed it at him. It hit his linen clad chest and rolled onto his lap. A portion of his sloppy calligraphy handwriting peeked out. "I hardly know what you would do if I wasn't here for you to boss around. If I don't come back, who'd get all these books for you?"

"Minh? Gabriel?" he asked in a bored tone, although inwardly he panicked for reasons he did not understand. He shrugged. "My faithful nursemaid lives to serve my every whim."

"Jackass!" she swore. The word was not muttered, but boldly proclaimed. She stomped her booted foot as if the curse alone was not enough to make the point that she was upset. "I think I liked it better when you couldn't talk."

Narrowing his eyes, he surveyed the small girl who stood with arms crossed possessively over her chest as he awaited an answer. She seemed as if she may ignite on the spot. Her foot tapped in the most irritating manner while her face turned an unhealthy scarlet hue It was overdramatic, as if she had rehearsed the entire scene for a play. He did not have relationships that demanded feelings and used arms and bodily gestures as grammatical lyric. It had to be the evolution of things. Women became drama queens in the new apathetic world.

She was so small and volatile. Compared to him, she was a child's size. He guessed they were close in age only because of her shape and speech. She may be tiny, but had the body of a woman. And she was sharp, but it was absurd that she dare take that kind of tone with him.

"I believe when you are done with my skills, I will be expendable," she added belatedly; as if the notion just popped into her head.

Jareth managed not to laugh aloud. It was so typical of her to say something both confusing and in retrospect. "I dare say you are not expendable." If anything, he was honest. "I need you. I could not have survived without your care. As much as I wax about my faithful servants, let us be truthful. They are profoundly absent as of late." The hard planes of Elizabet's face softened as she seemed to gauge the sincerity of his words, and her arms relaxed. "I have not had the pleasure of their company since you arrived. That leaves me in your care. Exclusively."

Jareth fidgeted slightly with the bed sheet as her demeanor was suddenly premature. The way she went doe eyed and hopeful was a mystery. It did something strange to his stomach. "I feel as though I know you," he admitted. "Impossible—I know, but I do."

He grimaced. Self-depreciating, for he was a man who knew a great many things. "I can still hear you speaking to me on the field where I lay dying. Your voice grounded me." He watched his fingers lift the heavy cover as he drew it further upward over the sheets. "You saved me."

"I have to go," she murmured. It was the softest he had ever heard her speak, and that made him lift his gaze to meet hers. He was sure she would say something further, but then the apparition faded in. The wormhole contracted near the doorway; it would only be seconds before Mrs. Wheatley fully appeared. Their privacy was about to be invaded.

Jareth closed his eyes, pinched the bridge of his nose and inhaled sharply. He allowed his head to rest back on the pillow. "Return tomorrow. Please. We can finish this discussion when there is more time." It smarted the way his voice sounded like a plea. He never begged. His lips turned downward into a frown.

"I'll come if I don't have too much work. I have other people who rely on me too. You know?" she said.

He peeked at her and she smiled to assure him she was not being difficult. She stepped away from the edge of the bed and turned away as the small circle of light opened wider. Mrs. Wheatley's form fully materialized in the center of the circle. Her wrinkled face appeared worried as she got her bearings and stepped from the portal. She gestured for Elizabet with a sweep of her arm. "Come, dear. Your grandmother is becoming suspicious." She turned to face Jareth. "All is well, my lord?"

He could tell she was rushing things and only asked to be polite. "Aye," he answered. His eyes were open a fraction. His heart raced as he lay there—slain by a mere conversation. He had the uneasy feeling that he had either said too little or too much and he was out of time to remedy it either way.

Mrs. Wheatley smiled and nodded, then slightly frowned. Her eyes narrowed as she stared at Elizabet's back. The girl had not moved an inch, but rather blinked stupidly at him.

"You'll have to change your dressing," she said, her sarcasm back in full force. "That is, if you can manage anything for yourself, my lord." The word 'lord' dripped from her mouth as though it was laden with poison.

Jareth pinched the bridge of this nose with a force that would hurt if he could feel it over the pounding of his heart. His jaw clamped and ground to a painful degree.

Regardless of Elizabet's rudeness, the faithful Mrs. Wheatley wrapped an affectionate arm around Elizabet and guided her to the portal's opening. She looked lovingly down on the girl who seemed on the edge of sticking her tongue out at the duke. "The correct method of address isn't 'my lord' for you, child. It's 'your grace'."

The last thing Jareth saw was the expression on Elizabet's face as the portal's round opening closed around them like a cinched purse string. Her eyes were round, questioning and a little wounded, perhaps from thinking she had been played false. Her confusion mingled with all the other emotions she must be experiencing, as well. That was the thing about Elizabet—her face exposed everything she felt.

She had no idea he was one of the most powerful men in the thirteenth century, and she still did not know his name. Even though she had just asked, he had not the chance to answer. How that escaped him, he did not know, but it pleased him greatly that he still had the upper hand. This meant she would be back tomorrow. She was not the type to let something like that go. Perhaps she should learn to be patient and listen rather than barrel through every conversation like a stubborn bull. He had a headache just thinking about following her idea patterns.

But Jareth smiled—the second real smile of the day as he scooped up the book at his side and began to read about the prevention of infection and gangrene in the surgical patient.

Chapter 3

JARETH INSPECTED THE TRANSLUCENT SKIN covering his healing wound. He ran his fingertips across its length, from under his heart to an inch below the navel. It had been deep enough to nick his bowel, but miraculously left his internal organs untouched. It was as if a skilled surgeon had made the wound with a jagged knife. It was still deep, but no longer required packing or debridement.

"Are you going to put your shirt down, or would you like some privacy?" Gabriel asked from the doorway, and leveled a stare toward Jareth's exposed abdomen.

Jareth carefully rolled his tunic over his wound and smoothed down the velvet cloth in a protective gesture. He tipped his chin toward his guest. "How long have you been standing there? Are you spying? Collecting data for the future me?"

"Both." Gabriel smiled and took a few steps forward. "It looks better five years from now." He gestured to the covered wound. Jareth frowned, to which Gabriel's smile widened. "Very roguish. All the rave for the ladies."

Jareth's lips drew into a straight, unimpressed line and he looked away, upward to the canopy over the bed. Gabriel's smile slowly vanished. "Minh sends well wishes."

"And the girl?" Jareth kept his voice abrupt; his hands were knurled into claws within the coverlet. "It's been a week since she visited."

Had she taken his offer and refused to return? He could hardly imagine that she went without a fight after the exit she made. Her curiosity was probably killing her somewhere in the twentieth century. The day after she left, Gabriel showed up. Jareth confided in him the conversation he had with Elizabet. That had been the last he saw of either of them until today.

"You wanted her gone. I took care of that."

"I said I wanted answers," Jareth said, and tried not to curse and smite Gabriel where he stood. "I had to get a servant to help change my dressing. Do you know how awkward that was? It is why it is unbound now. I will not have anyone know how wounded I became, but I cannot dress it properly myself."

"You said she caused you unrest." Gabriel took a seat in the chair near the bed without invite. "And we both know you need your rest." He adjusted his sword to fit comfortably by his side and gazed down on at Jareth. "That's what I do. Take care of you."

Jareth allowed his lips to twist, and rolled his head to the side so their eyes could clash.

"Before you go all royal on me . . ." Gabriel made a cutting gesture with his hand. "We have things besides women to discuss."

Jareth merely stared at Gabriel. He drummed the fingers of his left hand while he waited, but maintained a stiffness that held a clawing motion. He still wanted to skin Gabriel alive for assuming he wanted to be free from Elizabet.

When Gabriel had finally appeared, Jareth bombarded him with questions, none of which garnered him any real answers. It seemed Jareth's minions were scheming against him. Taking the secrecy thing to a new level that included even him. Jareth did not like it.

Besides that, a person could have too much rest. That was partially his problem. He was tired of lying abed all day and night, waited on hand and foot as if he was an ill child, in terrible pain. Without even an entertaining chit to boss around.

"I never discuss women," Jareth said.

"Not now," Gabriel replied under his breath.

"What was that?" Jareth asked. With his head slanted, he awaited another low reply.

"Nothing."

"Precisely."

Gabriel's eyes flickered to Jareth's face for a brief second. He wondered if Gabriel noticed what he'd seen in the reflecting glass—the tightness around his mouth and the flaring of nostrils as he breathed.

Most probably. Even though Gabriel spoke with clear inflection, his body could not lie.

"I apologize, your grace. I wouldn't have come unless I had to. It's obvious you are in pain."

"Apologies will not be necessary," Jareth stated with a negligent wave of his hand. "I grow tired of synthetic medicine, but my travail comes and goes." He inhaled deeply and closed his eyes. "I must beg your forgiveness, my friend. It would seem I am not myself today."

"It's to be expected."

Jareth's head dipped slightly. "A nobleman's lack of manners should never be excused. To agree with such nonsense is a travesty. You provide me a grave injustice."

"You are always a gentleman, your grace."

"That is the problem, is it not?" Jareth asked with a rueful half grin. "I am a duke with massive lands and responsibility. I am expected to rule for King and Country with a mighty fist, yet I find the company of orphans more palatable than the presence of the Black Prince himself. I make judgments based on biblical principle rather than the law of the king." He looked away and out the small, narrow window that was thrown open to allow a breeze to enter his chambers. "And I find my heart increasingly absent from my duties. Why is that, Gabriel? Do you care to tell me why I find myself in this predicament?"

He followed Gabriel's gaze as it lowered to his worn leather boots. There was a smear of blood left on one. Gabriel's vision seemed focused on that speck of red.

"Are you still translating?"

"You know the answer to that," Jareth snapped. He loathed the way his basic question was ignored and sidetracked. It was classic Gabriel style.

"And you realize this hobby of yours could get you killed?"

"And you realize that this hobby of mine, as you fondly refer to my *calling and election*, is the primary reason I am head of the Amalgam?"

"I don't mean to be insolent, your grace."

Jareth allowed his voice to turn irritable. "Ah, but you are, Gabriel."

Gabriel's teeth clenched at his tone, and he changed the subject. "Then I will be quick and be out of your way. I'm here to give report."

A bark of laughter left Jareth's lips. "Then I shall put misery far from you. You are wondering about the Huns, I presume?" He shook his head, a *tsk* riding under his breath. "Of course you are not here to hear my problematic ranting on why I find my life burdensome. Nor do you have a care that the work I do is crucial to the survival of true Christianity."

"You presume incorrectly. I do care for you, your majesty. I support your ties with the Church. I just don't always understand them. But I was hoping you had insight on the attack. The future your grace has no clue. We are finding that time jumping is causing hazy memories. For us of all. Some are totally hidden. Other memories have some definition, but huge holes are missing. I think there's been a breach somewhere. I count all seven travel stones, but that doesn't explain the Huns and how they got here. It has to be alchemy . . . or we are missing something."

"I do not know, Gabriel," Jareth suddenly felt as weary as he appeared. "Why would an Asian army attack a free people who are at peace with their enemies? The harbor has been safe since the last crusade. The French are quiet, even if they are not allied with England." He shrugged. "You say that the travel stone is one mined near Russia?"

"You think that is related?"

"The Huns are kindred to their neighbors, if I recall history correctly." Gabriel nodded. "Then, why is it that I—my future person—have not discovered the breach and diffused it before it reached this caliber?"

Gabriel stared at his bloodied boots again. He seemed unable to meet Jareth's questioning gaze. "You are not available. Family problems."

Jareth was intrigued by his future. The mention of family interested him as currently, he had none. "Family problems?"

A smile curved on Gabriel's mouth as he looked up. "You're a daddy."

Jareth's brows became lopsided as one climbed until it could go no higher.

"Would you like to know what you named your son?" Gabriel asked.

"Nay," Jareth said. His hands batted the air to thwart any other announcement that might change his course. His heart was near ready to explode at the news Gabriel leaked out so blatantly. "No," he corrected. "Enough."

"You asked why your future self didn't figure this whole mess out. I'm just answering questions."

"Perhaps I should ask then, what are *your* questions?" Jareth asked. "Why did you come if not to torment me?"

Gabriel cleared his throat, but his amusement ended when he noticed the tears in the corners of Jareth's eyes.

"My questions seem irrelevant now." Gabriel hinged at the waist and leaned forward, closer to the side of the bed. He put his hand on the mattress, inches from Jareth's hand that was fisted in the covers. "Your grace, are you in great pain? Withdrawing from the pain medication? Let me fetch you a doctor. A real one. I fear Elizabet has missed something. I can handle this problem with the Huns—it's what I'm trained for. It has been over a month since you allowed Harrow to visit and he grows anxious. He doesn't believe us when we tell him Elizabet was able to heal you adequately."

"She missed nothing, because it was I who instructed my care." He blinked twice, three times, and then closed his eyes. "And it is not physical pain as much as my very soul that ails me. How will Harrow heal that part of me? He is a physician, not a magician. No, Gabriel. I am not ready to see Harrow."

"Is there something I can bring, then? Something that will get you out of this muck you've buried yourself in?"

Jareth glanced around the room that was usually orderly and noticed the books strewn about, propped open by their spines in various places—by the window seat, on the bedside table, near the hearth. He saw the room in whole now. His restlessness was evident not only in his physical bearing. He was a man who prided himself on orderly conduct and strength of mind and body. He was possibly one of the greatest minds of all time and here he stood—or rather lay—pale and downtrodden. The room was a cluttered mess.

"No," he replied. He reached for the abandoned book that lay face down next to him. He avoided touching Gabriel's nearby hand. "I want to be left alone. I will have your answers when you return. You have given me much to think about."

"But you don't know the questions."

Jareth sighed. "You want to know why Huns are charging medieval Dover—so do I. You question their use of firearms and the magnitude of their army—so do I. You want to know if I have acquired the travel stones and my answer is not as of today, no. I have not met the strange urchin you speak of, the man who will pawn the stones for the health of his only child."

"And we know this will happen soon," Gabriel said. He pulled back, sitting upright once again and fisting his hands on his lap. "You meet Gyula the Mad sometime in the winter months of 1312. Winter is upon this time now."

Jareth nodded vaguely, paying more attention to the book than to the visitor. "Goodnight, Gabriel. May God bless and keep you."

Gabriel would realize he had been dismissed. It would be pointless to try to keep a conversation flowing, and Gabriel was smart enough to not make the attempt. When Jareth was done, he was done. The fair-haired Spartan rose to his considerable height, untwisted the silver bracelet from his wrist and tossed it in the air.

The portal expanded and opened with a flash of light.

"Gabriel," Jareth called just as he stepped into the circle of light. Gabriel paused to look over his shoulder, then turned. "I have one question that I require an answer for. There is something that brings me extreme curiosity and I must admit that I cannot bear not knowing for another day." He shook his head. "Nay, another hour."

Gabriel nodded his consent. Theirs was such a bond that he would understand the question before it was formed. He answered without prompting.

"She's your wife. The person who will introduce you to your first, most powerful host. The mother of your children. Three boys and a girl—so far. And you love her to distraction." Gabriel shrugged as Jareth felt himself pale. His mouth hung slightly open from the question that never had a chance to leave. "It's sorta disgusting, truth be told. Elizabet has you wrapped. Nothing happens unless the duchess wills it."

A strangling noise gurgled up from Jareth's throat before he could stop it, and his mouth snapped shut. He looked away in a combination of embarrassment and shock.

"Anything else? Am I free to go now? I've got a grocery list the duchess gave me and there's ice cream on the list. She loves her ice cream, especially when she's nursing."

Jareth waved his hand in the air. He winced as if the duchess might suddenly appear—nursing, God forbid—at any moment. "By all means, see to your list."

Gabriel bowed, just barely hiding his grin before he stepped into the wormhole and disappeared eight centuries into the future.

"I REQUIRE A MOUNT, PERCIVAL," Jareth said to his squire as he entered the stables. A group of squires and a traveling minstrel congregated there, playing some sort of game involving gleaming rocks. He did not remember what the game was called, because he did not partake in games. The only sport he had been allowed as a child was that which included battle strategy or foreign translation.

He was sure to fold his cape over his torso, even though curious eyes were roving now, inspecting his person for injury and weakness. The minstrel, who had failed to be introduced, did not seem familiar. Jareth's hand idly circled the pommel of his sword that was sheathed and belted at his side.

He spoke not a word as Percival saddled a strange brown gelding. The mount, he assumed, was a spoil of the recent battle, although he wondered what use a Hun made of a horse when they arrived by ship? It must have been an uncomfortable journey for the animal.

Nor did he question why he was saddling an unfamiliar steed and not his own horse, Veritas. The last he remembered of the battle was the black stallion going down and taking him to the ground after a cannon hit. He wanted to believe that his squire was being sensitive to his current bodily situation by saddling a gelding, but that was unlikely.

Veritas was dead.

"Your majesty." The minstrel bowed slightly, but kept his eyes fastened on Jareth. The correct address was to lower the gaze as well. The boy wanted more than a greeting. He wanted a story. It was in his brown eyes, the way they traveled over his cloak and hovered just where the wound was hidden. There were people who would be interested in knowing the depths of Jareth's wounds, and whether he was able to protect the English Channel from Britain's foes.

Was the wound causing any stain to his cloak? He did not dare glance; he used the satchel he carried to cover the area.

Jareth looked away and refused a proper greeting. His mind was on the gelding, his squire, where he was traveling and why, and an obscure girl who would be his duchess. Somewhere between today and a month from now, his destiny would be set. Events beyond his control would begin his journey to the Amalgam, and to be honest, he was eager. Even setting out on a mundane errand had him anxious, as if his life were on hold. It was no wonder a noisy minstrel could not fluster him. His future seemed more important than the safety of all of England. He felt selfish, but did not care.

It was a cold night. A thin layer of snow covered the ground and allowed the reflection of the moon to light the paths that were worn from travel. If he searched, he could see spot patches of ice that could only mean one thing.

"Have the widows and children been accounted for?" he asked.

"Eighty-seven, your grace." Percival spoke plainly in modern English. He was one of the insiders. One of the chosen who knew and understood what was happening. If he could not trust the squire who had been with him since he was eleven, it was time to distrust all people.

"Eighty-seven," he murmured as he steered his mount back onto the path. The horse had a mind to tarry. Unusual for a gelding, but not so much for an animal of the Huns. An ache went through his heart; he missed his horse, but the greater pain was for the orphans.

"Aye," Percival said. Jareth glanced over and met his eyes. Percival smiled and shrugged. "Yes. I mean yes."

"Better." Jareth turned away. He exhaled softly to let out the pain balled up under his ribs. His breath came from his mouth as smoke into the air. He glanced to see Percival watching him as their horses kept in time along the icy road. "So, did you meet her?" he asked.

Percival kept eye contact only briefly before he looked away, straight ahead into the glum before them. "Yes, I did." He did not pretend that he did not know whom Jareth was speaking of. His eyes blinked rapidly against the cold . . . or maybe it was a nervous gesture. "She asked me to set her free once when I went up to bring supplies for your dressing." His eyes peeked sideways at Jareth. "It was during the early days, your grace. Before she was accustomed to our time period. "

Jareth let a smile tug on the corner of mouth. He was not positive if his smile was sarcastic or real, but he could not stop it. Percival was nervous. Elizabet could do that to a person. "That was very brave of her."

"Her grace said—"

"*Her grace?*" Jareth interrupted. He all but stilled his mount as he turned to gape at his squire. The movement twisted the wound and caused the sutures to become taunt and pinching. So, the nerves were of a different nature. The squire felt guilty. "You know who she is to be?"

Percival nudged his horse into a trot, thereby hiding his expression. "No one said a word to her, your grace. She does not know."

Jareth's lips flattened as a flash of red passed before him. He could not distinguish whether it was anger or pain. "But you know, and I want to know how it is that you were privy to this information when I, myself, have only just been let in on the joyful news." It was not lost on Jareth that he gave the word *joyful* a full measure of sarcasm.

Percival's shoulders broadened, stiffened as he sat taller in the saddle. "Mrs. Wheatley, your grace. She thought I should know since I was tending to the supplies."

"Ah, but of course. The tenacious do-gooder nursemaid of my youth." Jareth smiled ruefully. "Must have killed her to keep it between only you two." A thought struck him and he swiveled in his saddle to face Percival again. "Please tell me the woman used discretion."

Percival grinned. "Yes, your majesty. 'Twas just me she told."

Relief unfurled within Jareth. So much relief that he deflated slightly in the saddle. "See that it remains thus, Percival. I will not have everyone 'her gracing' Elizabet before the proper time." He gazed at the road ahead. "I am not quite sure it shall come to pass. It remains unseen. Time and free will is a mystery."

Who did he think he was fooling? Usually, his mind stayed on facts and small details. Repetition soothed, and there were topics he found he could not leave alone no matter how hard he tried. He had obsessions, and it was increasingly evident that Elizabet could be added to the few, as well. He was obsessed with her. In the turning season, he was reminded of multi-colored hair and brown eyes.

Quite silly, but there it was. He was thinking of the girl and he could not stop. A short, abstentious chit who would be given the title of his duchess. His mind kept returning to her lack of height, her strange colored hair and the freckle she had below her left eye. The topic of her kept creeping into all of his conversations. It was irritating. He decided it was best that he kept silent, in fear that he might give words to his thoughts and forever lose the respect of his squire.

They rode into the village with only the sounds of winter between them. It was late, but a town like this was restless and slumber was infrequent. Most of the activity was indoors due to the time of night and the weather, but nonetheless, the town was alive. The village tavern's windows were aglow from the lit hearth within, and sounds of singing and merriment wafted into the street as they passed. Jareth took a moment to peer through the muddy, sooty window to see a small crowd unruffled by the clamor.

The lord of the manor's presence would not raise suspicion. Jareth often made the journey into the village to visit the orphanage. It was another of his obsessions. He tended to gravitate toward those less fortunate than himself. They were not as complicated and quite frankly, more honest than adults. It was refreshing to be about persons who wanted nothing from him.

The orphanage stood alone. It was a large stone building with massive steps leading to the entry door which was a dull red with large metal knockers. The location could have been better, but Jareth's preference had been considered naught when the Black Prince stepped forward and demanded that no one wanted to behold the orphans. They were best kept out of the way and only seen when it was productive or necessary, which was never.

It was not only the children that called to Jareth, but also the castle he was given, the providence, and the very people whose charge he was entrusted with. He had been only thirteen, and an orphan of sorts himself. Entitled Duke of Dover by the king when titles were new to the English. It was a custom of the French and some Scottish. Even

Prince Edward, the Black Prince, had only recently been given the title of Duke of Cambridge. Titles were given only to royalty—which was the crux of Jareth's birth.

Whose son was he? How was he the only duke of England who was not a royal?

His Scottish mother would not look at him, so she had not the civility to tell him who his father was. Instead, the rumors abounded and when he was given lands and title, a sort of legend spread. Was he a son of the king? Even he did not know for sure, but he had his suspicions. He had deep suspicions.

Visiting the orphanage had a dual purpose. He was making a delivery. Across his breast was a satchel that contained precious cargo. Recently, he had completed another chapter of translation for John Wycliffe, a reformer being held at Oxford University under house arrest. It was of grave importance that he deliver the documents into the hands of the local priest who had access to Wycliffe's guarded room.

"Your grace, spare ye a moment?" a deep voice thick with foreign burr begged from the darkness. It came from near the stone gate of the orphanage, where a knight stood in watch over the yearlings' home.

Jareth pulled the reigns tightly, clamped his thighs around the girth of the horse and came to a complete stop as to not run over the man. His eyes searched the darkness until the hooded, cloaked figure stepped up to his mount. The contour of the garment was odd, misshapen. The man was hiding something.

Jareth said nothing. The plans of his night were thwarted. His heart beat in his throat; anxiety had crept up and settled under his breastbone. Suddenly, he forgot about the orphans and the translations. Adrenaline made his thoughts swim as if he were entering battle. He said nothing, because his tongue refused to move. The entire world as he knew it was spinning toward a single moment in time that would change his life forever. Fate was knocking on his proverbial door. It was no longer a wait for a month to pass. The time was here. The awareness of that made the air around him sizzle. This was the moment Gabriel and Minh had prepared him for.

Percival steered his horse between them, leveraging himself as a protective divergent between him and the unknown person. Jareth craned his neck to see over the large horse. The veiled person did not move, nor was he intimidated by the squire's defensive stance.

"Be gone, ye beggar." Percival touched the pommel of his sword, then shook the blade free from its scabbard to bare the steel. He spoke French, regardless that the man spoke in clear English.

"I am no beggar," the stranger growled.

Jareth stood in the stirrups for a better look.

"Tis a strange tongue ye speak," Percival said. He glanced over his shoulder to the duke. His lips turned downward at the corners when he saw the duke's curious stance. "What business have ye?" He reached with his free hand and fumbled at the coin purse tied to his waist.

"I don't want money," the man spat—both in words and physically near the hooves of the horse that was sidestepping dangerously close to him.

Jareth swung off his mount, ignored the pinch of the sutures and the grueling pain it brought. "Do you have the stones?"

"Yes," the man answered quickly. He came forward.

They met at the rear of Percival's horse. Jareth looked down to the lump in the man's cloak. "Give me the stones first, and then I will see to your boy."

"I see someone has been playing with time." Gyula shook his head and thrust his arms forward as if to show it was impossible to hand anything over but the load he was hiding.

Jareth gripped the man's lapels to tear back the cloak. Gyula took a step back, but Jareth advanced, and leaned forward with narrowed eyes to peer into the ashen face of a dying child. The boy's skin was so pale it reflected the moon's light with an eerie glow; his lips were rimmed in blue. Vibrant baby fine red hair was plastered to the child's skull. He touched the boy's cheek. "How long has he been unconscious?"

"A while," Gyula answered. He spoke briskly as his dull eyes searched the duke's face.

Jareth gazed up into the face of the worried father. He glanced over the rough features of Gyula the Mad, a famed warrior who once rode in the last crusade, or so was said. He was named mad for the fact he smiled while killing the heathen. It was also said he had such a great hatred for non-believers that he could not help but be joyful when one fell at his hand in battle.

Not that he was a religious man, but rather mean and spiteful. The man's face was mutilated, as if someone had taken a blade to the left side of it. Even if the scars had not been present, he was still a strange, ugly man. He was short, broad shouldered, and appeared to waddle when he walked.

"You have the gift of the future." Jareth referred to what he knew as fact in the man's language. "Why not save me some time and tell me what ails the boy."

"Meningitis," Gyula responded. His arms shifted as though the burden he carried had suddenly become too heavy to bear. Perhaps it was his heart and his soul failing at the mere thought this child could die. The disease process seemed to be advanced by the looks of the fevered child. "But it's evident that you, your grace, also have the gift of the future. Do you judge me because I dare use it to my advantage?"

Touché.

"Percival," Jareth said, his eyes on Gyula. He took in the harsh lines around the man's mouth. "Ride before us and prepare a place in the infirmary. We will follow at a slow pace. I have yet to pay my visit to Friar Ephraim."

Gyula stiffened. "You dare risk the life of my only son for a Church that will see you burn?"

Jareth stepped back, his hand protectively touching the satchel that hung over his shoulder, the strap across his heart. He felt it to be sure it was still safe and secure. "What do you know of this?" he asked. His eyes flickered to the orphanage where his contact awaited. "What do you know of my standing with the Church? Speak or so help me, I will kill you first and then watch your child die at your side."

"The gossip about you is true," Gyula sneered. "How eager you are to kill, even those who live in your province. I'm your servant, my lord. Why would you kill someone who is in service to you and your castle?"

"Tell me what you know. Or shall I show you that the stories are true?" Jareth could not let that slip by, even though a child was literally dying before him. He considered his relationship to the Church his greatest secret, not that he was a guardian of the future Amalgam. Not even the fact he was soon to be an avid time traveler held a candle to the idea that he was aiding a great reformation. Innocent people could be killed just for being linked to him.

"We are running out of time and you are my only hope," Gyula said. His voice quivered slightly—the only sign that he was remorseful for his verbal attack. He looked around in the darkness as if searching for another to help him if Jareth refused. "You must take him to Dover or he'll die. I've seen his death, your majesty. It's why I'm willing to make this exchange with you. The stones for the boy's life. It's all I ask."

"Precisely so," Jareth said. "You had better speak quickly, then, Gyula the Mad, or his blood is on your hands. I grow weary of begging your compliance. What do you know of my relations to the Church of Rome?"

Gyula seemed to gauge the opposition, his gaze traveling between Jareth and Percival. Jareth's spine straightened to full length. Percival's face hardened; his hand rested on his sword's grip. Both dared him to make a move he would be sure to regret. They did not leave room for escape or for treason.

Jareth's deep voice boomed through the night air like gunshot. "What do you know of me?" he repeated. He used force to attain the man's compliance. An invisible timer had begun for the boy's life and Jareth was not heartless, but neither was he stupid.

Gyula's gaze darted around, panicked but also rebellious as he appeared to gauge the distance between squire and knight, and then to the orphanage. Did he wonder if he could possibly get away with his life if he ran? But then his face dropped and his lips quivered as the truth seemed to dawn on him. No one could save his son's life except the man before him.

"Forgive me," Gyula blurted. He bowed low and held his son close. "Your majesty, I speak out of order. I'm a simple man whose only child is dying." He held his arms out. "Please, have mercy on your servant. Do not hold my foolish ramblings against me. I beg you. Take the stones. Save my son."

"Mercy is what is keeping me from taking your life," Jareth said. He gazed at Gyula's bowed stance; his lip was curled in anger, but his heart was pliant. He did not want the boy to die, but would allow it if it came to protecting the future of the Protestant Church. "You have failed to answer my question. Must I keep repeating myself, vassal? What do you know of my relation to the Church?"

Gyula's gaze darted to Percival, but he received no aid there, so he bowed again, so deep this time that his son almost tumbled to the ground. His eyes narrowed as he tightened his hold on the boy. "I know that you translate scripture."

Jareth waited a beat to see if he would reveal more, and when nothing came, he prodded. "Go on."

Gyula licked his lips as he straightened. He glanced at Percival, who spurred his horse forward and bared his sword in the moonlight. He would find no mercy with the squire, either. "It is true, your majesty. I jump time. I know of your league. Is that your concern?" Jareth shook his head slowly, his eyes narrowing. Gyula looked unsure of what was being asked of him. "I know you are aiding the Church in translation."

"The Church that is forming is not the Church as God intended," Jareth said. It was a sore spot for him. He always felt the need to defend his position when the topic was breached. No matter that this man probably could not care less about Church error. "It is most certainly not the Church that I help."

"Of course," Gyula sputtered. Jareth could almost see the wheels of his mind turning, searching for the proper response that would not get him and his son found buried. "What I meant to say was that you are tied to early reform. The reformation of the Church. Wycliffe and his Lollards." He smiled weakly and shrugged. "It's legendary, sire. I didn't mean harm. Please . . ." He held out his arms that held his limp son and his voice cracked. "He's dying. I can't bear to lose him. "

Jareth's head tilted a fraction; his gaze briefly paused on the boy's now wan appearance. "Do I have your allegiance? Will you swear an oath to the flag of Dover?"

"I'm giving you something of great price," Gyula nearly growled. He took a heavy step forward and thrust the boy's body against Jareth. "How can you ask for more, you selfish bastard? I don't care what you believe or what you teach your mutant freaks. Isn't it enough that I'm giving you your destiny?"

The squire had dismounted when Gyula's tone changed. He stood next to Jareth, ready with sword drawn. "I request permission to execute, your majesty."

Jareth's jaw stiffened as he gazed at Gyula. The man was enraged, but so was he. The travel stones were useless if his election was thwarted. There was no life for him if he did not complete what he started for the future of Christianity. It was vital to him—as essential as the life of this man's son was to him.

They were at an impasse and Jareth prided himself on being a good judge of character. One gift he felt he had been given was one of discernment. He lifted his hand. "No, Percival." He shook his head as he pressed his squire back until he was a safe distance from striking Gyula. "I believe he means us no harm. He has spoken with honesty. He is stupid, but he is frightened. His son is dying." He leveled a stare at Gyula. "I will have your allegiance, however, or I will not cure your son. " He made a chopping motion with his hand. "No compromise. Take it or leave it."

"So be it," Gyula agreed and dipped his head in reverence. His voice held a semblance of humbleness, but lacked conviction. The words tumbled from his mouth like rapid rain, the rebellion of them thinly veiled. He made his oath rapidly and without apparent thought. "I swear my allegiance to the Duke of Dover, to the crown of England, to the flag that bears Dover Duke's colors and mark."

Jareth removed the satchel and slipped it onto the blade Percival held. His eyes stayed on Gyula in weighed thought. "See it to the hands of Friar Ephraim." He did not like the way the oath tumbled from Gyula. Also, he had an answer to a previous question presented to him by Gabriel. Gyula was Hun—he was sure of it. He had the look and the manner. The breach of the Huns had started with this man; he would bet on it.

An alliance with Gyula was the only way Huns would have access to twentieth century firepower. It troubled him that he was entering a deal with someone who would wage war on his people, but it was necessary. He needed the travel stones to form the Amalgam. The future needed the League to create a balance and refuge for host. Gyula was merely an end to his means.

"Your majesty," Percival responded with his chin touching his chest, his bow was so pronounced. He rose swiftly and gave Gyula a severe warning look. "I will deliver it into the hands of thy servant or die. And then, I shall be your rear guard."

Jareth waited until Percival was on his way before he held out his hand.

Gyula's mouth twisted. "My hands are full, your majesty." He shifted the boy in his arms and thrust out his right arm from under the folds of the cloak. "But you can have a look. They're here. All seven."

Jareth's eyes touched on the seven bracelets; a smile curved his mouth. "Yes. I can count. How thoughtful of you to be precise." He looked into Gyula's eyes. "Just so you know. I shall kill you and your son if you ever break treaty." He reached out and removed the bracelets from Gyula's wrist. They slipped off with some effort.

"I can teach you how to use them. The travel essence is stronger in your country, particularly Dover," Gyula said. "I don't know why this is, but it is so. I can travel to any time in Dover, ancient or modern." His weight shifted under the weight of the child he held. "After you save my son, I'll do whatever you ask."

"No need." Jareth peered at the boy whose breathing was becoming erratic. He had wasted enough time. He held a vast amount of information concerning the travel stones that would shock Gyula. Dover was the main conduit of the wormholes, which was information he was not willing to share. It was time to save a life. He slipped the seven bracelets onto his right wrist. "I have been properly trained in their use. As you so rightly ascertained, I am a man of the future."

Chapter 4

Vermilion Parish, Southern Louisiana. Present time.

THERE WAS NOTHING MORE TO do but change the hydraulic hose—again. Elizabet kicked the side of the motor and silently cursed whatever fate caused the demise of crawfish boat motors. Somewhere in a heavenly place, a flock of beings was laughing hysterically. The irony that she actually could diagnose what was wrong with a broken crawfish boat was not lost on her. Being a seventeen-year-old female who could double as a middle aged farmer did not appeal to her.

"Broke again?" Grandma hollered from the levy. Elizabet was knee deep in the crawfish pond, where the boat had died.

Her grandmother should not be out in the field inebriated. She could tell by the way her words slurred and how she hitched up her robe so it would not drag in the mud. The flowered mint green house coat was knee length. Her perception was drowned out by an excess of beer. It was early in the day, but today was Tuesday, and Grandma played cards at the city Senior Center tonight. She always got a head start, saying it made her more sociable.

Elizabet wiped the sweat from her face with the back of her hand, careful not to smudge grease over the bridge of her nose. "Yeah," she replied. She heaved out a breath as Grandma stumbled closer and teetered near the edge of the pond. It would not be the first time she would have to fish her out of the water if she fell in.

"I'll call Eli—"

"No," Elizabet bit out. "You won't. We can't pay him for the last time, and he'll be wanting his pay for this time *and* that one." She regretted the way she spoke the second she saw Grandma's face pale and then look heavenward. The money they had was limited, and it came sporadically with farming. Crawfish season was their money making season—when the boats all ran properly.

And Grandma was having difficulty enough standing upright,

much less comprehending money matters. Her breathing was erratic, as though it was an exertion. The walk from the house was only about thirty feet, but that was a marathon for a person with chronic COPD. A drunken COPD was twice the charm.

"I'll call Phil," Grandma said. She spoke hesitantly, as though she was a child asking permission, her voice strained and winded. Phil, Elizabet's dad, was a last resort, though. He was too busy chasing girls half his age to be bothered with things like helping family.

"I'll fix it," Elizabet insisted. She motioned to the motor. "And if I can't, then we call Phil." She refused to call him Dad. The title gave the impression of respect and love. She did not want to give the wrong vibes, and Grandma would second that motion. Phil was a horrible son-in-law, except when he dealt with the farm animals.

It took the usual fifteen minutes to persuade Grandma that she had things under control. Elizabet placated her by talking of soap operas and politics, anything to keep her mind off of the fact they could go belly up at any minute. Finally, Grandma had heard enough chit chat and disappeared into the house to watch said soap operas.

Elizabet managed to change the hydraulic hose without getting the boat to the bank. By the time she moved on to repairing a levy breach, she was agitated and tired. Hard work was easy for her. It made time slip by quicker. That way she didn't have to think about how much her life truly sucked. She could do this all day and still have time to feel sorry for herself way into the night.

She sank the shovel head into the soft dirt with a shove and yanked a glove off using her teeth. It was times like these that they had come to her; when she was working outside. If she daydreamed hard enough, she could imagine them appearing. There were times they insisted she come with them and there were times they merely came to harass her to keep quiet.

She whirled around to peer at the tractor as she had multiple times before, as if being on her toes could conjure them from nothing. The hairs on her arms prickled. They were coated in sweat, so they could not stand to attention, but they wanted to. The heat had her hallucinating, or it was tricking her. Or perhaps she wanted something to happen so badly that she imagined she had seen a flash of light in her peripheral vision.

She thought about the lie she had told the knight, claiming apathy as the reason she was not freaked out. The truth was that she had known Mrs. Wheatley since she was a child. The lady had been friends with her mother. Seeing the wormhole appear with a flash of light was nothing new to her. She guessed she had been about seven years old the first time she witnessed it. Her mother had told her to never be afraid of Mrs. Wheatley, and that one day she would come for her and she must go without question.

It was then that her mother insisted she learn all there was about veterinary medicine. It was clear why now, although what she had needed was a human anatomy course instead. But she guessed her mom decided that was the most logical course considering she had access to a doctor of animals. It also meant that her mother knew why they would come for her, but kept that detail from her. That was irritating.

Elizabet frowned as she cleared her mind. Something changed the last time she was back in time. There had been something final about it. No one was coming for her. It was just wishful thinking, but it was over. They had used her and that was it. She spit the glove from between her teeth and bit at the other. All the while she kept an eye on the lone tractor whose engine was hitched to the canal as it pumped water to fill the pond. The glove dangled from her teeth as she whipped around to retrieve the shovel.

As if on cue, the engine silenced; it choked off just as she turned her back to it. It was not the sound of engine failure—which would be her luck today, but a distinct switch. She gripped the shovel handle and the air left her lungs in a noisy exhalation. Alarm crippled her—a deep-set fear that someone was there. Or even worse, that *no one* was there. The chance that this could be a simple farm mishap sat in her mind unwelcome.

They had left her alone for the past month. She had no clue how the knight was faring, whether his wound was closing properly or if infection had become a factor. He had ordered a book on gangrene, which meant he worried about sepsis. Perhaps he had succumbed to the disease and that was the end of things.

Your grace.

It was foolish to be timid and nearly hyperventilate over a tractor shutting off. It could be the switch. It had been faulty before. However, they had always come for her like this. If she were honest, she had been working sunup to sundown in hopes they would come and take her away again to a place where she mattered. A place she could smell if she thought hard enough—like the sea, cloves, and something citrus.

Your grace.

She gripped the shovel handle tight enough that it busted the blister wedged in the crease of her palm. "Are you there?" She lifted her dirty chin. She waited for the blink of three and then let her chin slowly fold to her chest. She felt foolish—stupid. It was over. No one expected anything of her other than sacks of crawfish. She was the girl who dropped out of school after she missed too many days because chores became vital to her life. It was work or starve. The adventure that had stolen her from this life had come to an end, and there was nothing she could do about it. The reprieve from farm life would never come for her. This was her lot.

It was not unusual where she was from, that kids dropped out of school. Louisiana remained one of the states where this was most common. Her mother would be disappointed, but she did not want to think about that. She wished she could speak to her mother one more time and ask her why people from the past wanted her. There was no certainty to it and it bothered her to think that it was all over. And it was evidently over. She heard nothing behind her. No footsteps, no rustling of leaves, no voices. She was alone.

Elizabet twisted her short legs together and lowered to sit on the muddy slope like a top winding down. She did not know if she did it out of exhaustion, or if it was out of aggravation that she was stuck forever working for something that had no prize. She would never own the land she worked, and she received no paycheck other than a bed to sleep in and food to eat. Her head dipped low as she blinked back tears. Her rubber boots were caked in mud as she sat there on the wet levy Indian style.

"Hello, Elizabet." A branch snapped under his foot as he approached. The sound was a punctuation mark to his words—an exclamation mark to be exact.

Her boots were pink with small red roses. The inane thought appeared as she pressed her hand to her chest to calm her racing heart. After days of working, watching, hoping—someone had come. Not just someone—*him*. It had never been him before.

"You turned off my tractor." She said the first thing that sprang to mind while she twisted to look over her shoulder. Her heart still pounded in her throat. His large form was showcased by the descending sun, which made it impossible to make out any facial expression, but something about his stance reeked arrogance and certainty. She spit out a fiber of glove left in her mouth and swiped at her lips with the back of her hand. She released the shovel with her other hand; it fell with a dull thump between them.

"It was tired," he replied with a lazy shrug. He stepped over the shovel and stood before her. He clasped his hands behind his back and stared down at her, waiting for her reply.

Elizabet smirked because it was all she could do to suppress the urge to scream. He just showed up and acted as if they had seen each other only yesterday. As if he had not disappeared into thin air without a goodbye or explanation.

He did not know how depressed she had been. How miserable she was when she thought of it all being over without any answers or closure. They had just left her without word—without excuse. She had walked around with a half-beating heart—a sick thud of a heartbeat that let her know she was hurting—and keen with the loss of an opportunity that was gone too quickly. They had left her with nothing—no promises, no clues to their return.

He had become her ideal, a crush if she were totally honest with herself. She knew no one who could compete with his elegant beauty or his intelligent ways. He was a genius, and part Greek god, obviously. His movements were predatory, like a sleek jungle cat. She had never seen him move before and she was glad, because if she had seen him the way he was now, she may have given in to silly girlish fantasies and made an idiot of herself.

And to hear him say her name with a fondness, a personal knowing, and the inflection of a British scholar . . . It did something to her stomach. She had almost forgotten what he sounded like. Not quite a modern Brit, but something else entirely. As though he belonged to a heritage of his own making; as if he were combining time periods and heritages to be uniquely himself. It was so unfair that she did not even know his name.

Your grace.

She squinted against the sun's rays. His face came into focus and she saw he was mirroring her smirk almost perfectly. She used her hand as a visor to shield her eyes. He looked really, really good. The gauntness and pale complexion were gone, replaced with a charged glow. The air practically crackled around him. It was most disturbing, and she hardly knew what to do with her limbs. It made her awkward and conscience of every breath she took. He was perfection personified and she simply was not.

"Tractors don't get tired. Just like time traveling 'your graces' don't just show up on a crawfish farm." Her eyes narrowed. "What the heck are you doing here? You've never come before. Are your henchmen too busy to fetch your slave?" Her voice sounded breathy, winded. She hated it. The fact she was ecstatic to see him was unnerving. She also despised how she could not help but attack. It was a habit of hers to act hostile to cover any weaknesses. It was far easier to argue than to come up with something interesting to say.

"I came to speak with you." He squatted down and as he did, she was able to make out the vivid hue of the royal blue tunic he wore. It made the light blue of his eyes pop in comparison. He had the palest eyes imaginable. He rested his forearms on his thighs. "My henchmen are otherwise involved." He smiled with half his mouth. "And you, most certainly, are not a slave." She remembered that smile, but fought the pull it had on her. He should use his charm on someone else. It was as if he read her mind, because the smile vanished. "Do you have a moment to spare? A few minutes of your time?" He waved a careless hand toward the flooded field. "I do believe it is appropriate to have the people you employ tend to such matters as this. I shall not tarry long. Summon your men of business to deal with this matter of moving soil."

Elizabet glanced around for witnesses who would see him in all his glory of medieval attire, and maybe for a man of business. She almost laughed out loud at that part, but instead she felt ill—nauseated. "There is nobody else. Just me. And my grandma," she said. "I guess you could say that I'm my own man of business."

"Are you an orphan?"

"We don't say orphan anymore."

"Any longer."

"Any more," she repeated, her lips taunt. Her chin jerked upward. "My mom died, but I have Grandma. And sometimes a dad, so I'm not an orphan." It was a sore point for her, and he seemed intent on honing in on it. She did not like feeling sorry for herself, and no one else was allowed to, either.

Jareth studied her face, his eyes making a perfect circle. His eyes roamed her face as he took in her features. He nodded and stood suddenly, looking away from her and out into the field. "Have it however you like." His hand reached out toward her, but he did not look in her direction. "I require a moment of your time. I have a few questions that I would like to ask you."

It was simple to reach out and grasp his large hand that was given in aid to help her rise, but she did not want his help. She stood as best she could on her own, using his hand only to steady herself as she rose to her feet, and then nearly fell over. The light contact with him brought her to the place they were now—they were starting over. It was awkward, as though they had not already spent hours alone together.

Elizabet curled her fingers into a fist. Her hand recoiled in the middle of his until he released her. Her fingers were numb. She clasped her hand with the other and massaged the palm while she stared up at him. He was tall. She was accustomed to seeing him lying in bed. Hiding under the covers had been a good six feet, six inches of solid man-boy. She was used to having to look up into people's faces, but he was gigantic compared to her.

She cleared her throat when he caught her staring. She did not waste any time, however, and pressed on even though she felt her face involuntarily warm. "Can I at least know your name?" Her thumb massaged her palm. "If you want a moment of my time, then I want a name. I refuse to call you my lord or your grace, so you better tell me or I'm gonna make one up." She allowed her lips to tilt in a slight grin, but then they trembled with her underlying nerves. "I'm thinking Jackass;

do you like the ring it has to it?"

"Jackass would better suit Gabriel, not I." He bowed slightly as if she had not just insulted him. "My name is Jareth. I will allow you use of my Christian name, but only do so when we are alone together. I must maintain a level of respect for my station, even in these times."

"Wow," Elizabet said, and rounded her eyes with mocking awe. He said 'these times' as if she were living in Sodom. He had offending down to an art, even while he pretended to charm. All that fantasizing she had done had left out the bluntness of his personality. "For a while there I expected your majesty would be your choice. You surprise me, Jareth." She uttered Jareth as if the word shared space with a clove of garlic in her mouth, and yet inwardly she rejoiced that his name was not Ralph or Victor.

She could not decide if she wanted to kiss him or slap him. It had been so easy to get him to tell her who he was that she was eager to ask more questions. He appeared to be oddly sociable even though he was being a jerk. While his words were appropriate, it was the way he held himself, the way his words sounded bored. He seemed to barely tolerate her.

They had reverted back to the bantering that accompanied their previous conversations. She felt most comfortable when she hid behind sarcasm and veiled complaining, while Jareth shot straight to the heart of things with seemingly little thought of feelings. He was practically a sledge hammer to her ego.

"Well." His thick eyebrows creased together as he reached up to touch a scar under his eye. His mouth curved into a grin that was bashful. "There is that."

"I was kidding," she said as her eyes widened. He was embarrassed because he had royal blood? Her lips turned downward as the magnitude of that fact sank in. "But, figures. That's just my luck. I guess you needed someone simple and from the working class." And was it not just perfect that he was a royal? It matched his demeanor with a whole new meaning of snobbery. She rolled her shoulders. "Can't imagine just anybody climbing into a wormhole with an old lady. Call me crazy." She would blacken his royal eye if he did.

One of Jareth's black brows arched. "I was given a title after squiring for the Prince of England, Edward. I am a duke. The Duke of Dover to be precise, but I believe history refers to me as the Bastard Duke, so do not get any romantic ideas."

"That is very hateful to be referred to as something you have no control over." She scowled at his overture of thinking romantic thoughts where he was concerned. "Even for you," she added. The word bastard was unexpected. It took her by surprise and made her soft to his pompous attitude. Her anger was gone just like that. No one deserved to be judged by the mishap of a parent. She had firsthand experience.

"Cruel, but precise. The cruelty of my birth has lost its sting long ago. The specifics of my birth remain a mystery even to me, and quite frankly, I do not have a care one way or another. My title was given to me because of my abilities. I can learn to speak another language overnight. It is a gift." He lifted one shoulder. "I am a translator by trade, a knight and duke by title given to me by the king."

"That's big of you, but I think you're lying. Words like bastard stir up bad feelings, no matter what century. Which century did you say you were from?"

"I did not say."

"Well, feel free." Elizabet propped her hand on her hip. "Spill it or get out." She wagged the other hand. The shell of uncertainty cracked away as their accustomed banter returned. She momentarily forgot that he was the best looking thing on two legs. Her self-confidence had a surge. "Leave. I don't care if you're the King of England. I do remember the two clues you left me with: England and medieval. But, I'm no longer willing to put up or shut up."

"But you do it so well," Jareth leaned forward mockingly. His eyes met hers even as he made the cynical gesture. She was forced to look away. The intensity and challenge she saw there were nerving.

"I see you brought the ugliness back," she said, and allowed her lips to twist. He had the nerve to be beautiful even with a condescending smirk firmly in place. "How I missed it. I wondered how long it would take you to revert back to being a jerk."

He turned his attention to the house, then to the barn, and finally back to her. His face clouded as if with confusion; his lips twisted as well.

"I digress. Is there a place acceptable for us to converse? A place where we will not be disturbed and I will not be on display, perhaps?"

Even while she was sparring with him, she felt protective. "We can go to the barn," she suggested. Far from the kitchen window where Grandma would be stationed while she watched her afternoon television. Her eyes trailed to where her thoughts were. It would not be good if Grandma became suspicious. There was still the lie she had told when she claimed she had run away. Grandma would be suspicious of a man-boy wearing weird clothing. "I can leave the doors open so it won't offend your lordly nostrils." Elizabet motioned for him to follow, and then hooked her thumbs into the belt loop of her jeans as she led the way. There was no sense in delaying and staying out in the open.

"I do own livestock," Jareth said. "My lordly nostrils are accustomed to putrid odors. I live in the medieval age. Normally, there is no plumbing and animals are housed in close proximity to living quarters."

She looked over her shoulder, and for a brief second her heart plummeted into her stomach at the sight of him following. "I love the middle ages." She rolled her shoulders as she looked ahead again and shook her head slightly. "Well, studying about it, at least. It wasn't so great playing doctor while I was there, though. I could've done without that part. I can't tell you how many times I wished I'd studied anatomy instead of vet science."

"You did remarkably well given the circumstances."

Elizabet tripped over thick thatch of dry grass and teetered to the side. Jareth reached out and steadied her, placing his hands on her hips to right her on the uneven levy.

"Don't touch me," she said immediately. She pulled away by stepping forward. Her slick boots caught in another slippery thatch of grass and she slid, but righted herself even as he went to help her. She batted his hands away. "I don't need your help."

Jareth's hands balled into fists as he drew back. He changed the subject. "What do you know of medieval England?"

Elizabet patted down her hips where he touched her, then skimmed her hands down her sides before she crossed her arms over her mid-section in a slight embrace. "My mom was a history teacher. She used to read me her old college textbooks." Her heart ached as she remembered her mother. She did not like speaking of her in past tense. Some things never got any easier. Losing a parent was one of those things. She motioned for him to follow before she began walking again—cautiously.

It was sweet the way he gave her an out. She had reacted badly when he merely helped her not to fall into the muddy waters of the crawfish pond. An awkward silence hung in the air as they walked up the three acres of levies to reach the barnyard. It was a good distance to cover in self-conscious quiet. She was thankful to come to the barn.

"I hope you weren't trying to make me feel better by saying your nose wasn't sensitive, because two of our hogs just gave birth." Her nose crinkled as she reached for the lever that held the door closed.

"May I?" Jareth stepped up to her side. He motioned to the door, one black eyebrow climbing up. It looked like a difficult task—to have only one eyebrow nearly disappear into his hairline. He did it often and she imagined it went with being an arrogant, overbearing lord of the manor. His vassals probably cowered in fear when that haughty eyebrow went north.

"Sure," she said, and her hand fell away from the lever. She stepped back. "Be my guest." So, he wanted to be a gentleman and prove that he would not be offended by barn smells. She almost roared with laughter as the smell hit him, but instead settled for a curt cough that resembled a cackle as she swept past him as he held the door.

Chapter 5

IT HAD BEEN HARD NOT to show his shock at having found her working like a serf. Seeing her toil over the land and repairing large machinery disturbed him. She would be his duchess, for goodness sake, but for now he reminded himself that she was just a girl. A peasant girl, if he assessed correctly.

He had come with the sole purpose of planting seeds about his future host, Jeremy Cameron. Someone needed to watch over Jeremy as the time of his turning approached. Jareth trusted Elizabet. It was getting her to trust him in return and being civil that seemed a good place to start in this journey. It had been a while since they were acquainted. Talking soothed Elizabet, which meant she was open the longer he kept her going. It was evident how she threw her soul into her words.

It was an easy task to lure her into conversation. They had been in the hot, enclosed stable for an hour and he had a complete history of her losing her mother to leukemia and how she was now resigned to a life of farm, field hand, and property mortgage. Jareth understood better than anyone the importance of land holding and maintenance, but he had not come to give a lecture on proper stewardship.

The more she talked, the more she relaxed in his presence. However, she still spoke with animation, volume, and the type of voice that boomed and sounded angry. He was forced to match her facial expressions to her tone to be certain she was not picking an argument instead of merely conversing. Even as he watched her, his mind wandered to thoughts other than the purpose of his visit. He wondered how this petite girl had his emotions in knots. In the past, whenever he considered marriage he imagined the girl in question would be ugly. His prospective wife would be someone he could confide in and beget heirs, but never more. For all of his goals, though, he would never marry, but rather dedicate his life to Church and country. As a duchess, Elizabet would never do. She was loud, bossy, and sassy. And she was pretty. That was unacceptable. The alliance could make him weak.

"Aren't you going to say anything?" Elizabet asked. She leaned forward over the bale of hay she was seated on. She grabbed a handful of rice hulls to toss to the chickens that scurried about.

Jareth leaned against a wooden beam, half of his weight supported. He forced the scattered thoughts from his mind. "I am under the impression you require words to put you at ease with my presence. I am merely allowing your leisure."

"Well, I'm under the impression that you aren't leaving until I answer the question you came for, but you let me talk my head off about all things me. Why?"

Clever girl. Jareth's mouth curved into a lopsided grin. "You speak in broken English. There are times I find it impossible to follow you. I say nothing because I am still deciphering your language."

"Liar. You didn't have that trouble before," she said. "You said you were a translator and I could point out that you spoke in cultured English, but definitely not Middle English the way you should be. Or is it French?" Elizabet smirked. "Which is it? And remember, I know these things because my mom was a history teacher. Don't change the subject."

"Right."

"You see . . ." she lifted the fistful of hulls and caused them to sprinkle around her as she spoke. "You say, 'right.' That is just wrong for you." Her lips flattened as he covered his face in exasperation. "You should be using thy and thou." She narrowed her eyes. "Or is it Norman French?"

"You are exhausting," Jareth muttered under his breath from behind the veil of fingers. He caught her irritated expression from between his fingers and smiled sheepishly. It was not the time to be on her bad side when he needed her help. "But actually—you are right. I hail from the twelfth century, so French is the prominent language for nobility. I speak four tongues fluently. Translation comes naturally to me." She nodded to encourage him to keep going. "But the language I speak is my own. It is a mixture of English. I am told by Gabriel that I will grow more British as my travels increase." His hand dropped away. "Which makes perfect sense. I am British by birth, so do not become too accustomed to my speech today as it will evolve." Elizabet opened her mouth, but Jareth cut the air with a chop of his hand. "I am not done yet. You have been given an adequate chance to have the floor, but it is my turn now."

"Slang," Elizabet cut in, as if she could not help herself. She wagged her finger. "You're using slang. 'Having the floor' is slang for—"

"I know what it is slang for—I was the one who used it. You say this as if you are surprised," Jareth said with a touch of irritation in his voice. He did not like the turn in the conversation or how she was picking at him. They had serious business to discuss and he was reduced to bickering about slang. "I am a time leaping progeny. Of course my language is strange. I no longer have a time that I call my own."

"I'm sorry," she said. She looked away, and appeared embarrassed that she could not keep her mouth shut. Her finger seized its accusatory wag and she dropped her hand to her side.

"I should not have to explain these things to you. Do you not remember the castle? The days and nights you spent giving me care? We had a clock, we spoke in your English, and wormholes abounded, for goodness sake. How can you question the way I speak—or live, for that matter?"

Elizabet shrugged but he barely left her sufficient time to come up with a smart quip. "It's a blur. I hardly remember it at all." She flapped her hands in the air as if waving her hazy memory away.

Jareth recalled her weak stomach for nursing a near fatal wound. Where she claimed to not have recollection of what happened between them, he wanted to collect each detail and study it. He wanted to dissect every word and each moment until he knew for sure what was between them, and at once, he knew she fibbed.

She wanted to know what was between them as badly as he. Something on her face told him he had figured her out. He was disappointed that she had dissembled, but he also realized she was nervous. There must be an allowance for feminine nerves. And they were almost fighting again, as if they could not help it. He did not understand how this happened.

Elizabet sighed, sort of snorted, and crossed her arms. She must realize she was caught. He did not need to utter the words that he was wise to her false claim.

"Why don't you just tell me why you are here?" She lifted her shoulders. "Obviously, I'll never keep my mouth shut long enough for you to get a word in elsewise," she murmured.

Personal conversation was difficult for Jareth as well, and he felt a twinge of remorse for becoming cross. He tilted his head and studied the way she flushed when she was nervous. She was having a difficult time meeting his gaze. He felt for her—something; probably mercy. "We are both inept at being civil," he murmured.

"You think?" she asked with a sarcastic bend to her lips.

"Yes," he said. "But I also believe we are getting better." His mouth curved upwards on one side. "You have not thrown anything at me, nor have you run screaming. You have not vomited once in my presence today. I think we are making progress."

"Maybe," she said, and her mouth also tipped into some semblance of good humor. She appraised him, up and down. "But I wouldn't say you're safe with the vomiting part yet. You could always flash your scar and I'd probably chuck all over your cute black boots."

Jareth smiled and shook his head. "I like these boots. Hoby." He tapped the heel of his left foot to his right toe. "They were a gift for my birthday from Minh. Please, do not . . ." His grin widened. "Chuck on my cute boots. It would break my heart." His hands folded over his chest, where his heart lay beating under his fingertips.

Elizabet laughed and lifted her hands. "Okay. I won't. Just keep all things gross to yourself and we should be good." Jareth nodded. His smile wavered as he turned to the stall where the hogs were kept. She cleared her throat. "So, tell me what you want. Why did you come here?"

His reply was swift. "I need your help."

"That's given. Just by showing up here you tell me it's serious. Might as well spill it. Give it to me. I'm all ears. You have the floor, your majesty." She bent at the waist in a slightly mocking gesture, and swept out her hand.

"There is a boy. His name is Jeremiah Cameron," Jareth said. "He would be about nine years old in this time."

"Whoa, whoa!" she said in a soft exhalation. Her surprise was obvious. She popped up, her head shaking. He had never seen that look on her before. "Slow down." Her face scrunched in confusion. "One minute we are talking about my vomit issues and the next, Jeremy?" She waved her hands toward him as if to spur him to speak. "I know Jeremy. What does he have to do with you?"

"You did give me the floor." He was spilling information, but she had asked for it. He needed to seize the moment while they were companionable. He had broken the ice by jesting with her. Jeremy was a topic he had to breach, and the time seemed appropriate. It was, however, upsetting that he could be as flighty as she when it came to ideas and topics. Elizabet motioned with her hands for him to continue. "And Jeremy has everything to do with me." He winced and looked away briefly, not liking the way she was staring at him with suspicion in her eyes. "He will need my protection soon, but I cannot interfere with his life as of yet. I need you to watch over him for me until the day I become necessary to his existence."

Elizabet narrowed her eyes. "What would you want with a little boy? How do I know you aren't here to hurt him?"

"You know him well enough to care for him?" Jareth would not think on why that made him ache in a way he never had before. What would it be like to garner someone's loyalty? For someone to protect him this way? Her guard was going up. She liked this boy. He sensed it.

"Of course," she said. "Everybody knows the Camerons. They are the only ministers in this parish who aren't regulated. They're like area pop stars, and they're Presbyterian. That makes them strange to this part of my country. Everyone else is Catholic. When the Great Regulation was passed, only the Pres's were left unregulated. The other minor religions were forced to either merge with them, comply with the government, or go Catholic and under jurisdiction with Roman religion. But you didn't answer me. What do you want with Jeremy?"

"I want to help him." Jareth said. "There are things I cannot tell you yet, but I need you. Can I count on you?" He knew he sounded like a lunatic. How was she supposed to trust him when she knew so little?

But Gabriel and Minh had not debriefed him on how much she should know at this time. The threads of time were delicate. He could change someone's destiny with one small wrong move. Lives could be erased.

"I'm just supposed to help you without knowing why?"

"Frankly, yes. It would be easier if you were to cooperate. I need your help. You are critical. Have I ever harmed you in any way?" He appealed to reason and logic.

"Hmm," was all she said.

"I sound quite mysterious, do I not?" he asked, but did not await a reply. The answer was written plainly on her face. "And I am bombarding you with my needs and begging for help. It must seem I speak in riddles and harbor secrets, and that is not all untrue. I am going somewhere with this, and I promise that one day you will know and understand it all."

"I get that what you are calls for big secrets." She smiled sardonically. "You carry a wormhole around your wrist and are as old as the dinosaurs. I just wonder how long you plan to string me along. It would make things better for me if I knew why I'm stupid enough to consider helping you."

"What a blessed lady you are," Jareth said, and his smile was sincere. "But I am not quite as old as the dinosaurs."

He did not even care that she knew the time travel capabilities lie in wormholes. Nor did he worry that it was he who had given away the information. He was becoming sloppy with her already, and barreling uninhibited to his demise without a care. The truth was, he would reveal whatever she wanted to know, but she did not need to know that at this precise moment. The only thing he could not tell her was exactly what Jeremy would be.

"I suggest we compromise." Her tone was strictly business. While he had been prattling on, apparently she had been calculating.

His smile faltered. "What is it you require?"

"Nothing earth shattering," she replied. Her shoulders rolled up a notch; her nose wrinkled. "For every one thing I agree to do for you, you have to tell me one of your secrets, or a little bit about you—"

"My choice," he interrupted. He knew where she was leading, and while he was open to honesty, he was medieval. Men set the course of things. She opened her mouth to disagree, but he swiped his hand through the air—so roughly that she stepped back. "I decide what you know. The more you know, the more vulnerable you become, and I cannot protect you while we are apart—in different times." It was ironic that she made a game of something he was willing to give freely. But this way, he had an excuse to keep some of his secrets.

"Okay," she conceded. But her posture remained stiff. "At least let me choose the topic."

"No."

Elizabet's face turned pink. "If it wasn't against my nature, I would call you a bastard. You're not being fair."

"Your nature is quite corrupt," Jareth said, "so do what you must. Call me a bastard at your leisure."

A sound of annoyance came from her mouth. "How rude! I'm not corrupt."

"That is where you are wrong," he argued. He leaned against the railing of the pig pen, his hands braced, his tall form at an incline. Now, this was a point he could debate with comfort. "We are all corrupt by nature of Adam. We need divine grace."

Her face scrunched up and a puff of air left her nostrils as they flared. "What are you? A man of the cloth?"

He gave her a smug smile. "Actually, yes. I am one of the early Church's first reformers. I aid The Morning Star of the Reformation to translate scripture." He crossed his ankles, and reclined heavily on the rail at his back. "Does this count for the first of my secrets?"

"It most certainly does not," she stammered. She looked as if she wanted to kick dirt on his expensive boots. "I didn't agree to let you decide."

Jareth laughed. A full belly laugh that both felt and sounded foreign. When was the last time he found anything that amusing? "They're not your secrets, so that would be unfair." His grin made it hard to speak. "But I will give you one concession. What will you ask of me?"

Elizabet smirked and looked away. Her shoulder drooped a bit. His laughter dwindled to a bemused snicker as she pivoted to him. Her gaze was intense. "I want to know, why me?" His smile immediately dropped from his face. "Why me, when there are millions of people who could help you. Your people came out of nowhere to get me. Why?"

His genetic makeup would have been an easy request. He could explain mild Asperger's in detail, the why and how of what made him the way he was. Or concepts of doctrine in early church history perhaps. He could expound on the laws of physics, chemistry, medicine, or most definitely theology, until she screamed in boredom. He did not wish to speak of things he barely understood. She was unfair, just as she had claimed him to be a second ago.

Jareth pushed away from the railing, his hands going to his temples where he raked his short-cut hair as he thought of something clever to say to appease her. He looked up into the rafters, and willed anything to come to mind.

"I know I'm not the brightest person," she said, her voice softer. "I'm not smart. I'm not rich. I don't come from a prominent family in time." She lifted one shoulder. "I'm confused. Why me?"

Jareth regarded her, took in her presence. She was muddy and probably smelled. Her hair was tangled and drooping and soggy with sweat. She had the strangest hair he had ever seen. It was yellow, brown, and even apricot in small strands. There was a smudge of dirt on her chin that he had not noticed earlier. How he missed a speck of uncleanliness was beyond him.

The girl scrambled the very essence of what made him tick. Choosing her would create a challenge. His life would become a series of compromise and heartache because he would have to protect someone other than himself. She lied when she was nervous and she talked too much. He had many enemies who would prey on that.

Elizabet brought her chin up slightly under his perusal. Her short legs stiffened as she planted her booted feet in a widened stance. She crossed her arms and glared at him as she waited. The silence stretched between them as he pondered a proper response that would not get him slapped. Everything about the way she stood let him know she realized exactly what was going through his mind and that she was under his scrutiny. He swallowed—and felt his pride slip down his throat.

"Time and chance, perhaps. Your location is vital to the future of the League I have organized. Jeremiah is from this area and he is an essential player in the future of things." He shrugged. "It is possible you are just in the right place at the right time."

"Or the wrong place," she replied, her lips a severe line. "It all depends on perspective."

Jareth was not ready to delve into every detail of the whys. Some things needed to be handled with great care, but he felt the need to clarify, too. "It is also because only you shall do," he said. His voice was a low, deep rumble in the space they shared. To his ears, he sounded weak. He did not like it, but soldiered on. It was necessary to be truthful. It was all the blasted girl would accept. Unlike her, he did not lie when he was under pressure. "You are, quite possibly, the only female who could stand the sight of me—as I am." He opened his arms. "You say that you are not smart, but I am not what I seem."

"You're a duke," Elizabet said, her brow furrowed.

Jareth gave a rueful grin. "The word bastard is the ugliest word, no matter what century. Your words, not mine."

"I don't care about that." His grin faded as she took a step toward him. Her arms remained crossed, but she closed the distance until they were only an inch apart. She had to flex her neck almost unnaturally to stare up at him. Her expression dared him to deny her loyalty. "I don't care if you're a bastard," she said slowly.

Jareth stared down at her, that pert nose of hers pointed up at him. "No, you do not," he agreed, just as slowly. The top of her head reached him at mid-chest. For the first time in his life, he had the urge to reach out and embrace someone. How precious and innocent, as a child, that she could toss aside propriety. That she could laugh in the face of his birth status. Her response was the answer to her own question, although he was too stunned to tell her this.

"My second question—" She was convinced that he believed her.

"No," Jareth said. He stepped back. His hand came up to ward her away; the trance she had over him was broken. "You had one question and I have answered it."

"Well, I have another and you're going to answer it or I'm not helping you." She jerked her chin up a notch. "I want to know what you plan to do with Jeremy. It sounds a little perverted to me that you would be interested in a young boy. You don't look like a predator, but I can't be sure unless you tell me why you want me to spy on a friend."

Jareth pulled a face. So, that was the wall she erected when he questioned her about Jeremy. "Is that what you think?" He sputtered something unintelligible, and briskly waved his hands he still held before him. "I want to help him. I am to be his guardian. How could you . . . do you . . . I would never hurt a child." He let his expression turn thunderously angry. "I am to be the only thing that stands between him and disaster. His guardian."

"You've said that," she said, and propped her hands on her hips. "But I'm not stupid. I need more information before I jump into this. Tell me why you want me to watch Jeremy Cameron."

Jareth lips twisted in irritation and in resignation. She was right. He needed to clarify things or it *did* sound creepy. He drew in a deep breath, and inhaled quite a bit of stale barn air. "Fine," he said, and leaned once more onto the rail of the stall behind him. This time it was not an arrogant pose, but a weary one. Life with Elizabet would be exhausting. "I will relent and answer your question."

"Sweet," Elizabet said with a smile unlike the word she used. It was diabolical.

"There are . . ." His hands rotated at the wrists as he searched for the right words. "Strange times coming to our world. Things that we never dreamed possible." He touched his chest with his fingertips. "Things I find troubling and bizarre. Full blown situations that will tear families apart and leave desolation in their wake. Things that will render society fearful and negligent unless intervention is made."

"And you are the intervention?" Elizabet asked. She was halfway making fun of him, but as he revealed more of who he was, she had to know this was big. Things were about to get real in her life. She seemed both terrified and excited.

"Yes. It is no coincidence that I am a reformer and this boy is an unregulated pastor's progeny. I believe in the providence of God, so yes, I will be the intervention. Jeremy will need guidance when he turns, and it will come from me."

"Turns?" Elizabet asked, her voice raising an octave. "Like what? Werewolf? Vampire?"

"You read too much fiction," Jareth scoffed. He shook his head and lowered his gaze to his feet. He didn't know how to proceed without giving it all away prematurely. He had forgotten that the world of the future was riddled with fictitious ideations. Jeremy would, in fact, turn into what some would call a monster, but it was nothing like fabled stories of old.

"Maybe," she agreed and shrugged with one shoulder. She seemed to want to do this, but only with her eyes wide open. "Apathy, movies, and all. My imagination doesn't just exist, it romps."

"Honestly, I do not know how much information I can relay to you at this time. It is still early for me, as well. Is it not enough that I am here asking *you* for help? Can you not ascertain that I have a level of trust for you? Why can you not extend the same to me?"

Elizabet tilted her head as he adjusted his stance to something more relaxed. She made a clicking noise with her tongue. "So, you don't care if I invent stories in my mind?"

"I have no control over your imagination." He was a bit sick that he had sounded as if he was begging. He never begged nor did he trust openly as he trusted her, but she would be married to him in the future. Surely, he could trust the person he would share his life with. "You need to think intelligently. This issue is one of DNA mutations. I do not understand it fully myself and I do not know if we ever shall. I am in the early stages of this, as well. It would behoove you to remember that."

"It's like that, huh?" She sounded disappointed that it was not something fantastic. Something unworldly. Her shoulders slightly drooped.

"I do apologize if I disappoint your romping imagination."

"Umm."

"I can see your mind churning," Jareth said. His finger twirled in the air. "Perhaps I should dumbfound you more often. You are almost charming when you say nothing."

Elizabet's lips turned down in the corners. "You're the rudest person I've ever met."

"Quite possibly." Jareth grinned. He was glad they were back on bickering terms and steering away from his momentary lapse in self-control. "Although I thought calling you charming was anything but rude." He braced both hands behind him on the railing. "So, is this a yes? Will you help me?"

Elizabet surprised him by gazing up at the rafters instead of going into a full eye roll. "You're crazy."

"You are the one who claimed lunacy," he said. "I am just a bastard."

"Stop calling yourself that. Okay? It makes me think of small medieval orphans. Like a bad Charles Dickens story."

Jareth was in awe of the sincere injustice she felt of his lack of birthright. He wanted to tally how many times she incited joy. It was remarkable. He was halfway convinced he could marry her on that merit alone. He wanted to squeeze her in a fierce hug each time she became indignant over his birth. "Do you realize that you are the most vexing person, yet I find conversing with you to be wonderful?"

Her nose crinkled. "Does that mean I get another question? Being wonderful has to get me something."

"It does not. No." He shook his head. "And I did not say that *you* are wonderful, merely that conversing with you is pleasurable."

"I'll make a deal with you."

Jareth crossed his arms. "No more deals. I have reached my quota of agreements for the day and I am running out of time. I have a castle to tend."

"Which castle would that be?" She clasped her hands behind her back, rocked onto her toes, and tilted her head as she waited.

Jareth allowed the silence to stretch as he weighed his options. To give her enough information for her to search things out would save time. It would give her access to knowledge of him—at least as far as Wikipedia could provide. He had not intended to play games. He had come here willing to bare all; this was her idea.

"Dover," he answered. "As I said before, I'm the Duke of Dover. You must have missed that because you were too busy prying. It is near Kent."

"You're right," she said thoughtfully. "You did say that." She hummed meaningfully. "Medieval, England, and now a definite location." She ticked each clue off with her fingers. "Any siblings, Sir Jareth."

"Yes," he said easily. "One half-sister named Agatha. And no one calls me sir. My title supersedes the necessity."

"What year?"

"Thirteen twelve."

"You're so easy." She seemed pleased at that.

"I am tired," he admitted. He faced her with a serious expression. "Much like your farming equipment, but you are the reason of my exhaustion. I find you tiring. I may be in need of a nap when I return home."

"Poor you."

"Poverty is not a disadvantage of mine," he said. "Although Gabriel does tell me that it will be a gradual accruing—my wealth." He tilted his head. "I will have to sell off quite a few artifacts."

She counted off another finger. "My thanks, but you'd better stop talking. My memory isn't the best and I wanna be sure I stalk you correctly." She waved her hand. "You may go now. Off to your castle. I have digging to do. The next time I see you, I plan to be prepared."

Chapter 6

Beneath the castle walls of Dover, 1312

JARETH THREADED THE FINAL SUTURE that closed the incision. One of his stewards had been afflicted with gallstones and it was past time for surgery. He looked forward to the day he could incorporate laparoscopy into his procedures. If he were to do that now, he feared the people he trusted would break under the pressure. It was one thing to stand aside and watch your duke during an operation, and another to observe him perform it using computer aided medicine in the early century. Most of his staff were superstitious and their faith weak. Even the solar panels it would take to run the equipment would raise a suspicion of witchcraft. And the Church would love to burn the young Duke of Dover at the stake for heresy against the faith he loved. They had been lying in wait to find something to kill him for. Ironic thing was they would have their proof if only they spoke to the right sources and pried in the right places.

He had built an infirmary in the tunnels beneath the castle and sealed it off with industrial locks that could only be opened by combination. Gabriel had brought the medical equipment after he took nearly a year to track down a smuggler they could trust.

New Orleans was a hotbed for traffickers looking to stick it to the government. Medical institutions were also regulated, like the churches. Dr. Harrow Mills was bent on vengeance against the system. Luckily for Jareth, Harrow was a professor at Tulane Medical Center, and a surgeon. In one day he gained both a mentor and a smuggler.

"I like the new retractors," Jareth commented. The surgical mask he wore made it difficult to breathe and he usually refrained from speaking, but some things needed to be acknowledged. "Left handed. Both practical and smooth. *Gratias tibi ago.*"

"You're very welcome. I thought you would appreciate them. It was my pleasure to lift them from the university surgical suite. Those bastards can ask the government for new ones," Harrow responded. Jareth often switched to Latin when he was in surgery or when he was distracted; it was a good thing Harrow understood the language. Learning anatomy and medical terminology from him had been a breeze. Harrow peered over the glasses that were perched on the end of his nose. The neat line of sutures reflected in the lenses. "And the scrubs? How do you like those?"

Jareth stepped back from the sterile field and removed his gloves. "Nice. A bit breezy, but I suppose I will grow accustomed to lighter materials. Modern fabric is cheaply made. Not well done." He frowned down at the emblem over the left pocket. "Gabriel tells me that you have secured identification and documents for my entry into medical school. Can I hope that it will not be an American university?"

"Ha! Speaking of not well done." Harrow went back to swabbing the wound with an anti-infective solution before he removed the sterile drapes. "Gabriel is a snitch."

"Is the snitch correct or is he merely teasing me?"

"The snitch is correct. Harrow removed his gloves and then pushed his bifocal glasses up the bridge of his nose. "But I was planning a better delivery. You're now a proud twenty-year-old elite Oxford Medical student. First year—with great letters of recommendations, I should add."

"Brilliant," Jareth said. He rubbed the crick in the back of his neck. "Can I trust that we have sufficient funds to complete the entire education?"

"The crown sold to a museum for a hefty price. It's rather like selling your birthright, eh?" Jareth merely shrugged, so he plowed on. "Minh purchased the cottage we selected in Kent, as per your request. And Gabriel set up a trust and bank fund in your name at the Royal Bank."

"And yet, I am trapped here," Jareth said. He motioned to the drugged body lying between them on the gurney. He grinned. It was something he rarely did, but it was becoming common practice and he did not want to think why. "Or in South Louisiana until the storm." He faked a shudder. "Ghastly."

Harrow laughed. "You'll get used to it. The humidity and heat is bearable when you realize you have access to the best cuisine in the world."

Jareth shuddered for real. "Shellfish? I would rather eat my own liver."

"Liver is a delicacy."

Jareth pretended to gag, which made Harrow laugh again.

"I think you better focus on learning to be normal and forget that you are destined to be in a place you'd rather not be. Besides, it'll only be for a short time."

"That, unfortunately, is untrue." Jareth grabbed hold of the stretcher to help Harrow roll the patient into the recovery area. "It seems I am to be married to a native of the area."

"Interesting," Harrow said. He grabbed the blood pressure cuff and stethoscope from a wooden table as they passed and tossed them both on the patient's legs. "The girl they brought over to nurse you, I presume?"

Jareth nodded. He didn't meet Harrow's gaze as they strolled the patient down the wide mouth of the north tunnel.

"Still don't understand why they didn't come get me instead," Harrow muttered under his breath. He glanced at Jareth, who let himself remain remarkably stiff and deaf. "Did she patch you up well enough?"

"Quite," Jareth bit out.

They reached the recovery area and parked the gurney against the wall. Jareth reached for the stethoscope that hung on the stone wall.

"They were under direct order by me," Jareth said. He placed the tips of the stethoscope in his ears and bent over to listen to the patient's heart and lung sounds. It was necessary for him to clear the air between him and his mentor. He liked Harrow and did not want a misunderstanding to stand in the way of their friendship. "They brought the girl to me because it is the way of things, the way the future is heading." He masterfully passed the stethoscope between lung fields. "It is my understanding that I can be rather nasty in the future."

Harrow waited for Jareth to complete the assessment, and then passed him the blood pressure cuff when he reached for it. "A bloodthirsty duke like yourself? Who'd have thought?"

Jareth ignored the comment. In fact, he chose that moment to remain silent for the duration of the recovery. It was a bit awkward because Harrow continued to attempt conversation. But Jareth was accustomed to being odd. He kept his tongue still. Somewhere deep in his heart he felt it was what he needed to do. Besides, what was the logical argument? Harrow had been only partially joking. His ability to slay opponents was legendary. It embarrassed him. He did not like docile people like Harrow to see him as anything but harmless and capable of healing.

Harrow eventually broke the silence. "Whatever will you do with Catherine?"

Jareth hid his eyes by gazing down at the patient. "I have never agreed to any betrothal," Jareth snapped. His hand gripped the gurney to the point his knuckles blanched. He did not like when his emotions switched so quickly, but this topic was a sure way to get him upset every time it was brought up. It had been at least six months since he heard Catherine's name spoken, yet it still hit a raw nerve. He had almost forgotten about her and their proposed betrothal. "Whatever was decided was decided without my consent."

"That won't hold up in royal court."

"I do not care what holds up in royal court. They can have my title and lands if they must. I will not marry Catherine of Torquay."

"Then you'd better get yourself hitched before they catch you with your pants down."

Jareth stood to his full six feet, six inches. He leveled a killer stare at Harrow. "I beg your pardon, good sir."

Harrow gave a short laugh. "Your *proverbial* pants, I should have said. You're so good with slang that I forget you don't know it all." He took off his glasses and pointed them at Jareth. "You need to be rid of that supposed betrothal if you plan to pursue this other girl."

"She is not the other girl," Jareth said. He relaxed, reached up, and idly massaged his neck. Some of his tension left him immediately as the subject changed from Catherine to Elizabet. "She is *the* girl. The one and only if I can ever figure out why I chose her."

"Wow!" Harrow's eyes popped wide with the single mocking word. "You've never said anything like that before. You're actually considering this girl as your future duchess? She's from Louisiana, man. She'll be like a fish out of water. She won't fit in. Even the serfs will know."

"She is irritating, short, and bossy."

"And she probably eats shellfish by the dozen," Harrow added. "I know how you love your bottom feeders." Jareth pretended to gag. "Most likely she's crude." Jareth shrugged. "And not as smart as you, and probably the lowest station known to mankind." Harrow used the hem of his scrub top to wipe the lens of his glasses. His head tipped to the side. "But she saved your life. There is that."

"Yes." His fingers slowed as he squeezed the stiff muscles of his shoulder and neck. "There is that." He imagined his expression waxed whimsical; he was nauseated just imagining it. It was a good thing there were no mirrors in the recovery area. "She has remarkable hands."

"Ummm," Harrow hummed. He paused in cleaning the lens and lifted his gaze. Jareth met his eyes in a look he imagined said, *Did I say that? Out loud?*

"I will go to the autoclave and be sure Percival understands the new system," Jareth said—almost as swiftly as he fled the room—leaving Harrow grinning after him.

"ART THOU TIRED, MY LORD?" Catherine of Torquay asked in eloquent French. Her speech flowed from her tongue with distinct proper form—as should any lady of her station.

She thought she loved the man before her. Certainly, she loved the way he looked—his commanding presence when he entered a room, the way his body moved with elegant grace. He resembled his Scottish mother, which made him dark when Englishmen were drably fair. All other focus was swallowed when he opened his gorgeous full mouth to speak. Jareth Tremaine was the stuff of legends. Odes and songs had been written by squires and maidens concerning his great beauty. He was strong, just, and currently popular due to his involvement with the Church. And he was of possible royal bloodline. Anyone tied to him would have great status—both monetary and social.

Catherine planned to marry him for all of those reasons. The Bastard Duke was her betrothed. She had to suppress the urge to squeal with glee as she gazed at him from across the room. He was majestic and altogether beautiful when he brooded.

"Only tired of keeping company with you, my lady." Jareth spoke in English simply to irritate her.

"How can one so great of beauty be so cruel?" Catherine pouted in the way of her mother when she wanted her way. She toyed with the edge of her veil that covered the crown of her head to get his attention. It angered her that he continued to stare out the window as he answered. His brooding, although magnificent, was aimed in a direction that was unappealing.

They should be out in the fresh air, enjoying the tourney taking place on the grounds of Dover Castle. It was why she was here—to watch her favorite knight perform and win the prize. Jareth commonly took championship of tourneys. It was widely known that he was best skilled with sword. This was his home, his castle and still he had not taken the field. Not for jousting nor blade games. He had not even gone to the lists to practice with his men, something that was unheard of during a tourney of this magnitude.

Instead, he was holed up in his solar absorbed in documents belonging to an old scholar Catherine personally hated. John Wycliffe would get Jareth into trouble. His time could not be filled with Church issues. It needed to be occupied with wedding plans, and quite frankly—her.

"Men do not aspire to be beautiful. We want to be known for our vigor and sensibility. Even being called bloodthirsty is better than being referred to as beautiful." She understood the English language, but chose not to use it. It was unrefined, and beneath her to speak such a flat language. He used it to make her go away.

Catherine made her laugh sound musical. She did not notice the scowl that crossed Jareth's face for she was too busy twisting her hands to match the laughter she had practiced. It took great skill to be a lady in waiting. "Why must thou speak strangely, my lord? I find it tiresome to follow. You know only paupers and the unrefined use the English language."

"Then leave, and listen no more to my chosen language." Jareth turned before she could hide the frown that betrayed her feigned laughter. "As I said, I grow tired of keeping your company." He bowed at the waist. "Good morrow to you."

"Thou art cruel, your majesty." Her body trembled with anger under her many layers of clothing and veils. How dare Jareth dismiss her! She would have an audience with him or she would summon her father and the king—not in that order.

"I can be crueler still, Catherine. Would you like to try? Give it a go? I assure you, the Bastard Duke is not just a name they call me beyond my ears' reach."

Catherine glanced to her maid who was keeping chaperone for them. If Sara was to sew any faster, she would prick her fingers with the darning needle. "Sara, I bid thou leave."

"No," Jareth said. He stepped from the dark shadow and into the glow of the candlelight, and pointed at Sara. "Nay," he corrected, for the sake of the servant. He motioned for her to stay seated when she went to rise. "Sara stays where she is. You will not catch me unaware. I will not be bullied into marrying you."

"*Bullied?* What orgin—" There was not even a word in French to match this. She was angry that she had to imitate the vile language he spoke. Her fingers snapped as she searched for something to say to keep him at bay . . . and under her thumb.

The large doors to the solar burst open, and Gabriel strode into the room. The clamor had Catherine and Sara jumping. He thrust his hat under his arm, his jaw set as he stared at Catherine.

"Your father is looking for you," he announced in Norman French. "If you don't make haste, you will be left to Jareth's charity." He glanced at Jareth and something of a smile tugged at the corner of his mouth—so he switched to English. "I've arrived just in time. As usual."

Catherine hopped to her feet and grabbed Sara's sleeve. "I shall have you both summoned to the king." She glanced over her shoulder at Jareth as she cut a wide swath around Gabriel and bustled toward the door. He wanted to crow that the aversion to his person had worked its charm yet again. For some reason, the sight of him seemed to cause her great unrest. She could not stand to be in the same room with him and he did not know why, but neither did he care. "My father shall hear of this."

"See that he does," Gabriel said. He stepped forward and caused her to move faster out the door.

Once she was gone, Jareth smiled at Gabriel and stepped forward into the solar. He put his hand out for a handshake. "It's good to see you, my friend."

"And not a minute to spare." Gabriel shut the wide, heavy doors. The outraged voices in high female falsetto were mercifully drowned by the thick wood. He shook Jareth's hand. "You really should marry quickly so you can be rid of that vulgar girl. Saving you is getting old. Besides, my French is amateur at best."

"She did not even bother to question," Jareth said. He seemed to find it hard to speak, he was smiling so much. "I find it very gratifying to make fools of the already foolish. It pleases me. And your French is more than acceptable." He indicated the length of the Gabriel's attire, particularly the hat. "I must say you are getting better at mixing modern attire with medieval clothing. I am almost convinced that you belong here."

"We both know that I don't belong here," Gabriel muttered. Jareth's face fell. "I'm not here to save your hide. That was merely a bonus." He grinned, and hoped it took the sting out of barreling onto the reason he was here. "Things are becoming jumbled and not as accurate. I have orders to desist visitation. The future is uncertain. Everything is changing. We're concerned that if we continue to jump time, things will be lost."

"Is this your final visit, then?" Jareth asked as he turned away and walked to the window he had abandoned. He would not look Gabriel in the eye. "I have come to enjoy our dealings; I counted on your visits to keep me on course. I do not know how I will fare not having a glance into the future. Those interactions will be sorely missed, not only for the information gained, but also for the friendship."

"I will be available until the storm." Gabriel said. Jareth turned to face him. They stood before the open window that overlooked the English Channel. The white cliffs gleamed under a full moon. The view mesmerized Gabriel as if he were seeing it for the first time. "That way Jeremy is safe and secure." His gaze left the open window and turned to Jareth. "You agree that you will need guidance in the course of the next few weeks."

Jareth sighed and shook his head. "It never gets old how you speak of me—to me—about me." His shoulders dropped "How will I know when the storm comes? I assume it is near. I have watched carefully the times we are in, both past and future."

"Elizabet will have that information. I trust you have the stones and you have made first contact with her?" Jareth nodded, his expression becoming vacant as if his mind was suddenly with the one they spoke of. Gabriel knew that look. He had seen it just an hour before on the same face that had barely aged in eight years. "And—?"

"And what?" Jareth asked, annoyance in his tone.

"Did she mention the approaching storm?"

"No." Jareth turned and shouldered the window frame, looking out over the moorings of the cliffs. "We did not speak of the storm. I did not get that far. I though it unwise. But we did speak of Jeremy."

"Jeremy is friends with her young cousin. The duchess is very protective of anyone close with members of her family."

Jareth glanced over his shoulder. "She did not mention a cousin. I only heard of a father and grandmother." He frowned; his eyes narrowed. "I forget that you know her—well."

"She is the wife of my best friend." Gabriel stressed the word best and ignored the jealousy in Jareth's voice. "The duchess is the gateway to your hard heart. I would be stupid not to take advantage of the fact she has you at her beck and call."

"That easy, am I?" Jareth asked dryly.

Gabriel laughed. "Only with her. With the rest of us, you remain an unyielding bastard." Jareth had no response other than a slight lift to his right shoulder. "How's the romance going, by the way? Are you totally smitten yet?"

Jareth grimaced and looked away. He leaned forward and gripped the window frame to bear his weight. The stance appeared as if he were readying to leap from the window. "To say that someone is smitten is equivalent to someone telling me I have gone daft."

"You're over thinking again, Jareth." Gabriel kept his voice low because he was embarrassed. Even in present time, he and Jareth did not sit around speaking of their feelings, and it seemed this was where their conversation was headed. He had merely asked to see where they were on the timeline. "I shouldn't speak of it, but I just left both of you in wedded bliss. Makes me a little sick, actually. Your life is so freaking perfect, it makes Hallmark look like a horror film."

Jareth pushed away from the window and turned to lean his back against the wall. "She is plain and short." He used his hand to show where the top of her head met the lower part of his chest. "I would have to stand in a hole to kiss her."

"Ah, but you have thought of kissing her," Gabriel said with a grin.

Jareth flung his arms out akimbo. "She is loud and a bit obnoxious."

Gabriel choked. He didn't know what to say. "Why do you want to do this?" He knew what Jareth was doing; he was counting the cost. It was the way of things in Jareth's mind. If he could make sense of something, then it was good. However, in this case, it was absurd that Jareth was making a case against his future bride.

"She is poor and has been abandoned by her father. What is wrong with her that even a parent flees?"

"The same could be said of yourself, your grace." Gabriel's eyebrows rose as Jareth bristled with the set down. "Her mother died when she was young. Can you honestly fault her height or the manner in which she was raised? You should consider it fortunate that she isn't Catholic. She's from South Louisiana, where nearly everybody's Catholic. It's like being French in the fifteenth century; it would be social suicide. What a chore that would be if you had to convert her *and* fall in love." Jareth's jaw stiffened as he turned away with a growl. "Ah," Gabriel grinned. "There is the Jareth I know and love."

"Check mate," Jareth replied.

"Point. Match. I win." Gabriel leaned his shoulder against the wall. He wanted to hug himself for his brilliance. "I mention Catholicism and finally you shut up. Some things never change." He waved his hand in the air. "But really, stop all of this doubt. Admit that you like the girl and move on. It'll save time."

Jareth smirked with half his mouth. "She mocks me by questioning my motives and wanting to play games when I was more than willing to provide her with answers." He flipped his hand in the air. "Except about Jeremy and you know she wants to know about him. Pries about him. If I tell her all there is, I may lose her. How can anyone be expected to believe something like that is possible?" He folded his arms over his chest again. "What say you?"

"Elizabet is braver than you give her credit for. You forget that she knows all about Jeremy." He thumbed over his shoulder. "I just left your house. He's there, babysitting your children. Does that sound like a woman who is going to freak when she discovers her fave cousin's friend is a living host for a hurricane?" He shrugged. "And she's your wife. You do know what that means—don't you? You did hear me mention children. Plural."

"Of course, I know the meaning of marriage." His biceps bowed as he gripped his arms . . . probably in an effort not to punch Gabriel. "I understand what the institution entails."

"Have you spoken to her about the *institution of marriage?*" Gabriel let his face show how appalled he was. "That will endear her to you, I'm sure. Sometimes it amazes me how different you are. And what I mean is, the person you are here and the man you are there. The one I just left was bouncing a baby on his hip and giving a toddler a pony ride on his back as he ordered me about." Gabriel shook his head. "You just delivered your own son last week because you wouldn't trust anyone else with your family and you hate obstetrics. You're a surgeon, not an obstetrician. I'm getting confused. You look like him, but use insults as a weapon."

"I was merely stating that I understand what the institution of marriage entails. You must not continue to drop these small facts of my future. I am beginning to see why your time here with me is becoming limited. You cause me great upset." Jareth's chin lifted a notch. "Therefore, let us get on with the briefing. How am I to approach Elizabet about the storm?"

Gabriel frowned. He hated when Jareth took that 'I'm your lord and master' tone of voice. "You ask her," he said pointedly, just to agitate Jareth. "Elizabet is not a girl who caves to being wooed or manipulated. Although a little wooing might go a long way, even with her. Have you tried to at least pretend you have a romantic bone in your body?"

"I shall travel to her home at first light of the morrow," Jareth said. His hand sliced the air. "No wooing. No romance. She knows not to expect it of me."

Gabriel knew when he was being dismissed. He yanked the time band from his wrist and tossed it open without preamble. "Cheeky jerk you are becoming, your grace. Please, hurry and grow up a little. I like the lovesick swain back home more than who I'm seeing today. I'm starting to hate you a little, myself." He bowed mockingly as the portal expanded with light behind him. It contracted slightly as it fully opened to receive its traveler. "A word of advice. Get rid of that other girl—Catherine. Posthaste. While I may not have the details, I do know that when she is spoken of by the duchess, it isn't favorable. She does something to the two of you that causes her to be banished from England."

Jareth sneered. "Capital news. I look forward to being the one who has her banished."

Chapter 7

Gueydan, Louisiana. Present Day.

JEREMY CAMERON WAS CONSIDERED WEIRD. Those who were acquainted with him thought he was mildly retarded when truthfully, he was an undiagnosed autistic. Asperger's Syndrome ran in the Cameron family. It was not common knowledge, but Elizabet knew the family on a personal level. They were her pastors, and she was a member of the choir. She had not shared that with Jareth because she was entitled to yet another secret of her own.

She observed as Jeremy led the congregation in the call to worship. Wednesday services were small and intimate, which was typical of a Presbyterian service. There was nothing, however, typical about Jeremy. He was a brilliant pianist. Even Catholics and people who were terrified of regulated religion buckers came to hear him play. It was his singular passion—music. As with most Asperger kids, his mind tended to primarily, obsessively, cling to a few narrow topics. His mother, Brenda, removed him from school when he was bullied and beaten, and now he was homeschooled because of his nature.

Over the years, he became a curiosity. He was not often seen outside of church service, and if one ran into him, they received few words. But when he was behind an instrument, it was evident he lost all insecurities. He wove a web with music that was tangible. One felt the passion he infused into the music.

Tonight, Elizabet was more spectator than member. Although what she was looking for was beyond her. Unless Jareth was seeking a new musician at church, he would be disappointed. Jeremy was boring when he was not singing or playing an instrument.

She sat in the last row, her eyes glued to the back of Jeremy's head. Watching nothing and everything at the same time, she was compelled to do whatever Jareth asked like some blind, love-struck ninny. Which was ridiculous, because Jeremy barely moved while Pastor Jed, Jeremy's father, gave the sermon—what there was of a sermon. There was a hurricane churning in the Gulf of Mexico, so his preaching naturally evolved into a local weather report.

Frankly, she was sick of hearing about it. Attending church was no different than visiting the local grocery store, which was precisely where she went after service. Benoit's Grocery was owned by her mother's twin sister, Gwen. It was a hub for information and where Jeremy could generally be found, because that was where Beau usually was. Beau was her first cousin and her best friend. Sad that a nine-year-old was her closest confident, but the truth was brutal.

Benoit's Grocery was not just a store and meeting place for collecting information. It was part Cajun restaurant, part drive-thru cigarette and liquor shop. Jeremy had painted a mural on the side of the tin building last summer, depicting a caricature of a crawfish sitting in a hot tub which was actually a steaming pot of boiling water. The building was old, and attached to it was the rickety, tin living quarters of the Benoit family.

"Is that a new piano?" Elizabet asked Jeremy. It looked the same, but sounded different. "Newly tuned, maybe?" Jeremy did not answer. "Okay. Whatever." She always felt awkward talking to Jeremy. It was mostly a one-way conversation. She tilted her Chocolate Soldier bottle in his direction in a salute before taking a long sip. She looked at him over the bottle as she drank, and waited for him to speak . . . or blink—anything. His eyes never left the untouched soda can directly in front of him on the red and white checked tablecloth.

Beau spun a bottle cap across the table. Flicked it as though she was skimming a rock across water. The top flew over the table and Frisbeed halfway across the room and onto an adjacent table. "I wish I could've been there."

"Then tell your parents to go blow," Elizabet said, and placed her drink on the table. She did not stop watching Jeremy. His eyes briefly flickered to where Beau's dad was perched on a stool behind the register. "I can take you on Sunday, but you have to ask them yourself. I'm not fighting that battle for you."

Beau's gaze followed the same path Jeremy's had taken. "Well, I guess I won't be going either." She stuck her tongue out at Elizabet.

"We should go," Jeremy said. He stood at the same time Elizabet opened her mouth to scold Beau. The backs of his knees hit the seat of his chair and it tipped over. Beau scrambled to right it before it hit the floor. "Your dad is listening." He dropped his voice, but his eyes remained focused on the can of soda as if it was his attentive audience.

Elizabet snorted and glanced at her uncle. She was frazzled from Jeremy's sudden movement and how fast Beau covered it up, but made herself slowly sip her drink. "Then we should talk a little louder. He's not a regulator. He can't dictate where we go to church." She twisted her lips before she took another sip of pop and spoke around the bottle. "He can't dictate nothing."

"You're going to get her in trouble," Jeremy said. He looked down on Elizabet. His black hair partially hid blue eyes, and those eyes were wide—threatening. "So shut up already."

It was quite possibly the boldest thing Elizabet had ever heard him say, which was why it plagued her throughout the ride home. He had looked directly at her and spoken clearly. She knew that Beau and Jeremy were close, but had never noticed the protectiveness he extended.

Beau was *her* closest friend and she was shocked that she could overlook something that crucial. It went without saying that she did not like being in competition with a boy who could barely string along a sentence unless it was a musical lyric. Jeremy obviously was as passionate about keeping Beau safe from her crazy family as he was about music.

She thought on this until the headlights of the farm truck caught on a figure standing against the barn when she turned into the driveway. He was dressed differently, but that stance could only belong to one person.

The Duke of Dover had returned.

JARETH DID NOT CARE FOR that material known as denim, but Gabriel assured him that the uncomfortable pants were acceptable for the time period he was traveling to. He referred to his new attire as a uniform he could don each time he hopped into a wormhole. The light colored denim and plain white cotton shirt were nothing compared to the boots, though. They were as stiff as a pair of silver gamblets. Definitely not made by Hoby. At least being overdressed was not a factor. Elizabet was wearing much the same. It would take time to become accustomed to women's tendencies to dress like men.

"I wondered when you were gonna pop up again," Elizabet said. She slammed the truck door and shoved the keys into the front pocket of her jeans. "How long have you been here?" She came around the truck and crossed her arms before her.

"Long enough to know you have a bandit problem." He pointed to the window under the porch eve. The lights were on and the curtains open. She could make the outline of her grandmother in a recliner watching the barn.

"Bandit?" She furrowed her brow.

Jareth made like he was wearing a mask, a grin spreading on his face. "Cute, furry creatures."

"Ah!" Elizabet nodded, understanding the sign language. "Coons. Yeah, they wreak havoc on the crawfish traps and feed supplies." She glanced at the barn. "Did you just watch them tear things up? You stood here and did nothing while they robbed me blind?"

Jareth ducked his head and swiped at his left ear as mosquitos swarmed. "I have read that in this time, people are protective of animals." He swiped at his other ear. "I did not want to offend."

"True," Elizabet replied. "But Grandma is old school. She shoots them from the porch. You're lucky the Saints are playing tonight, otherwise a stray bullet . . ." She looked meaningfully at him.

Jareth's hand paused above his ear.

A laugh bubbled up and out of Elizabet's mouth. "Nah, the old lady's pretty good with a rifle. She'd only hit you if she was aiming for you." She uncrossed her arms to shove her hands into her back pockets.

"I suppose now would be the time to let you know I have a blade on my person," Jareth said. His hair was a mess from his attempts at ridding the air of the flying pests and for the first time he looked his age. He was rumpled and dressed down. And adorable.

"Thanks for the warning." She frowned irritably at her prior thoughts. He would assume she was scowling at him for merely existing. It needed to stay that way. Only a few days had passed since he visited and she had not expected him to return so quickly. "What brings you back so soon?"

"I have questions." He pushed away from the post, sliced his hand next to his ear, and continued to frown at the swarm bent on sucking his blood.

Elizabet nodded. It made sense that he would be back for more information. Time traveling dukes must have serious business. "And I have answers, for a change. Let's go up to the house. I'm sure Grandma spotted us and is wondering who you are. You're lucky she didn't take a shot at you, coons or not, with you hiding behind the post like that."

Jareth looked over his shoulder at the post he had just vacated. "I was not hiding."

"Not like you could anyway," she said. He looked back at her. She smirked. He seemed out of sorts and she liked him that way. He was flushed, and annoyed over small creatures she was quite accustomed to. "You've filled out since your injury. Every time I see you, I swear you get bigger."

"And you grow shorter."

"Oh!" she exclaimed. She put her hands on her hips, aggravated that he brought that up. The boots she wore gave her a two-and-a-half-inch advantage she did not normally have. "Big bad wolf gonna blow my house down?" Her lips turned down in the corners. "I wondered how long you would play nice." She shook her head and let her disgust show in her expression. "I should've known."

"What?" She'd managed to baffle him.

"I'm short. I can't help it."

"What?"

His cute, bewildered face gave him away. She sighed. She could not even pick at him to offend him. "It's the wolf thing that has you fixated—not that you insulted me?" He still looked confused. "Never mind." She winged her arm toward him and began to walk. She wanted to punch him in the arm as she passed, but she refrained.

"You insulted me first. I have no reason to hide, and I most certainly do not lurk about."

"Boo-hoo!" she said. He was not following; she turned to look back, and motioned with her hand. "Come on. Grandma with a gun—staring at us. Granddaughter with strange man in driveway. Hello?"

He took a few steps and she continued walking toward the house. She refused to watch the lazy lope in which he strode. When she was a child, she had been fascinated with panthers. That was what came to mind as she watched him move. He was calculated and loose at the same time, alert and attentive, but seeming about to pounce. It peeved her to admit he was attractive. To him, she was nothing but a means to an end. A spy. Someone who could give him the information he needed for his 'host.' They were friends. Period. She needed to become accustomed to the idea that he only wanted one thing, and that was what she could do for him and his host. The fact she was drawn to him must remain a secret

"It wasn't an insult," Elizabet said. "What I meant was that you look better—healthier. I didn't mean you were a creeper or anything. It came out wrong." She glanced back, much to her detriment. "What I meant was that you don't look like the angel of death is hovering over you anymore." Contrary, actually; he looked like a teenage dream. Something unreal and frightfully beautiful at the same time. She rolled her eyes in the darkness, thankful that her thoughts were not hooked to a microphone.

"I have you to thank for that."

Elizabet stopped and turned to him. "Did you just thank me?"

He was walking with his gaze lowered and nearly slammed into her. Elizabet stepped back quickly to avoid the crash. "I believe I did," he said. "And I apologize if mentioning your height causes you discomfort. Forgive me."

She narrowed her eyes. "I forgive you."

"Thank you."

"Impressive. You said that twice in one day." She turned back and proceeded to walk toward the house again. "So, what should I tell my grandma about you?"

"The truth," he said, and paused before he followed. "But only what is necessary."

"Hey, Grandma," Elizabet mocked. "This is Jareth, the Duke of Dover. He just stopped by, passing through our century through a wormhole, and he's asking questions about a young boy in the area.

Yeah. Sounds perf. Next idea. I don't want to be locked away in nut house just because you've got a conscience."

"Just Jareth will do," Jareth said. "You may tell her that I am new to the Presbyterian congregation. A traveling minister, if you will."

"Honestly, you're brilliant. Grandma is Catholic. She'll never step foot in a Pres church." She kicked at a rock that was too large to ignore. "And actually, I just left there. Spied on Jeremy. Proud of me?"

"That's my girl," he murmured. There was a twinge of awe in his voice.

Elizabet stumbled over her own feet, but righted before she made a twit out of herself. She refused to look back, terrified that he would be laughing at her. "Well, you owe me, because tonight wasn't an average service. It was more one weather announcement after another." She shook her head and frowned. "Who's bringing the taco dip and soda for the evacuation? I almost fell asleep. It was awful."

"Evacuation?"

"There is a mega storm in the Gulf of Mexico, headed straight this way. It's a hurricane. Ever heard of that sort of thing?"

"Yes."

She began walking again, motioning with her hand to nothing in particular as she spoke. "It happens all the time around here. We prepare for the worst and sometimes it happens. Other times—nothing. Storms have gotten worse over the past few years. They happen more often and earlier in the summer season, but we don't have the special occurrences like those hyper tsunamis and monsoons. Just hurricanes. Thank God for small favors."

"How long have these special occurrences been in existence?" he asked.

"A while. Years. I remember the first mega hurricane. My mom was already sick by then. We went to Dad's office, spent the night while the storm blew through. It was horrible. I can't stand hurricanes. You can't hide from them." She made a shivering motion. "Nasty things. We haven't stayed since. We go up to North Louisiana and stay with Dad's family. They own a horse breeding ranch. It's big and safe. Far enough away, and most of the time, the storms turn before they reach us." She hated the way her stomach did a somersault when she glanced at him over her shoulder. He needed to stay medieval. It was easier to ignore that he was gorgeous when he was wearing a tunic. "This will cost you, you know? I'm racking up the points. You'll owe me."

"I have noted that you mentioned your mother," Jareth said. He continued speaking even though she kept walking. "And I want to hear more of her, but after we speak of the necessary. I am not opposed to answering your questions. I have some as well."

"You don't have to be nice to get me to talk. I've already decided to help you. I don't go back on my word."

"It is not kindness that prompts me. I am curious." Jareth quieted as they reached the porch and together ascended the three small steps. The porch was narrow but long. It spanned the width of the wooden house that was as old as her grandma.

"I think it might be best if we go inside," Elizabet suggested, but stopped and turned to him with a questioning expression. She smiled and tilted her head. "You're different. And it's not just the clothes. There is something new about you."

"I assure you, it is the clothing. It is irritating." He shifted to show his discomfort under her scrutiny. There was something in her gaze that he had seen before on another's face. He was accustomed to the perusal of ladies and he recognized it easily enough. He motioned to the screen door. "Invite me into your home. I want to meet your grandmother."

Elizabet's eyes traveled the length of him. "Where is your weapon?"

His eyes widened. "I assure you, it is for your protection as well as my own." Jareth said. He reached down and lifted the hem of his left pants leg. The handle to a bowie knife peeked out above his leather boot.

"Just like knowing what I'm up against."

"You are not up against anything," he assured her, and shook his pants into place. He reached for the door handle. "I would never hurt you. In any way."

She pursed her lips and made a *harrumph* noise. "You say that like you mean it."

"I do." He twisted the knob and opened the door a fraction. "Is it so difficult to believe I am not the abductor you thought me to be?"

Elizabet laughed. "That's cute." She wagged her finger at him.

"You remembered."

"It is rather hard to forget being accused of kidnapping."

"Well, just remember that Grandma thought I was a missing person, so let's keep this as a private joke." She mimed locking her lips closed and then jerked the door until he released it. She swung it wider and stepped ahead of him. "Stay right behind me. I'll not be responsible if she talks your ears off."

Jareth remained relatively silent, though polite, during introductions and she attempted to view the scene through the eyes of a stranger. It would not take him long to understand the family dynamics. Grandma was an alcoholic, who was currently intoxicated. An oxygen tank leaned against the wall in the corner, and the ashtray was full of cigarette butts. Not that he needed to see an ashtray. The lingering odor and stained walls told the complete story.

"Who's your parents?" Grandma asked as she dug between the cushion and arm of the chair for the remote control to the television. The woman was large with a pendulous belly. Her worn calico print house dress was stained on the right breast and from where Jareth was standing, he was sure to spot the food crumbs pooling in the area of her lap. She found the remote and muted the television. It was apparent that she was not happy with the interruption of the football game and news she was viewing in a split screen.

"He's not from around here," Elizabet said quickly.

"My parents . . ." Jareth said at the same time. He looked at Elizabet. She flushed and glanced away. "I have been on my own for quite a while. I am studying medicine at the University of New Orleans. I was invited this evening by the Camerons to give an exposition on the Book of Solomon for the local Presbyterian congregation. I am an expert in that particular book of the Bible."

"Never heard of it," Grandma said, looking unimpressed. Her legs were covered with a Saint's blanket. Her eyes tapered. "You aren't from around here. You talk funny."

"He's from England, Grandma."

"I am British born and raised," Jareth said.

"Umm," Grandma hummed. She fumbled with the remote, pressed the mute button so the sound resumed—and loudly.

They were dismissed. Elizabet smiled pitifully at him and jerked her chin toward the hallway.

"It was a pleasure." Jareth bowed.

Grandma frowned. "Umm," she repeated.

"We can talk privately in my room." Elizabet headed for a single long hallway. She motioned him along with the sweep of her arm. The house was narrow and efficient. It was old and smelled of fried food, most likely seafood-shellfish and bottom feeders. The medley of smells was nauseating; a mixture of stale cigarette smoke and various food odors.

"Do you think that is wise?" Jareth asked. He followed her anyway; the volume of the television had risen to an obnoxious level.

Elizabet kept walking and did not look back. She motioned again with her hand for him to follow, flapping it slightly over her head; annoyed now. "We're not going to roll around in the bed if that's what you're crying about. I have chairs."

"It is inappropriate." Jareth frowned and shook his head. "I will not compromise who I am for the sake of being modern. There are some things that are not done."

Elizabet stopped, braced her hands on the narrow walls of the hallway and peeked under her left arm. "You do understand that Grandma will be able to hear everything we say."

Jareth's right eyebrow arched upward. "I highly doubt she can hear her own breathing over the television, and that says volumes."

Elizabet let out an exasperated breath. "It's here, the porch, or the kitchen." She marched onward up the hallway, and paused before her bedroom door. "The porch—we'll get eaten by mosquitoes. The kitchen—we won't be able to hear over the Weather Channel and the Saint's game. Here . . ." She reached for the door knob. ". . . We'll have peace and quiet." She made a face. "Come on; we'll leave the door open." The door hit the opposite wall with a resounding thump as if to emphasize her point that it would stay open.

"No."

"Look," Elizabet said with a huff. "I seem to remember being locked away—alone—with you for days on end."

"Shhh," Jareth said as he stepped forward. He glanced back and she peered behind him at Grandma, who was on the edge of her recliner reaching for the can of beer on the side table.

"If we leave the door open, the inside of the room will still be visible."

"All right. All right. Agreed. The door stays open."

She rolled her eyes. "You're so bossy. Honestly, you act as if I'm about to jump you. You must be quite the catch back where you come from."

Jareth concluded the remaining three steps in long strides. "It would be an honor bestowed onto a maiden to be offered my suit."

Elizabet's lips slid to one side in a smirk. "Poor maidens. I bet you just melt hearts wherever you go. Good thing I'm no maiden, so that makes me, like, immune to your charms."

Jareth mirrored her smirked expression as he brought his body almost flush against hers. She tilted her face upward and tried not be shocked or awed by his proximity and boldness. A mere inch separated their bodies. Heat radiating from him, and he smelled of Dover, a distinct citrusy smell mixed with a spray of the sea.

"How very clever of you to point out that you are not a maiden. In fact, you are equivalent to a serf. Peasant. If we were to be introduced, the *king* would have me shun you—publically. I am, after all, a duke."

Heat crept up over Elizabet's face. She kept eye contact with him for as long as she could and then lowered her gaze to the floor. Her mind churned for something malicious to say.

"Forgive me," he begged. His words were rushed as he exhaled in a whoosh.

Her head jerked up and she gazed at him; her top lip quivered as she fought to keep a smirk in place.

"All I do is forgive you," Elizabet said. Her face felt as though she'd been working in the fields mid-summer. She blew a piece of her hair that fell onto her face. "You have no idea . . ."

"Hush," he pleaded, and then his fingertips were over her mouth. The contact jolted her, and she took a step back. The back of her head hit the door frame.

"Don't touch me!" She gripped the door frame behind her with both hands. The movement brought her heaving chest forward as she forced deep breaths to remain calm.

Jareth stared at the hand that had touched her and then regarded her with a puzzled expression.

"Keep your hands to yourself," she warned. She sidestepped to fully enter the bedroom, and narrowed her eyes when he looked down at his hand again. "I get that you are royalty and I'm beneath you. I. Get. It. You don't have to rub my face in it." She shifted her weight to one side. "I'm helping you, so please, don't get all snooty on me and remind me that I'm nothing, when I'm all you've got right now."

Jareth said nothing. Instead, after they stared at each other for precisely one minute, he walked into the room, grabbed a chair, carried it to the open doorway and placed it there.

Elizabet kept a stiff stance, even as he walked around her, and watched him position his perch in the doorway. She had conflicting emotions. Part of her was immensely relieved that he did not have the chance to bring up the problem of Grandma. The other part was, well, a mixture of aggravation and embarrassment. He was being a jerk and she didn't understand how he could go from being nice to telling her she was basically dirt. "Aren't you going to say anything?"

Jareth brushed off the seat of the folding chair. Lint and bread crumbs fell to the floor. He stood for a beat, made eye contact with her, and then sat, legs slightly bent, his hands resting on his knees. "You are right. I treated you badly and I am sorry."

"That's it?" she asked. People did not drop that kind of innuendo and merely say, 'sorry, my bad.' This required a foot washing service with a possible public declaration.

Jareth turned his palms upward in a questioning pose, and then returned to cover his knees. He did not seem to know what to say. "That is all, yes. There are no words that can make up for what I said. It was not well done of me."

"Well . . ." she drawled, though she wasn't yet convinced. " . . . If you're really sorry."

Jareth leaned forward and dropped his head into his hands, resting his elbows on his knees. "I am extremely repentant." He grabbed a handful of his hair. "Why do you vex me so?" He looked up, and his hands fell away. "I do not understand. Why is it you cause my pride to flair? You are only a girl."

Elizabet rubbed both palms down the fronts of her thighs, drying them on the denim. She allowed her expression to turn cynical. "Is that what you say to all the girls you apologize to?"

"No, no, no," Jareth said, shaking his head. He straightened, his hair disheveled, and struck the chair back with such force that it slid back an inch toward the hallway. "I am mucking things up again." He frowned, and lifted his gaze to the ceiling. His lips moved silently for a beat before he spoke again. It looked distinctly as if he mouthed *Here I go*. "What I want to say is that I like you."

Elizabet had been reaching for a chair. She paused and gaped at him. "You *like* me?"

He nodded and closed his eyes on a sigh that almost seemed exasperated. "Very much, I am afraid."

"Oh," she said, and grasped the back of the chair to drag it next to his. "When did you come to that conclusion? Before or after you called me a serf?"

"I liked you the first time I heard your voice."

"Oh," she repeated, but this time it was unfeigned. He had surprised her.

"It is a lovely memory," he admitted. "No one had ever shown such a kindness to me as you did. I shall never forget what you have done for me. I owe you my life."

"Well," she said as she sat slowly, keeping her eyes on him. "That is very—"

"Sweet," Jareth offered dryly, his lips bending. He muttered something under his breath and shook his head.

"I guess you could say that," Elizabet agreed.

"Please, forgive me," he repeated.

"Forgiven for the hundredth time today," she said with a wave of her hand as she crossed her legs. She gave him a pointed look. "Mostly, I forgive you for being a jerk. Don't remind me that I'm gum beneath your shoe. I don't like it."

Chapter 8

JARETH GLANCED AROUND THE ROOM. "Gabriel informed me that time travel was emotional. He said that I would find it troublesome." He rolled his shoulders, leaned forward and laced his fingers together, his elbows on his knees. "And I am, by no means, an emotional individual." His mouth pursed sardonically. "Or sweet. I am a knight. Known for justice that is best executed by sword."

"Yet you also plan to be a doctor?"

"Caught that, did you?"

"Oh, yeah. I've Googled you."

"Nice. And very convenient."

"You know what Googling is?"

"Of course. I know many things pertaining to your modern world." He made a stirring motion with his finger. "But let us get on the fascination you have with my life. Where did Google lead you?"

"I wouldn't say fascination . . ."

"I daresay I would." He grinned.

Elizabet scowled. "You gave me the information and said 'happy hunting.' Of course I Googled you."

Jareth shrugged one shoulder. "Saves time. We will not have to play your silly little game anymore. Besides, I am willing to tell you whatever it is you would like to know. Games are not necessary."

Elizabet made an unladylike growl. "Do you know how many websites I searched through? And you'll *tell* me whatever I want to know?"

"Precisely." Jareth smiled. "With the exception of Jeremy. I have to insist that the details of what happens to him stay forbidden for a while longer." He tilted his head; his eyes sparkled with what closely resembled glee. "Tell me all about me. I am almost afraid to ask, however.

Am I a bloodthirsty knight who is a religious zealot, or am I a simple lord who leads his people with kindness. It will vary by perception. That is most unfortunate."

"I will tell you who you are not," Elizabet said. Her sudden cheery demeanor seemed to make Jareth uneasy. His shoulders slumped and his jaw became rigid. "You are not the Casanova you claim to be. The man to one wife and father of a slew of kids. So before you go bragging about what a fantastic catch you are, just know that you've been caught."

"Really?" His eyes tapered. "Did they happen to name the lucky girl?"

"Elisabeth Tremaine, the first Duchess of Dover," she replied. She wrinkled her nose and stuck her tongue out sideways. "Of great beauty and all that nonsense."

"It does not sound like nonsense to me." Jareth's grin was predatory, which appalled Elizabet. She felt the heat of a flush again, and looked away.

"You're ridiculous," she muttered.

"Perhaps," he replied. She gazed back at him. A bored expression fell over his face. "But I have never heard of an *Elisabeth*. She must be a ravishing beauty to *catch me*, as you so fondly call it. I cannot wait to meet the woman who ensnares me."

"I'm sure it's all a matter of time . . ." She gave him a pointed look. ". . . Before you meet her and she snares you up."

"*Dubium*," he said with a sniff. He motioned to the small television in the corner of the room. "May we get on to business now? I would like to see more of this storm."

"You want to watch The Weather Channel?" she asked incredulously. "Honestly, you switch subjects as often as I do. Drives Grandma nuts."

He smiled and murmured something she couldn't quite hear. "Is there something else you would like to talk about?"

"What did you just say? That wasn't English."

He touched his fingertips lightly to his chest *"Ignosce mihi."* He executed a slight bow even though he remained seated. "Please forgive me; I think in Latin and sometimes it overflows my mouth." He tilted his head. "I think I said something to the effect of 'without doubt'."

"You think in Latin?"

"Yes. It is the language I am most comfortable with. Does this offend you?"

Elizabet stared at him. She made sure to blink every so often just to let him know she had not turned to stone. "I'm so out of my league," she mumbled and then shook her head. "No. It's totally cool that you can do that. I guess it's like speaking Cajun French around here. Nothing special where you come from, but crazy cool to me."

"You speak another language?"

"Only the curse words," she admitted with a bashful smile. "Grandma speaks it perfectly, though. It's her original language." She motioned to him. "But I want to talk more about you, not just your woman." She let a scowl cross her face and Jareth grinned again. "I read that you work for the Church—"

His grin faded. "No," he interrupted. "I do not work for the Church. I translate scripture. There is a difference. A vast difference. I would never ally with an institution that lacks the basis for biblical truth." The timbre of his voice deepened and a feeling of uneasiness swept over her.

"Does the name John Wycliffe ring a bell?"

Jareth crossed his arms; one of his hands went to his face, where he stroked the shadow of beard appearing around his mouth and cheeks. "What did you discover?"

"That you almost die for your little side job of translating. A Lady Catherine has you questioned by the Archbishop of Canterbury. She orders your execution."

"Really?" He straightened in seeming surprise. His hand paused over his upper lip. He pointed at her with that hand. "Did it say when? Did it explain what happened to this lady?" She noted that he said the word lady with vehemence. At once, she was aware that he knew this woman who wanted his life.

"No," she answered honestly. "I couldn't find anything else on your life other than the names of your children, your legacy with the Church . . . the date that you die."

Jareth grimaced and he waved his fingers before dropping his hand. "This topic has come to an end. I think perhaps there are a good many things I do not need to know."

"Agreed." She leaned forward to rest her elbows on her knees. "And okay, I get it. No information that speaks of your demise." He nodded and appeared relieved. "So, you want to watch TV, you said? The Weather Channel?"

"Please."

"Why?"

Jareth's lips slid to one side. "That question was foreseen. Somehow, I knew you would question that." He motioned to the television.

She smiled. "Okay." She rolled her eyes and reached for the remote that was on her fluorescent green bedspread. "I'll give a little, but we are going to talk about all sorts of stuff while you watch TV. You did say that you'd tell me whatever I wanted to know."

"*Dibium.*"

"Without a doubt," she said over her shoulder as she switched on the television. He smiled at her before he faced the small screen.

The hand that held the remote trembled as Elizabet placed it carefully next to her on the bedside table. He could be so charming, but he was not for her. He belonged to some girl named Elisabeth, and she needed to remember that. He should save his lethal smiles for his wife, anything else was a waste of time—her time, to be precise.

She took advantage of his inattentiveness to absorb him—the way his large body made the small folding chair seem as doll furniture beneath him. Although he was not for her, she could not help herself. His dark hair was cut short, not the way she imagined a knight's hair would be styled. It curled slightly at the neckline of his T-shirt. It was a recent, modern change. And his new clothing made him familiar. He was more approachable, more touchable. It was an understatement to say he was attractive. The man practically reeked pheromones that called to every eligible female within a hundred-mile radius.

He gave her a good thirty minutes to study him and she did not become bored with it. His face remained unmoved as his eyes roved the screen, studying the red mass that covered the entire Gulf of Mexico. It was a terrible thing coming straight for them, but she could not muster up the fear to care. If Hurricane Libby blew through the house this second, she would die with a smile on her face. He was that lovely to watch.

"This track is giving us under a week to make arrangements? According to this . . ." Jareth waved his hand toward the small, flat screen, " . . . I have six days to prepare for the worst."

"Give or take," Elizabet said. She came out of her pheromone induced fog to glance at the screen and see that the latest coordinates were indeed closer. The hurricane had gained both strength and speed. The millibars were low. That was never a good sign. "What do you mean by us and having to prepare?"

"This storm that approaches has a great deal to do with Jeremy. I will need your help to secure him. I need to be introduced to the people important to Jeremy. Gain trust before I swoop in and . . ." He motioned to the television. "Can you stop the television, please, Elizabet? I find it distracting and I have the gist of the report. They are merely repeating themselves."

Elizabet fumbled slightly with the remote due to the way her named rolled out of his eloquent mouth. She was terrified he would be laughing at her when she faced him.

He was not. "Elizabet," he repeated her name, and she had the same squishy feeling again. "Ask your questions."

A gush of air left her lungs. They were so much alike when it came to a disjointed thought process, yet when he did it, she found herself fumbling for footing. "You sound so rushed." He looked at her with a grave expression that did not bode well in the pit of her stomach. She brushed her bangs from her eyes and bit the inside of her cheek. "I don't know where to start." She shook her head. "I have so many. Any suggestions? I'm sure you can tell me what I want to know most."

Jareth scooted to the edge of his chair and reached out his hand. Elizabet stared at his outstretched palm. "You say that I sound rushed." He wiggled his fingers. She thrust out her hand, and felt awkward even as his warm hand covered her clammy one. She did not have a feminine bone in her body, and it had never been more evident than in that moment. She wanted to weep. She wanted to be a lady and refined instead of a girl with calloused hands which she had just jammed at him like a ham hock. "I am rushed. We are running out of time. I must answer your questions so we can get down to business, per se."

He made her smile. "You use slang so easily."

"I read a book on slang," he said, no humor in his voice, only urgency. He squeezed her fingers. The pressure had an odd effect on parts of her body other than her fingers. "Quickly, love, list your questions and I will answer them all."

Everything within her stilled. Elizabet's mind could not wrap around why he would call her such a thing as 'love,' but his urgency opened a floodgate of speech that lasted into the night. They spoke of the Amalgam, of Gabriel and Minh, and Castle Dover. He told her everything, except the fate of Jeremy. But even then, he gave her any answers she asked for that concerned Jeremy's safety. He kept his voice lowered, and it became hypnotic as he told her of unspoken things she was now privy to.

Gabriel was a Spartan warrior and Minh was an Asian assassin. She could hardly believe it, yet it made perfect sense. His openness gave her a level of trust for him she did not have before. She told him about Mrs. Wheatley visiting her mother when she was a child. Admitted that it was not apathy that made her compliant, but years of being groomed by seeing time travel first hand, and the knowledge that one day she would be asked to travel the wormhole. They spoke of his future as a surgeon, how it benefited host without giving too much information as to what host actually was. And he gave her what he called a bonus secret.

He admitted he suffered from a mild case of Asperger's, the same as all host. Asperger's and autism were wildly prevalent among host and some guardians. Jareth believed that this genetic link was what led to their turnings. That was unexpected.

Jareth did not release her sweaty hand until Grandma called out to say she was going to bed. They stood to make their way to the kitchen where they could continue their conversation and still be adherent, somewhat, to Jareth's moral code.

Jareth stepped aside and allowed her to exit the room first. He stayed a few paces behind to view the pictures hanging in the hallway and give her time to speak with Grandma privately.

"Grandma," Elizabet let her voice carry ahead of them as Jareth paused to look closer at a picture of her younger self. "I promise he won't stay much longer. We just have some Church things to talk about. That's all."

"You know how I feel about strangers in my house," Grandma said. The walk from her chair to the kitchen had left her short of breath. She did not need to mention how she felt about Elizabet's church activities; that was an old fight, and it went on and on like a broken record.

She lowered her voice. "He's harmless. He's really nice. I'll be okay."

Grandma made a noise that said what she did not verbalize: she was not impressed with her granddaughter's guest. "Make sure you put away the cash, you hear?"

"Why don't you go to bed? I'll bring you a beer after he leaves."

"Well," Grandma said after a beat of silence. "As long as you keep an eye on the crawfish money. It's in the coffee tin under the sink."

"I promise," Elizabet said. Grandma grumbled all the way to her room off the kitchen. "Goodnight," Elizabet called. She peered over her shoulder as Jareth appeared.

"Don't forget the beer," Grandma hollered before she closed her bedroom door with a loud thump.

Elizabet closed her eyes briefly on the word beer and winced in embarrassment. She then smiled pathetically and tugged on the hem of her shirt as if she could hide. How she dreaded this part. The part where Jareth discovered what a mess her family was. "We've covered just about everything tonight, except Grandma. Any questions?"

He joined her in the kitchen. "I could say you fit the Louisianan stereotype perfectly, but I hesitate. I have studied your traditions and the social functions of your people."

Elizabet leaned her weight on the back of a chair that belonged to the only table in the house. The kitchen was a cluttered mess. The paneling on the walls was stained from grease and cigarette smoke. There were outlines on the walls where pictures had once hung. "How weird is that? I mention the oversized elephant in the room that is my verbally abusive, alcoholic grandma and you say I'm a stereotype."

"It must be said, and I already discerned your family situation. As I said before, I have obsessions just as many Asperger's cases. I figure things out quickly." He looked down at her. He was close enough that he could touch her if he wanted. "When were you going to tell me that you sing?"

"That's not relevant," Elizabet said. She shook her head. "And stop flying off to different subjects. Are we talking about stereotypes, Grandma, or me singing?"

"Your grandmother is an alcoholic. I knew that the moment I met her. She is grossly overweight, gray in color but blue about her lips, and rude. She did not bother to stand when greeting me earlier, so I assumed she also has COPD." Jareth's head tilted. "My mother was the king's mistress, Elizabet. Do you know what that means?" Elizabet nodded. Even though she claimed to understand, he went on anyway. "She was nothing more than a glorified whore. Paid for a service with jewels, housing, and clothing. I have even heard that she was quite good at it. Virtual professional at pleasing a man."

"Jareth." Elizabet reached out. He stepped away and her hand grasped at the air between them. "You don't have to explain. I get it. We are both screwed up family-wise."

"Next subject then: stereotypes. You are classically Cajun, right down to your cute accent. When you sing, is your accent pronounced?"

"I don't have an accent. You—"

"Yes, we both do." Jareth raised his finger in the air to silence her interruptions. He wagged that finger back and forth. "So, now we have covered Grandma and my mother in greater depth. Do you feel better?"

Elizabet's lips flattened. "I guess so." He was being kind to lessen the sting of her embarrassment. He was deflecting her pain for his own. No one had ever done that for her before. He was being sweet again. A smile curved on her face despite that fact he looked serious enough to give her some type of language lesson like a stern professor. Speaking of his mother had hurt him. It was in his tone, and a shadow of shame covered his face at the mention of her.

"Good," he said. He added one nod that seemed more like a jerk. "I feel better, as well. Confession is good for the soul."

Elizabet remembered something. "Wait a minute. How did you know I sing?"

"I read the awards on the wall in your room."

"Oh."

"Does that embarrass you?"

She shook her head and turned away. Walking to the refrigerator, she opened it and grabbed the pitcher of sweet tea. Being hospitable gave her something to do other than appear foolish like a love sick admirer. Looking up at him, right into his thick eyelashes, was intoxicating and would leave her stupefied if she did not find something to divert her attentions. "No. Of course not. It's just that I don't sing anymore."

"Why not?"

Elizabet grabbed two plastic glasses from the drain board in the sink, and sandwiched the rims between two fingers of her free hand. She walked to the table, motioned with the cups for him to choose a seat, and placed the pitcher between them on the table.

"It was something I did with my mom."

"It was forward of me to pry."

"Don't think about it," she said with a shrug. She poured the glasses full of cold tea, yanked out the chair opposite him, and sat down. "It's been a long time, and if you and I are going to get along, I guess we need to know these things." She rested her elbows on the table, ignored the tea she poured for herself, and watched as Jareth looked into the green plastic cup in front of him. "So, speaking of stereotypes, how do you fit the whole knight thingy? I know that you fight, but you aren't good at it. I did see your ripped up body, remember?"

"I am very good at it, actually." he said, frowning into the brown liquid. "My injuries were caused by weapons—" He pointed to the cup. "What is this?"

"Tea."

Jareth glanced back at the cup before him. "I am told I will be quite fond of tea."

Elizabet reached into the basket in the middle of the table and pulled out two straws—one pink and one yellow. She stuck the yellow straw into his cup. "Well, I'm not surprised. You brag enough about being British. Stereotypes abound for us both."

"They have ground," Jareth said. He touched the tip of the straw with his finger and circled the rim. "Social functions of certain people who live in close proximity have been proven to have similar beliefs and convictions. It is the way of things." He looked up at her. "I do not like to fight. I have been trained to fight and it is something I do very well. Stereotypical. Your grandmother is a crack shot, and I am excellent with sword and shield. I am also quite fond of jousting."

"Is there anything you don't do well, oh gifted one?" she asked. She sipped her tea, and somehow managed to smirk around the straw.

Jareth leaned forward and put his lips to the straw as she did, but nothing happened.

"You have to suck," she instructed when he only hovered and did not drink.

He pressed back, appalled. "I will not," he flipped his hand toward the beverage, "pull liquid into my mouth by means of this conduit."

Elizabet purposely pulled hard on the straw, and her cheeks caved in. She didn't stop until the annoying slurp of an empty glass echoed.

"Dreadful."

"It's a straw." Elizabet wiped her mouth with her wrist. Her eyebrows rose a notch. "I take it this is the first you've seen one?"

He nodded and turned away from the cup as if by not looking at it, it would vanish. After a while, she understood that was what exactly he expected to happen.

She refused to move the cup. "It's just a straw. It makes drinking easier."

Jareth turned a haughty expression on her. "Must everything be easy? I have noticed a trend with modern inventions. Impatience must be a new virtue amidst your people."

Elizabet narrowed her eyes. "So, you don't like straws. We speak of Google and you have access to all there is to know, yet straws cause you nightmares. You don't like to fight, but you're good at it. You're a bastard—" She paused, but his expression remained unchanged. She sighed and sat back with a huff, and rubbed her eyes with the heels of her hands. "What were you planning to say about weapons?" She paused and peeked between her hands. "You stopped mid-sentence to be horrified over the straw. It's getting late and even though I am sure Grandma is passed out—your immaculate reputation won't allow us to stay up alone. You're running out of time, Romeo. It's way past my bedtime and, unlike you, I have a job."

Jareth glanced down at the straw in question and shuddered—in a manly, lordly sort of way. Elizabet offered a slight smile while she plucked a piece of lint from her black shirt, and then leaned forward on her elbows again and gave him her complete attention.

"The weapons being used at the battle that day by our opponents were not from the proper time period, nor were they expected." He used the tip of his index finger to slide the glass away and into the middle of the table. "I suspect they were Huns."

Elizabet's brow crinkled. "Huns aren't an enemy of England in your century. They're all dead. Extinct. How is that possible?"

"The traveling stones," Jareth said. "I am sure of it."

"Spartans. An assassin from the Ming Dynasty. Huns." Elizabet sat back and waved at him. "You're practically a doctor already, doing surgery on your own." She shook her head. "You might as well tell me about Jeremy, too—what happens to him, because I think I have it partly figured out." She flattened her palms on the table, on the blue plastic place mat. "You're oddly obsessed with the weather."

Jareth leaned back and laid his hands on the table in a mirror image of hers. "All right. I will give you another bonus and give you honesty if you answer correctly. Give me your best guess."

"Jeremy is about to die in the hurricane that is coming."

Jareth shook his head, his gaze trained on his hands before him. He pressed the jagged edge of the tablecloth down and followed the seam with his averted eyes.

"Okay." She followed her simple word with a sigh of exhaustion. Jareth was freakishly concerned with the condition of the dollar store place mats. "How about he gets abducted or something? By this storm? He goes up in the clouds . . ." She let out a growl of frustration when Jareth did not budge or give anything away. He kept tracing the square mat as though it was profoundly interesting. She rambled out what she thought were logical theories, but obviously her imagination was less than brilliant. "That's all I have. I give up."

Jareth looked up then. He slid back the chair and stood.

Elizabet shook her head. "I know. I know. I sound crazy. I guess I'm not as sharp as I thought."

Jareth stood by her chair, grasped the back of it and folded down next to her. They were eye level now, but she did not turn to him.

"There is something I want to tell you." She faced him then, brows raised. He shook his head and a jaunty grin spread on his face. "It is not about Jeremy, but this affects you profoundly and I want you to know of it. I want to give you the chance to consider the future, so you may have a choice." He reached up and moved a piece of her hair that had fallen into her face.

Elizabet's breath caught and she turned away. "What is it?" she whispered. She was unable to find the volume of her voice. He was too close, looking as if he might see her as more than a friend. She wanted to guard her heart from splintering into a million pieces. People like Jareth shattered souls. He could break her. She had warned herself of the facts over and over. They were contacts, associates—friends at best. But he was too close, robbing the air of oxygen. It made her weak and want things from him she could never have.

"The website you got your information from was wrong."

"What are you talking about?" She sounded a little hysterical, even to her own ears. He wanted to talk about websites when she was expecting something life changing. Her heart was beating in her throat as she gazed at him, her eye twitching because he was so close that her vision blurred, and he was bringing up random websites? The effect he had on her was like an allergy.

He leaned forward, pressed his forehead to her arm. "The name of my duchess. There is no S in her name, and they need to drop the H."

Elizabet screwed up her face as she tried to unscramble what he was saying. It was hard to concentrate when he touched her and was kneeling there unaffected and speaking so clearly she wanted to push him away so he was as shaken as she was. Instead, she stared at the top of his head. His hair was so black it had a bluish hue under the bright light hanging over the table. Even that part of him was angelic. "What are you talking about? I don't understand."

"There is no Elisabeth. Only you. *You* are my duchess, Elizabet."

Elizabet's arm jerked and Jareth's head flipped back. He braced his hands around the arm of her chair and managed to keep from toppling over. "*What?*" she hissed. It had been a reflex to shove him away and now she felt stupid. He eyed her as if he did not know what to do with her; as if she were a skittish animal that needed to be bridled.

Jareth blinked a few times. "I thought I was fairly clear." He motioned between them. "You and I will be married. You are my duchess."

"I heard you," she said in what came out sounding more like a growl than words. Her face was on fire. "How could you tell me this? *Why* did you tell me this?"

"I want you to have a choice." He shrugged and reached for her hand, but she batted him away. "I want you to have time to consider what this means."

"What choice do I have if it's already in the history books?" She groaned, rolled her eyes, and dropped her head into her hands. "We were just talking about my guesses of what happens to Jeremy and you come up with this? You're going to kill me before it's all over with." She shook her head as her hands dropped to the arms of her chair and she slumped.

Jareth's hand lifted to her face and cupped her cheek, even as she fought to press away. He went to his knees and raised his other hand to frame her face. "Stop. Listen to me. You have a choice. There is always free will. What is written can be changed." Her gaze was frantic; he captured it and held it with a steady gaze of his own. Some of her tension lessened and she reached up to grasp one of his hands and press it into her cheek as though she desperately needed to be grounded. "If being married to a bastard disgust you—"

"Is that what you think?" she asked. She squeezed his hand. "You're crazy. Look at you." He looked confused, so she said, "Look at me. I'm not in *your* league. I'm practically a farmer. A serf—remember? I'm a social retard. At least that is what everyone calls me, and I agree. I have one friend and that's my nine-year-old cousin."

"I spoke churlishly. Having to work hard to live should be held against no one."

"There are things about me that you don't know," she said quietly. "Things you might not like."

"An alcoholic grandparent? A father who chases girls rather than women his age? You are poor? What, Elizabet? What can you possibly tell me that I would hold against you?" She dropped his hand to turn away, but he held her there. "You saved me. You traveled to another time knowing nothing but what you were told. You stayed with me when I would have died or my enemies would have taken advantage of my wounded state. You were all that stood between Dover and a hostile takeover. You hid me and kept me safe. How can you speak of the lady who holds my deepest affection in such a way? I will take it personally if you say anything other than, 'Yes, Jareth. I will consider a future with you.'"

Elizabet lowered her gaze to where their hands were entwined. Even that looked out of place. His hands were strong and dark with long fingers that curved around her stubby, nail chewed paws. The urge to pull her hand away and wipe the clammy moisture was overwhelming. Tears pricked her eyes as she sucked her lower lip into her mouth to keep from going into a full ugly cry. Why, Why? Why would he say things that would cause false hope of a better life with *him*?

"I don't understand what changed," she said. She swiped at her nose with her free hand, but did not lift her gaze. "Why would you say such a thing? I mean, are you sure? How do you know it's me? There could be an Elisabeth somewhere out there that you haven't met yet."

Jareth ran his index finger along her jaw and caught a stray tear she had been unable to stop. "My mind cannot comprehend it, but my heart fully recognizes you. It has not beaten the same since I met you." He tipped her face up. "Why are you crying? If being married to a bastard is not it, then what is it?"

"You'll be disappointed in me," she said. "Eventually, everyone is."

"No," Jareth said, his voice firm. He covered her hand with both of his. "It does not work that way. We will work through our differences—"

"You don't understand," she interrupted. "You don't know everything about me."

"I know enough," he insisted. "I know you are brave and kind."

"That's not enough. There has to be more. You have to know everything." Her parents had a lovely marriage. Phil had not always been a loser. Once upon a time he had been in love and was a great father. She remembered laughter, date nights, whispers after dark and family vacations filled with good memories. Once upon a time, her life had been almost perfect.

Elizabet wanted what her mother had. Someone who loved her even when she was transparent. Phil had known everything about her mom and loved her anyway. He even thought her snoring was cute. Elizabet regarded Jareth through her blurry vision and wondered if he was capable of accepting flaws. He was so perfect—a progeny. There were none like him in his time period when it came to academic genius.

"All right, then." He smashed her hand between his one final time before he released her. "You can tell me everything, but not tonight. I have to go soon; we both need some time to process what this means for us."

Elizabet was taken aback. "You just said that your heart . . ." She looked away, her face heating. She didn't know how to repeat what he said without sounding like a desperate idiot who was clinging to his words. "You sounded like you were all for this."

"I am," he said quickly. So quickly, she looked back as if prompted. The expression he wore made it seem as if his eyes were smiling. "I will not change my mind. I am tenacious when I want something." He tapped her nose with his finger. "But I will give you space and time. We do not need to speak of this again until you are ready."

Elizabet's nose twitched. "How much time?" Dare she tell him that she was terrified he would never return? He was leaving after dropping that bomb? Well, she needed time parameters so she would not get depressed again.

"We have all the time you need," he said. He brought his wrist that held the time bands up between them and rotated it. The bands shifted until the leather strap revealed the odd metal piece beneath. "All I want to hear from you now is that you will consider it."

Elizabet never considered herself a fickle person. She knew what she wanted. "Then, yes. I'll consider a future with you. But come back in few days. I'll see Jeremy again on Sunday. I can tell you what he's up to."

"I do not need a report of his whereabouts. I need you to be his friend. He needs to trust someone close to me so when I come for him, his transition will go well."

She nodded. "I can do that. We're friends already." As friendly as Jeremy could be with anyone. If she was a social retard, he was a social quadriplegic.

"All right, then," he said. "Look for me in four days' time."

Chapter 9

"THEY ARE DEAD, YOUR MAJESTY," Perceval said. His voice was void of emotional inflection.

Jareth glanced up at the burned bodies hanging from the stone fence that led to Kent. His fence. Two men, one woman, and three young children.

The last of it was unacceptable. When innocent children were murdered as pawns, Jareth became angry. Sir James of Torquay would pay with his life. The slaying of children was something he never overlooked.

"I can see that," he said. He wiped the sweat from his brow before it ran down into his eyes. "I am not blind." He motioned to the bodies. "Have them removed, identified, and given a proper religious burial."

Perceval bowed and then turned to do his bidding.

Jareth looked behind him to the line of his men that stood as statues. "Well?" His voice was hoarse and loud. "Are you planning to ask me to dance or do we ride into Torquay?"

Half of the men headed for their horses, while those remaining appeared apprehensive. They looked to one another, each of them not daring to make eye contact with Jareth who stared them down with a brooding that did not bode well.

Jacob, a knight older than Jareth by ten years, spoke. "The moon approaches and the horses are tired and hungry. We cannot ride into Torquay in this state. We have only returned from Windsor Castle. May we have time with our wives and children before taking up this cause too?" He spoke in Norman French, which irritated Jareth.

Among his men, only Percival knew of his ability to travel time. It rankled that he must fall back into a language he considered ugly when he could practice modern English and slang.

"My wrath is nigh, Jacob," Jareth said with a leering grin. "Do you have a care for your very life?" His French was refined and punctual, where most that surrounded him used it in the fashion of a child. "You worry for your family that is alive, while these bodies have only just lost their spirits and souls." He waved negligently toward the fence behind him; he didn't dare to look back at the innocent stares of the children who were strung up like garbage. His hands curled into fists as his mind fought to keep the images at bay. "I shall not rest until I have vengeance in their names."

"She is not worth it, Jareth," Jacob said in whisper as he stepped forward. He glanced around as the other men mumbled and motioned to the ember remains of Sir James' flag strewn among the bodies. Some, hearing the measure of Jareth's tone, began to make their way to their horses—ready to ride anywhere he led. Jacob shook his head, and his blond hair twisted with the movement. "Let your actions be the end of her. Will not the fact she has been put off be enough revenge? Her father will never find a proper husband for her now that she was refused—"

"By a bastard duke?" Jareth finished. His lip curled in anger as he pointed to the bodies with his sword. "Yes. Poor, dear girl. She was scorned and hurt, so she had innocent people killed to alleviate her suffering." He tipped his chin forward to Jacob's horse. "I have seen you kill a man for insulting Zeus, yet these innocents you would have me forget and pardon their murderer? If that shrew has children killed because she has lost a suitor, what does that say of her character? Should I forget that I knew these families?" He closed his eyes briefly with a passing memory. A few months ago, he allowed one of the lads to ride Veritas into Kent. The family had gone to the village for supplies and to visit the orphanage at immunization time. Jareth had secretly given them the smallpox vaccine. Now, they were all dead—even his horse. He was furious.

"Catherine was the conduit," Jacob said. "We will avenge these people, but by hunting for the men responsible for their slaying."

"They shall die as well." Jareth seethed and noted that Jacob put more distance between his steed and Jareth's sword. Jareth turned to where Perceval awaited with his dun gelding. "Right after I slit

Catherine's throat so she may never spill lies and judgment on any other man or woman."

He glanced at the small bodies whose forms still singed; smoke rose from their charred flesh. "Or child." Unbidden tears surged into his vision. He stayed steady as he grabbed the bridle from Perceval and swung up into the saddle. Crying was for women and children. He refused to see those small bodies again. He turned his horse in the opposite direction.

Jareth was known for making decisions based on fact, never emotion. Seeing children cut down, however, evoked madness in him that he did not want to name. His justice was clouded by vengeance, yet if he were to think hard on it, he knew that justice for those people meant the death of Catherine of Torquay.

And anyone else who perjured themselves for the sake of revenge.

Five years into the future of Dover

"HE REFUSED HER?" MRS. WHEATLEY asked in a seeming mixture of shock and glee. She grasped her apron strings and yanked.

"Yes, he refused her, but not without cost," Gabriel said from where he sat at the large, splintered table in the main kitchen. "There were children among the slain."

Mrs. Wheatley's fingers flew in the sign of the cross and then tore her apron from about her neck. It sailed through the air and landed in a heap on the floor. "That witch!"

"I was thinking in other terms," Minh said as he scooped up the fallen apron and draped it over one of the chairs surrounding the table. His tall, lanky form moved lightly across the kitchen. He was bred to be smooth and it showed in everything he did. Even scooping up mislaid aprons by aging nursemaids. "But witch will do—for now."

Mrs. Wheatley reached for a fresh apron. "Does the duchess know?"

Gabriel lifted one of his shoulders. "Elizabet is forbidden to us."

Minh rolled his eyes.

"My mind is not what it used to be," Mrs. Wheatley murmured as she looked down at the clean apron in her hands and then to where she had abandoned the other. She searched with wide eyes until she realized Minh had removed it from the floor. She shrugged and put on the fresh apron. "I cannot remember that there were children." She looked up at Gabriel, tears in her eyes. "Why can I not remember? How many?"

"Three," Gabriel said flatly. "Jareth says that time jumping will do this. We will forget things and become foggy minded." He looked away, over to Minh who shifted from one foot to the other. The sounds of baby garble along with the lovely voice of the lady of the manor grew louder as they approached. Gabriel caught the eye of both Minh and Mrs. Wheatley, put a finger to his lips, and shook his head.

Minh's mouth became a hard line. Mrs. Wheatley looked away, swiping at the tear coursing down her wrinkled cheek.

It was technically five years since the slayings, and although they were seated in Dover Castle, everything was different. The castle had an acting duchess, an heir, a spare, a daughter, and one child on the way.

"Ah, there you are," Elizabet said as she spotted the lot of them brooding in the dark kitchen. It was early morning and dreary with only the fire in the hearth oven to offer a glow. As always, the young heir and his twin were two steps behind their mother, quietly following wherever she went. The black haired spare was perched on her hip. "Jareth said to fetch you." She smiled at Gabriel. "Jeremy is talking. He's talking!"

Before Gabriel could respond, the royal pack of hounds came bounding into the kitchen. They leaped at the hen that was hanging, plucked, awaiting the pot. Mrs. Wheatley swatted at them, scolding in brisk French. She tended to lapse when she was upset.

The twins giggled and dove straight into the rambunctious pack, squealing with delight as the animals licked their faces and bounded upon their small bodies.

"Did you tell them?" Jareth brought up the rear of the hounds. His hair was wild, as if he had been in a wind storm, which was entirely possible. He had just finished a tutoring session with Jeremy. He grasped Elizabet's shoulder and leaned in to kiss her cheek. Gabriel and Minh glanced at each other and just as swiftly looked away. Minh rolled his eyes to the ceiling again.

"Jeremy has spoken," Jareth announced. "He asked for apples." Gabriel avoided Minh's glance, but when Jareth noticed, his joyful tone dropped. He looked between the two of them and then to Mrs. Wheatley. She turned to the large simmering pot, muttering that something was burning. Jareth braced himself, his arms crossed. "What is it?" Jareth demanded.

"Nothing," Gabriel answered.

Minh sniffed and stared out the narrow window above the hearth, looking for all the world as if he were daydreaming and had not a care. Mrs. Wheatley mopped at her tears, stirring the broth with wide turns.

"Nothing that you'd allow me to do anything about, anyway." Jareth grimaced and rolled his shoulders.

The conversation could barely be heard over the ruckus the children and dogs were making. Jareth made a chopping motion in the air with his hand. "Quiet!" he roared.

The leaping hounds seized into the sounds of canine whimpering and toenails scraping against the stone floors. The twins looked up, confused by their father's harsh tone. Jareth stared at Abigail, the only girl of the family, until she smiled adoringly at her daddy, apparently satisfied that his tone was not meant for her.

He placed his hands on his hips and eyed Gabriel. "Out with it. I know it has to do with past events." He jerked his chin toward Minh. "I saw Minh cleaning his sword and I know of no battles."

"It was a poacher," Minh said. He turned to Jareth. "His knife was found in the belly of a serf in Kent. I recognized his mark. It wasn't one of ours."

"Very good," Jareth said, his voice soft. "I trust your judgment." He glanced at his children, grinned again at his daughter, whose idolizing eyes were still fixed on him. "Elizabet, can you take Peter to see the hounds out? I promised him I would allow him that before his nap."

The black haired toddler on the duchess's hip smiled a toothy grin at hearing his name. "Of course," Elizabet said. She passed Minh and Gabriel a look. "I will have Percival help." She narrowed her eyes as she turned back to Jareth. "You'll call me if you need anything?"

"All is right, my love," Jareth said. "Go see to your children." He leaned in to kiss her on the cheek as if he could not help himself, and smiled down at her.

It was an artificial smile that Gabriel recognized. Jareth was internally seething. He knew Gabriel and Minh well enough to know that something was not right—and he had his memories. He was probably calculating what had happened in relation to where they were in time. He would recall the deaths of his vassals. Still, he released no words or bellows until the duchess, her children, and the royal hounds all filed out, with Mrs. Wheatley leading the procession. There was no sense in speaking of killing while the children and Elizabet were about.

Jareth's eyes narrowed on them just as the doors clanged shut. The sound echoed through the halls. "Last I calculated, we were in the beginning phase and you were concerned I would be unable to rid myself of the lecherous Lady Catherine." He smiled that ghost of a smile he gave when he was not happy. Gabriel frowned and looked away. "I can safely assume that I was more than able. Am I locked up in the dungeon of Torquay?"

"Nay," Minh said. He turned to face Jareth, his brow furrowed. "Your clan rides eastward to Torquay. You haven't arrived as of yet."

"Oh, I guarantee, I am locked up in the belly of Torre Abbey even as we speak." Jareth's hands skimmed to his sides in a relaxed pose. He gestured to the bottle in the middle of the table. "Shall we have port before making war, boys? That is, after all, where this is heading."

"Boys?" Gabriel scoffed. "You're the only boy I see."

Jareth grinned as he pulled a chair and sat adjacent to Gabriel. He gestured for Minh to grab a chair. "It will be a long few days."

"James of Torquay is an avid naval captain, Jareth," Minh said as he pulled a chair and sat. "He is responsible for the peace of England's shores. "And he loves that thing he calls a daughter. Vicious witch."

"It will be fine," Jareth assured him. He reached for the apple port and uncorked the bottle. He poured a healthy portion into a glass and slid it to Minh.

"Enlighten us," Gabriel said. He leaned forward on his forearms and tapped the table with his finger. The sound ricocheted in the quiet room. "Because I saw blood in Dover not an hour ago and it had 'Vengeance is mine' splattered everywhere."

"I shall have my vengeance, there is no doubt." Jareth passed Gabriel a glass before pouring his own. "But it is obvious to me that you are not truly listening."

"Call me stupid, but last I heard, James of Torquay was a crazy bastard who single handedly won the crusades—if history be true," Gabriel said.

"History is most certainly . . ." Jareth raised his glass in salute, " . . . Interesting." He sipped the port and placed his glass on the table, tracing the stem with his fingers.

Gabriel picked up his glass with a salute. "I hear a *but* coming." He drained the port in one gulp and grimaced as he slammed the glass to the table. "I definitely heard a sardonic pause from the bastard Duke."

"Jareth?" Minh asked hopefully.

"We have Jeremy. History does not know about him, and he is ready." Jareth raised his glass again and saluted with it. "He is speaking, and that means he can communicate when he dissipates. Our host is ready, boys. Let the war begin. We cannot lose. May God have mercy on Catherine of Torquay, for I shall not."

Torre Abbey, Torquay, England 1312

SIR JAMES OF TORQUAY HAD rounded up all of the Duke of Dover's men, save for one who managed to ride off. "Do not hang him," he ordered to a group of his naval officers. Jareth understood it was an allowance on their part. Someone needed to warn the people of Kent that their duke was not coming home. "Wait a while. We shall see what King George has to say about his appointed duke. Do you think he shall spare his life? The life of a bastard?"

Laughter rang.

Jareth spit at the ground from where he lay at James' feet. It was more blood than spittle, and splattered the soft half boots he wore. James used that same booted foot to kick Jareth in the mouth.

"You disgusting piece of dung! It was a privilege for me to offer my daughter's hand in marriage. I did it for the alliance, not because I believed you worthy. Filthy bastard."

Jareth wiped his mouth on his shoulder. His hands were tied, as were his feet. He was strung up like a Christmas goose. "You do love that word," Jareth said in modern English. The crowd hushed. Everyone glanced around with narrowed brow, wondering if anyone understood what the prisoner was saying. Jareth licked his teeth to clear the blood from them and spit again, but had no particular aim this time. He spoke next in Latin. "Catherine never held my affection. They lie with another."

James' top lip curled in disdain and he kicked Jareth in the mouth again. "I can do this all day, Sir Jareth." He uttered the title mockingly. "Make a mess of your pretty face, so not even your beloved will desire you." His face puckered and he delivered another blow, but it landed on the side of his face as Jareth quickly turned away. "How dare you speak of another when my daughter—my *daughter*—is the most coveted of the land."

Jareth's head throbbed, his mouth was full of blood, and he figured about three of his ribs were cracked. It was amazing that he kept all of his teeth through the ordeal, but the day was young. He passed his tongue along his teeth, counted them and checked for breakage. Vain bastard, he was; Elizabet would laugh if she heard of this. Percival fought wildly against his ties, but Jareth made eye contact with him and shook his head. The effort sent a piercing pain through his temple.

James took the gleeful opportunity to kick Jareth again, this time not stopping until he rendered the sorry duke unconscious. Percival reared up until he stood, hunched over, and plowed into the stomach of the nearest man. James' men rang with laughter as he fell to the ground in a heap at the feet of the man he tried to take down.

"Pick him up," James barked, and kicked Jareth in his left kidney. There was no movement. "Cage him and his men." He gestured to Percival. "See this one beaten before we hang him from the shackles in the Abbey's rear."

Sir James' current home was Torre Abbey. Although it was a working monastery, he had no qualms about housing his family in the best living quarters. He was merely waiting for his title and castle. Like Jareth, he had been a young squire of the Black Prince. He never understood why Jareth was given a title and he had not.

It wasn't as if a bastard deserved a title and lands, but a rumor circulated that Jareth was a bastard of the king. Suddenly, Sir James determined that Jareth was the marrying type—and his daughter would make a perfect bride. It was too bad the duke was infatuated with seeing the Church disputed, or that was what he believed at first. He had no idea Jareth had a sweetheart.

How could Jareth's manhood be as important as translating scripture text for a house arrested scholar in Oxford? Catherine had merely acted out—a woman scorned and all that. The girl would go mad when she discovered she was not only fighting the Church, but a lover too. She wanted to marry a duke, and Jareth was that duke. Fair maidens all across England had dreams of the Bastard Duke and his handsome face. His daughter was no different except that he had the means to see her dreams come true.

Jareth deserved what he was getting. It had been easy to capture him when he was so selfless where his men were concerned. Jareth Tremaine would never leave his men to a fate he was not willing to travel first. The trap had been foolproof. Kill a few of his people and he would come. And here he was, but what to do with him? The stubborn duke was still refusing to wed his daughter and that was something he *must* do. Catherine would have her way or his entire family would not hear the end of it. He had a headache just thinking about it.

Sir James noted that Samuel, his chief man of the waters, did not aid in the removal of men, but instead waited until they were alone. As Samuel approached, James observed the agitation the day had brought forth. Samuel slowed and talked as one speaking with someone who held a knife to his throat. "Sir James, I would have a word." James inclined his head for him to go on. "The Black Prince is nigh. We can have word to him by nightfall and his answer by daybreak as to the king's wishes."

James was surprised. "Edward? Near our shores?"

Samuel nodded. "Aye."

James looked heavenward and thanked the fates for his luck. He was not a religious man, but he did believe in signs. "Grab that squire Jareth esteems. Do not merely beat him, but break his legs, as well, and then tether him to his horse and dispatch him to the prince. Let's see what happens then, shall we?"

Percival meets with England's gallant prince, England 1312

"'TIS A MATTER OF THE Church," Edward, the Black Prince, said with a wave of his hand.

Percival wished his legs worked so he could ride out and save Jareth. It would seem the royal family had no inclination to step forward. With all the babbling about the will of the Church and broken betrothals, Jareth was in a bad way—unless he produced a bride in a day's time and denounced all of his dealings with John Wycliffe. Both of which were highly unlikely. Catherine had dragged the Church into things—unfortunate, that. Things could get bloody quickly. She had notified the Archbishop of Canterbury of Jareth's dealings with Wycliffe.

The Black Prince would capitalize on Jareth's predicament to be rid of a more pressing problem than Catherine of Torquay. The Church was demanding Jareth's head on a platter or his translation pen—either would do, but with his knowledge of the Church, Percival rather guessed they preferred his head. Edward had washed his hands of the matter once the Church was involved. He would rather deal with heathens than puffed up archbishops and priests.

Harrow set the bones and wrapped casts around each of Percival's legs. The trip to see the Black Prince had ended with only words and no care. If it had not been for one of Dover's men traveling with the prince for protection; Percival might have ended up dead on the side of the roadway.

"You are lucky I was in the neighborhood," Dr. Harrow said as he put the final touches on cast number two. He tipped his chin to see above the bifocals he wore.

"Aye," Percival said, and then lowered his voice. "Nay. I do not believe in luck."

"Spoken like a minion of Jareth," Harrow said. "Does he have a plan?"

"Nay."

"He's just gonna wing it? Be left with his pants down?"

Percival's face scrunched up. "His grace has britches, sir!"

"Why does that saying gets you fellas all crazy?" Harrow asked with a grin. He looked through the bifocals of his lenses as he wrapped the final piece of plaster. "This will be ghastly to explain to the serfs, Percival. Good luck with that." He offered a smile. "While you explain this monstrosity of artwork you are wearing; I will see to fetching his grace a wife. What do you say to that?"

Gueydan, Louisiana. Present day.

GABRIEL CAREFULLY ROLLED THE CIGARETTE between his fingers. He had quit smoking a month ago, but the ritual of it soothed him. He hated feeling like a stalker. Watching for the duchess to emerge from the hardware store she had just entered—with someone who had to be young Jeremy and a girl his age—was very . . . *stalkerish*. Plus, he did not like small towns like Gueydan. His people had been clannish and it reminded him of betrayal. Which was why he stalked and rolled a cigarette between his fingers to help him forget.

A stout lady trundled past the bench on which he sat and smiled as she passed. It was the sort of smile that resembled sweetness, but was a cover for fear. Gabriel glanced down at his attire. Perhaps not the best for this task, but it was conducive to traveling. Leather seldom complained. Jareth hated leather—unless it was in the form of gambeson. He and Minh wore leather simply to irritate Jareth.

The bell on the door chimed as the trio exited the store. Jeremy carried a paper sack. Elizabet looked up and down the walkway as she fumbled for her keys in her front pocket. She was watchful—alert.

There was no sense beating around the bush. Harrow had found him and explained they needed to find Jareth a wife. He agreed and here he was. He put two fingers in his mouth and whistled.

Elizabet's head jerked his way. Her eyes widened with recognition, then narrowed to snake-like slits.

"That's adorable, duchess." He laughed. It was rather loud because she was still a few feet away, although her short legs were moving fast and the distance was closing. "You always say first impressions matter. You could try to look happy to see me."

"This isn't our first meeting," she declared through clenched teeth. She glanced behind her as the two kids caught up. "Beau, take the keys.

I won't be long." She smiled to soothe them as they looked suspiciously at Gabriel. Elizabet's hands trembled as she communicated to them with her eyes. Her expression promised she would handle this stranger and keep them safe.

Gabriel watched the exchange. He smiled and waved; the young girl scowled. He would recognize that fierce look anywhere.

"That's Beau?" he asked once the children were walking away. The girl in question glanced back before she picked up her speed and grabbed Jeremy by the arm. Gabriel tipped his head back and lifted his sunglasses to rest on his brow. Beau broke into jog. That made him laugh. "She's cute," he said. "All young and . . . little."

"She's none of your concern."

"She will be. Everyone involved in the Amalgam is my concern." His eyes briefly—very briefly—traveled down the length of the duchess. He valued his life. One never knew when Jareth would pop up and thrash someone for insubordination. "You . . . you are small too. Have you been dieting?"

Her face flushed. "I'm short. Tell me something I don't know, such as why you're here?"

"You are a bit stout when I come from," he said. Without touching her, he used his hands to measure the girth of her hips and expanded them. He shrugged. "Probably from all those babies you have."

Elizabet's mouth opened. And then shut it audibly.

Gabriel smiled. "Did you just growl at me?"

"Look," she said, her face the same red color as her shirt. "You are drawing a suspicious crowd. They probably think you're a bounty hunter from reality TV." Her hair hung from the back of her head, much as a horse's tail. It bobbed as she passed his attire a disgusted glance downward. "I understand I'll be contacted from time to time, but we need to set boundaries. Why didn't Jareth come himself? It's been over four days—"

"Don't get your pants in a knot, duchess—"

"Stop calling me that."

"Jareth needs you." He pressed his fingers to his chest. "*I* need you. You must come with me or Jareth will either be married or dead by nightfall."

"Married or dead?" She looked confused and more than slightly hysterical now. Her arms straightened at her sides; her hands balled into fists. "That's a broad spectrum, isn't it? Is that why he didn't show up on Sunday?"

"Uh huh," Gabriel affirmed. "He's being held without ransom for breaking a betrothal. If the King of England doesn't speak on his behalf by two nightfalls, they will either kill him or force him to keep his promise and marry."

"He never mentioned that he was promised," Elizabet said. She glanced over her shoulder and watched until Beau and Jeremy were safely in the truck. "I've never heard of this." Turning back, she crossed her arms. "What can I do? If he's promised, he needs to keep his word. That's what they do in his time. If the people can't trust his word, then anarchy will start. I will, in no way, become part of a love triangle. Read the book—it never ends well, and it aggravates me. I hate love triangles. If she wants him, she can have him."

"Oh, Catherine wants him."

Elizabet stiffened. Gabriel wanted to laugh, but he did not. She looked as though she wanted to hit something, and he preferred it not be him. The ancient warrior in him was still not tame—he may return the parry, to his destruction.

"She is all that is detestable. Liar. Mean-spirited. Cold. All the things Jareth is not. He never agreed to the betrothal. It was imposed by the Black Prince. They are trying to join the shores of England in wedded bliss. Don't get so offended. It's not as though Jareth asked for any of this."

"I'm not offended," she insisted.

"Hurt?"

"Why would I be hurt?" she asked, yet she attempted to hide her shaking hands by clenching them repeatedly. "I hardly know him."

"Hardly," Gabriel parroted. "Did you happen to see the name of his wife? Perhaps in a history book? Google?"

Elizabet's jaw tensed. "I didn't have to Google it. Jareth told me." She looked away, up into the tree behind the bench where he sat. "Google was wrong anyway," she muttered.

Gabriel did laugh then. "Prickly little thing, aren't you?"

"What do you want me to do?" Her face had turned both stony and red. She was adorable.

"Harrow has an idea. He's a medical doctor who—"

"I know who he is," Elizabet said.

Gabriel frowned at being interrupted, but he was impressed. Jareth had been talkative; that was a good sign. "Harrow says if we can prove Jareth was already betrothed or married, then the betrothal will be void. As if it was never made. It will make the Black Prince out to be a fool, but who cares? He's in a constant state of wrath anyway. Minh is developing a plan. If it works, we won't need the king's intervention."

"So, you show up here and you haven't got a plan?"

"We're working on it, sweetheart," Gabriel drawled. He tucked the cigarette between his lips.

She lowered her voice. "Don't call me that," she said—in threat-like fashion. "What do you want me to do?" she repeated.

"I want you to come with me. Today." He shrugged, bit the cigarette and smiled. "We aren't sure if we'll present you as his bride—all properly married—or if we will have you show up as his dearly betrothed. Haven't decided yet."

"Lovely."

"Catherine has had her sights on Jareth since they were children." Gabriel took the cigarette from his mouth and eyed it with fondness before he stuck it behind his ear. "She won't go without a fight. She's upset; had a bunch of Jareth's serfs butchered to get his attention. She's trying to scare him into marrying her. Her daddy had him ambushed and is keeping him trussed up somewhere in Torre Abbey."

"How awful," Elizabet said. She did not appear as hysterical suddenly, but concerned. "How is he?"

"I'd love to answer that question, but I can't. He's a prisoner and is being held for breach of contract—remember, princess?"

"Don't call me that," she replied automatically. She brought her index finger to her mouth and chewed at the cuticle. "Is he hurt?"

Gabriel rolled his shoulders. "Probably. Sir James is a di—" He smiled. "Known for his brutality."

She spit the cuticle from her mouth and lowered her hand to prop it on her hip. Her stance changed, shifted to sassy. This was the duchess he was accustomed to. "This Sir James is Catherine's dad?" Gabriel nodded. "He did point out what a catch he is," Elizabet said matter-of-factly.

"Sounds like Jareth was trying to get you jealous," Gabriel said. "But then again, he wasn't exaggerating either. Handsome, decorated war hero, a castle, title. I could go on, but I'm sure you get the picture."

"You left out bastard."

Gabriel feigned shock, his hand pressed to his chest. "And here I thought I nearly had you. What else do you know? Or are you only familiar with the juicy tidbits?"

"I know that history believes he is a son of the King of England. But he's still a bastard."

"The nature of his birthing will not hold him down. He was made for greatness. And you just said it yourself—he's a prince. That part is true."

Elizabet looked down, all the way to her scuffed, dirty boots. "What do you want me to do? Marry him?"

He let his smile lift on one side. "Well, technically, if Minh was successful, you may already have married him some five hundred years ago."

"Right." Her spine straightened. She brought her hands together and twisted them. "Don't I have any say at all?"

"We need you to be there, in Torquay, when we ask for his pardon. It is essential that you are physically there." He lifted his shoulders. "I don't care one way or the other, princess, whether it's as a wife or as a betrothed. But I will have you there if I have to toss you over my shoulder and haul you there."

"How rude."

"We thought of having you go—the present duchess who is already happily married to Jareth—but he said that wouldn't work. It had to be young you." He softened his eyes when he faced her. "We did try to spare you the inconvenience."

"Why?" she asked. He lowered his brows and regarded her through his confusion. She shook her head. "Why couldn't the older me go?"

"Because you are currently pregnant. About to deliver any day, and we can't take the chance. You're small and require advanced medical care when you labor. We must ride there, at least partially, and not use the time stones. Jareth is getting all crazy about us traveling. Says it has something to do with flimsy fibers of time." He waved his hand in the air as if to dismiss Jareth's concerns.

"It's a bit overwhelming," she said. She shook her head and glanced back to the truck where Jeremy and Beau's faces were pasted to the window, and then pressed her thumb and forefinger to the bridge of her nose. "But I'll do it." She turned back and nodded. "I'll do it. It sounds crazy, but I'm having his baby, for goodness sake. It's the least I can do."

Chapter 10

ELIZABET SAT ATOP THE HORSE she shared with Gabriel because he claimed she could not ride to save her life—a true statement—how utterly in the dark they were concerning her. They had both made fun of her because they knew her paternal grandparents owned a horse farm; though what they didn't realize was that her life was breathing oxymoron on so many levels. If they knew of the horse farm, what else were they holding back? She narrowed her eyes as Minh lit a cigarette.

"Put it out," Gabriel said.

"No," Minh replied. Smoke curled out of his mouth as he spoke. He used the cigarette as a pointer. "She doesn't mind."

Elizabet tipped her head back as Gabriel looked down on her.

"I don't," she said, but coughed the words. "My dad smokes."

"Idiot," Gabriel said.

"Oh, you know him?" she asked.

Minh smiled. "We haven't had the pleasure. Jareth keeps his in-laws away from time portals."

"Oh," she repeated. She crossed her arms. It was awkward being enveloped in Gabriel's embrace. She did not know what to do. Sit poker straight or relax back onto the wall of muscle behind her? She sat up taller. "How much longer to this place we are going?"

Minh shrugged. "A few hours."

Gabriel scoffed. "I'm sick of this. What are the perks of having alchemy if we can't use it? We could be there by now, saving Jareth's life instead of prancing around on ponies."

"Time is not something to be trifled with," Minh said, his voice obviously mimicking someone. He sounded an awful lot like Jareth.

He grinned; smoke trailed out the corner of his mouth. "He never lets us practice any of the good stuff. I almost forgot how to inflict certain torture laws to those in need of little honesty." His smile widened. "Almost."

"Mr. Minister of War," Elizabet said, and then smirked at Minh when he looked about to fall off his horse. "Yes, yes. I know all about you." She looked over her shoulder at Gabriel when she felt him stiffen. "You too, Mr. I am Sparta."

Gabriel laughed at that. "Sounds like trouble."

"Methinks Jareth has a big blabbermouth," Minh mumbled. He drew on the cigarette. "Sounds like a breach of classified information."

"No sense in standing on ceremony, eh?" Gabriel flicked the reins to his left hand. "She is Jareth's duchess."

"I do have a memory of a short chit who likes to scold people," Minh said. He looked her over, his lips sliding to the side and his expression becoming cocky. "Sort of looks a bit like you—I suppose. Do you have an overactive gag reflex? It's the only way to tell really."

"You really do know a lot about me." It was embarrassing that they knew of her gift. It was not as though she asked for a strong gag reflex as a super power, or as though she wished for a weak stomach.

"Yep," Gabriel said. "I'm not surprised Jareth told you about us. You're like everyone's little pet. We watch out for you. Make sure no one checkmate's the duchess."

"It's what we do," Minh said, and tossed his cigarette aside. He reached into his coat pocket and pulled out a pack of gum. "As if we need to state the obvious, though. Here we are. Watching you. Bringing you gift wrapped to Jareth."

"You told me not to bring anything that could tie me to the future," Elizabet said. The words 'little pet' vibrated in her mind. The sight of the gum was like waving a red flag in front of the face of a bull. She had left home with barely the clothes on her back due to their rules. They had made her strip, leave her clothes behind a bush somewhere between here and Dover and had given her a scratchy gown of some sort to wear. And they were allowed factory packaged cigarettes and gum? She clawed at her neck where there was sure to be an abrasion while she glared at Minh.

"You're wearing a watch." Gabriel pronounced each word like a sentencing of death.

"I want to keep up with the time," she said with a sniff. She pulled down the cloak's sleeve over the silver watch and rotated her shoulders to loosen the dress. They would be appalled if they knew what else she was hiding—what she had not allowed them to see when she changed into this hideous garment. "To keep grounded."

"We're here to keep you grounded, your grace. You don't need a watch," Minh said. He folded the piece of gum into his mouth and bit down on it with a smile. "What part of the chess game do you not understand?"

"Ignore Prince of Persia over there. He's missing his internet access. His phone has no service," Gabriel said. "The smoking, the gum chewing is all to aggravate us into letting him have his way. Manipulative bastard."

"I have no service," Minh defended, "As you have so quaintly pointed out." He shrugged and blew a pitiful bubble. It was small and popped immediately. He sucked the gum back into his mouth. "But I can still play Candy Crush."

"Pathetic," Gabriel said. He looked up and squinted at the sky that was darkening.

Elizabet watched the scenery as they rode in silence. It was beautiful and she did not want to miss it this time. Knowing she was seeing medieval England was sublime. She sniffed the air, enjoyed the raindrops that were scattered, and pushed her face into the breeze to memorize every smell and detail she could absorb. She had missed out on much while here before; technically, not knowing where she was. The knowing changed everything.

"Do you think he's lost his way?" Minh asked. Thunder rumbled in the distance. "Looks like he's over Plymouth."

"Who?" She gazed ahead at the dirt road. The sky was darkening. The clouds cast a greenish glow around them. She looked inquisitively to Minh. "There is nobody here on the road but us."

"The host is moving quickly," Gabriel said, and spurred their horse into a faster pace. "If he speeds up anymore, we'll be forced to use the time band. I'm not taking any chances with the duchess. This goes on the record as me disagreeing with Jareth. The host was not ready. He's volatile." He looked over his shoulder at Minh's lagging stride. "Hurry on, Prince of Persia. Times wasting."

Minh's expression was amused as he caught up to them, their mounts' heads together as they galloped along the path. "I wish I were a prince, then I would trump you." Elizabet clung to Gabriel's forearm for stability. Her scenic view was ruined. "Have you seen the popular movie about his people?" Minh asked. "The one with the ab display and all the models posturing like a pack of bulls?"

"Actors, Minh," Gabriel said. It sounded as though he was smiling, but she did not want to turn around again to confirm it. She was more concerned with staying on the horse. "They're actors."

"Oh, yes." Minh said, rolling rolled his eyes a bit. "They are actors, because we all have six pack abs like that. Finely made men who portray a dead tribe of warriors. Of course, you all must have been wildly handsome and buff just because you were elite warriors." He said 'elite' with a chuckle.

Gabriel snickered. "I'm not ugly, and we *were* rather large. And speak for yourself, I have abs."

"Can you guys stop for a minute?" she interrupted. The pace had increased until her bottom was coming off the horse's back and she was struggling to hold on. They were talking as if they were at a tea party, not going a hundred miles an hour on horseback. She lifted her gaze skyward. "The rain is getting worse. Shouldn't we stop until it passes?"

"No," they said in unison. Gabriel pulled on the reigns to slow the pace, though. "Listen, duchess, this weather is going to get really, *really*, bad in about—"

"Three minutes," Minh offered.

"Three minutes," Gabriel agreed. "And we're practically there. Just hold tight."

Thunder rumbled closer. They were near the eastern coast of England. The waves were rowdy with the approaching storm. The skyline was hazy, almost black where the storm brewed. It looked ominous and not harmless. Elizabet turned her face back to the sky and frowned. Even as they approached the dense clouds, it seemed as if the clouds were coming toward them even faster.

Lightening flashed and spooked the horses. The crash of thunder followed almost immediately to mingle with the neighing of the horses.

"He's closing in on us," Gabriel shouted to Minh as he fought for control of his mount. The horse danced to the side, tossing its head to be free from the bit. "We'll have to ride hard if we want to make it there before he is totally unleashed."

Minh nodded as he covered his head with the hood of his cloak. He motioned with an outstretched arm for Gabriel to lead the way.

Elizabet's study of England did not include their weather. She was confused—stumped—that Gabriel and Minh could appear apprehensive over a bit of lightening and rain, but as their journey progressed, so did the storm. When they reached Torre Abbey, speaking was no longer an option. Words must be shouted to be heard.

Something was not right, and she got the distinct impression that she was the only one surprised by this sudden turn in the weather. They were moving in sync with one another as if they had done this a million times before. The storm was upon the small town of Tourqauy like an epic scene from a Greek tragedy. Any minute, she expected they would be slain or sucked into an abyss.

Gabriel brought his cloak over Elizabet once they dismounted. "We need to run," he said as he bent down against the rain and covered her with his body. "We have to make it to the abbey or we will be caught in the surge."

"He'll be swift," Minh said. He was next to Elizabet, bracing her between them. The men picked her up; each grabbed under an elbow and lifted. A few times, she felt her toes scrape the soft, wet ground, but mostly, she kept her feet tucked so they would not catch on something and trip them all.

They carried her along until they came to a thatched roof animal shelter. Gabriel shoved her into a mound of hay while Minh secured the door. He unsheathed his sword and studied the parameter of the barn. "Don't move, do you hear me?" he said to her over his shoulder without looking at her.

Elizabet nodded vigorously. The space was tattered; there were no animals, but the smell of them lingered. She allowed her eyes to dart around the dilapidated space. How would it hold up in a storm of this magnitude? This was no regular passing thunderstorm.

"They'll have him in the lower east end." Minh threw back the hood of his cloak, reached for his quiver and pulled out a bow. "As long as Jeremy keeps them occupied, we should be able to move quickly. I'll look for their water source. I don't think plan A will work, but let's keep to schedule and cover all the bases anyway. You stay here with the duchess."

"I didn't see any guards or archers at the lookout post," Gabriel said. "If he doesn't go easy, we'll have to go with an alternate plan." He shook his head. "He was only supposed to distract and disarm so we could get inside with no trouble and have an audience with that naval bastard."

Minh said not a word, but snuck out the opposite door that led to the abbey.

"Are you talking about Jeremy Cameron?" Elizabet asked. She hunkered down as best as she was able in the heavy dress. Her fingers trembled as she ran them over the frog closures of her cloak. There was a bite of frost in the air and although there was some protection in the shelter, the storm was loud and vicious. She frowned up at the ceiling. The wind screeched through the holes in the thatching. A gap was beginning to form in the roof over the hay bales.

"Smell that?" She faced Gabriel and let her eyes narrow even as her expression hardened. "I've smelled that before." All at once, she knew. It dawned on her like the lightening outside. "This is Jeremy," she bit out. She gestured to the bowing doors of the barn. "I'd know that smell anywhere. It's tropical, yet we're in England." She stood, and kicked at clumps of hay in her path. *"England!"* she said again, and pointed to the ground. "This is no storm. It's a hurricane. He's turned into a *hurricane.*"

"What gives you that impression?" Gabriel stopped searching for weaknesses in the structure and turned to her.

She twisted her face in derision. It was ridiculous they were having this conversation—now of all times. Things were nasty outside. "I don't know. I'm only guessing. *Argh!* I'm not stupid, you know."

Minh busted through the door. "It's him," he said to her before looking at Gabriel. "They're using a simple well. I used the whole vial." He glared at Elizabet. *"Do not* drink the water here! It's been poisoned."

Gabriel pointed the tip of his sword at Minh. "We should leave this to Jareth . . ." His words cut off as the barn gave a heave under the strain of the winds and the doors splintered open. Gabriel charged forward to protect her with his body.

Minh strode about the interior perimeter as if chaos did not surround them. He shouldered the great door and wrestled it closed, then leaned back against the splintering wood to keep it shut and shelter them from flying debris. "He's usually so precise." His expression was perplexed.

"He wasn't ready," Gabriel snarled. "He's too young."

Elizabet covered her ears as she hunkered into the shelter Gabriel provided. "I knew it," she screamed over the noise. "Turning? Is that what you call a DNA mutation like this? Why didn't you tell me? I would've been prepared for a fricking hurricane instead of coming here like it was going to be a joy ride in Hyde Park."

"We have to keep moving," Gabriel said. She wrenched away when he grasped her face and forced her to look at him, to concentrate on what he was saying over the noise. "Let's find your husband and he will tell you the rest. Jeremy will be protecting his guardian. It's how they're trained. When we find Jareth, we'll find refuge in the calm eye of the storm."

THINGS WERE NOT BETTER.

Jareth was being held in a rat infested dungeon that was filling with water from the storm surge. Rats crawled up ropes that hung from the walls, looking for refuge. The room was built into the elevated hill of the abbey, but was still below sea level. It was evident that Jeremy was not mature enough to protect his guardian. At least here, however, they were safe from flying debris the wind kicked up.

A rat fell on Elizabet's head and her ear piercing scream rent the air.

"I got it." Minh used an arrow to skewer the rodent. He tossed the carcass and the arrow into the rising flood.

"Don't let them get me," she cried. There was misery in her voice. She ran her fingers through her hair and with shaking hands, lifted the hood of her cloak and held it tightly to conform to her head. She did not sign up for this. Marry the duke and become a duchess—that was what she agreed to. Not storms made by a superhuman, and most definitely not rats. If there was a refund to be had, she wanted it.

"I've got them," Minh said, just as she felt another swipe near the back of her neck. She cringed, held still and closed her eyes. Her stomach rolled twice before settling.

"Gabriel! Minh!" A familiar voice called from deep within the cavern they had breached.

"There!" Gabriel pointed with his sword. "To the back."

"Aw, screw it," Minh muttered. He reached for his cell phone and used the flashlight app to light a path to where they had heard the voice. "I'm sick of guessing what's a rat and what's my imagination."

"Really?" Gabriel scoffed.

"You can thank me when we are out of this rat trap." The beam of light rested on a wooden cage, filled with men. The cage was covered with the long-tailed rodents scampering for higher, dryer ground. "Ugh," he breathed. The light flickered as his hand shook. "I hate rats. Why couldn't it be snakes or spiders?"

"Something just touched my foot!" Elizabet hollered. She sprang upward and wrapped her arms around Gabriel, climbing his body like a tree.

"Swimmers," Minh said, and pointed the light into the rising flood. He peeled off his cloak and swatted the rats away from their feet while Gabriel swayed to regain his footing with the extra weight he bore.

Minh swaddled the cloak around an arrow and used his cigarette lighter to ignite it into a torch. "It's a good thing this wasn't my designer cloak. Leather just doesn't say torch me quite like cotton blend."

"Honestly," Gabriel said. His voice boomed in the cramped surroundings. "You're giving us a fashion lesson now?"

"I wish you boys would stop quibbling and get me out of here."

Minh waved the torch in the direction of the cage. Jareth was a bloody mess, but a welcome sight. And he was standing on his own accord and being bossy; things were better after all.

"We aren't boys," Gabriel bit out as he turned to Jareth. He bounced Elizabet on his back so he wouldn't drop her as he neared the enclosure.

Jareth gripped the bars of the prison. His eyes narrowed when he saw who Gabriel was carrying. "I thought I heard your voice." He did not sound pleased.

"My squeal, you mean?" She blew a piece of hair from her eyes, but wasn't willing to release her hold. "And before you get all nasty with me—" Jareth started to say something, but she silenced him by pointing at him. With her other arm she held Gabriel's neck in a basic head lock. "Let me tell you one thing. I'm your wife now, buddy."

Jareth was too tall to stand straight in the cage that was filled with men, but still he tried. "This is my rescue?" he asked, sharing a look between Gabriel and Minh. "You brought a weak girl along with you? Are you both mad?"

"We had a plan," Minh said. He looked at Gabriel who was twisting Elizabet's arm from his throat. "But it isn't panning out the way we expected." He approached the cage and began torching the rats from the top. They fell with heavy splashes around the enclosure. "Just go with it."

"For once," Gabriel muttered under his breath. He tipped his head to see how she was faring and then used force to pull her off his person.

Jareth's lips curved even though she did nothing to hide her anger. She glared at him, her jaw rigid.

"Let's have the outline, for curiosity sake," Jareth urged, his voice deceptively smooth.

"Oh, I don't know," Minh hedged as he kicked a swarm of rodents from the door of the cage. "We thought we'd use Jeremy as a mask, get it in here, bust you out. If that failed, we have your wifey here to verify that you are unable to be betrothed to another." He shrugged. "I also wanted to use a bit of poison, just to make it original. It seemed logical at the time."

"And I presume the boy is responsible for the storm?" Jareth asked.

"You're so bloody smart." Minh smiled. He set the torch aside, fumbled in his cloak, and produced a long needle. He began to work on the rickety lock, but not before he got a good look at Jareth's bloodied and bruised face. "So, while I pick this lock in record breaking time, was it James who quite messed up your pretty face?"

Jareth nodded and frowned at Minh's choice of words. He also seemed peeved over the mere idea that they thought using Elizabet was acceptable. "It is nothing." His chin jerked to the man two others were holding above the water line now at their knees. "I have a man who needs medical attention more than I do. Pneumothorax. I released the tension, but I must get him to stable ground."

Jareth met her gaze. His eyes roamed over her from head to toe. She could tell he did not like her being here. It was dangerous. Her eyes narrowed and her chin raised a notch in defiance.

"Bingo," Minh's voice broke their stare as the lock sprang open. "Fifteen seconds. Someone needs to give me a gold medal." It took brawn to open the decrepit iron barred door. He inclined his head when the men rushed the door. "His grace first."

Jareth grasped Minh's shoulder and squeezed. "Thank you, my brother."

"Your majesty." Minh bowed at the waist. "Let me see to your wounds, to ensure they are really nothing. Your eye is nearly swollen shut."

"We must get these people out." Jareth gestured around him but gazed at his wife as he spoke. "I would not want harm to come to those I care for while I am managed as one would a child."

"We must remove ourselves from this tomb," Gabriel said. "I don't think the host is stable. He will bury us alive unless we move quickly." He glanced around the space they were in. "If any area should be secure, it would be here with you, and it is not. If we get to the barn, there's a breach in the gates there. It's not ideal, but it's higher ground. Protection from debris."

Jareth breached the gap between himself and Gabriel, then gestured to Elizabet. "Come." He turned. "Get on my back. There is something infinitely wrong with you being tangled around my henchman's back. I'll carry you out of this mess." He peered at Gabriel. "I say we clear the barn and be rid of this place. The host should recognize our retreat and we will be free—not holed up on enemy territory like cowards."

There was something in his expression that kept her from contesting his command. She switched handlers, and clamped her legs around Jareth like a vice, careful not to allow her feet to touch the rising waters. She made not a sound of protest.

Jareth pivoted around to check the location of his men, then glanced at the cage to be sure it was empty. He ignored the glare Gabriel was shooting his way.

"Are you sure you got me?" Elizabet asked. She was cold. She shivered as she adjusted her weight and clung to him.

"I have you," he said. He jerked his chin to Minh. "Lead the way out."

Chapter 11

A FIGHT AWAITED THEM AT the exit from the underground. Sir James's men were stationed there, swords drawn and ready for a battle.

Gabriel and Minh made a way for Jareth to slip through to lead Elizabet to a place of refuge. The exit led to a courtyard that was surrounded by the walls of the abbey. He ran the length of the yard, putting as much distance between her and the battle as possible.

Elizabet slid from his back when he reached the far side and ducked behind a stone pillar. She stepped back in the shadows and grasped her arms, running her hands up and down for warmth. She already missed the heat he provided.

Jareth grabbed her chin with his forefinger and thumb and lifted her face. "You are scared and cold, but you must be brave—all right?"

She shook her head. Her eyes were wide and watery. "Stay with me and I'll be whatever you want me to be."

"I must fight—"

"Don't leave me," she pleaded. She shook her head until his fingers no longer held her still. "I came here because of you. You can't leave me now."

Jareth closed his eyes for the beat of two seconds, then exhaled sharply. "I have to go. You will be safe. I promise. I will protect your hiding place. You have to trust me."

Elizabet's lip quivered as she stepped back and away from him. His words worked their magic. "I trust you," she whispered, for it was all she could get out. Her breath had left her. The words 'trust me' curled around her heart; it was what she had to do.

Jareth inclined his head briefly. Something fierce crossed his features before he turned and walked beyond the pillar and into the battle.

She could do nothing but watch him leave.

MINH AND GABRIEL FOUGHT DIRTY. It was the first time Jareth was in battle with them that he could remember. He was aware this would be the norm in the future, but this was the first time he had to trust them to ally with him. They used tactics that were both odd and not chivalrous.

They used their heads to smack the guards, they tripped and took advantage where they ought not, kicked kidneys when they had someone down, and Jareth was pretty sure he witnessed a bite of teeth, as well. Still, they were losing. War was real, not romanticized as it was in fiction. Jareth was tired and sore, which made him slow. He was also preoccupied that Elizabet was a mere stone's throw away from where he was killing people.

The man wounded while escaping Dover Castle was dead, as were the men who carried him from the tunnel—each of them except the one named Quill. Quill continued to fight with a broken sword, yet he was out numbered. The boy was a lowly armor bearer and lacked battle skills. It was not just a battle, but a storm. It was at their backs, their fronts, between their fingers and in their ears. It made fighting difficult. It weighed down each movement and hindered hearing; surprise was working against them.

Jareth was normally a careful soldier, but today he was different. He wanted blood and retribution for the people slain for the sole unfortunate reason that they were his. Each time a soldier approached, he pictured the family whose bodies had been strung on his fence in charred ruins. It was easy to make the choice to kill rather than maim. He sliced through flesh, arteries, and bone. That dark place in his mind took over and allowed him to function as a machine. Never in his life had he felt the insistent urge to be so violent on purpose. It was both troubling and exhilarating—but he had no time to tarry on it, which pleased him. Perhaps it was both. He only relented when he kept watch over Elizabet's hiding place. For the thousandth time, he glanced to where she was hidden and did not see her. He turned in a circle, his eyes searching the perimeter.

Gabriel was killing an archer; he held the young boy's body upright and ran his sword through him. Minh was yanking an arrow from the neck of another and already drawing back to strike again. Quill was holding off Sir James and three others with his broken half sword.

Bang

Jareth whirled just in time to spot a knight approaching from behind, his sword raised. Jareth lifted his sword overhead, then lowered it to slice the soldier's midriff and continued his arc. His body reeled with agony from his earlier beating and now the grueling task he gave it. He picked up the newly fallen soldier's sword and turned back into the battle with two blades. His arms trembled with the weight of two weapons. He did not know how much longer he could hold out.

Having Jeremy hovering over him compelled him, however. He would never view mere wind the same, and although it was a nuisance to fight in, it was also lethal and it fueled him. Knowing it was the host he was responsible for empowered him—as though he was invincible with Jeremy surrounding him like a wind kissed blanket. If he was attentive, he could hear the boy's voice riding in the winds. The host was communicating with him, to protect what was his and honor what had been taken from him. If only his bride would stay put so he could focus on what was at hand.

Bang

"She's got a pistol," Minh called.

Jareth's eyes frantically searched until they found her. He saw her then—Elizabet—stationed at the helm of the battle. She was cutting through the crowd, aiming and taking fire at each foe she crossed. Her pale face was illuminated with raindrops, but ashen in appearance. She aimed and fired straight at the kneecap of the archer aiming for Minh. Another archer who had scaled the abbey's wall was sighted on her, but Minh drew back and sailed an arrow into his heart. The body fell silently to the ground.

Bang

"Elizabet," Jareth called. He used his shoulder to press a knight back and then skewered him with his sword. "Aim higher. *Kill* them."

She shook her head, her nose wrinkling.

Gabriel thrust a dead knight from his sword. "Aim for their chest."

"No!" she called. She squeezed her eyes shut as she pulled the trigger.

Bang

Another knight fell, clutching his knee. Blood sputtered and hit the hem of her cloak. She sidestepped him as he reached for her. Minh shot an arrow that penned the man's arm to the muddy ground. She stepped over it and stopped to reload.

Jareth noticed the way her hand trembled; a few bullets fell to the ground. She bit her lip, sucked in a deep breath, and swayed on her feet. He knew that look. It was the look she got before she spewed her guts. Something drew his attention; he looked up. Sir James was poised behind her, advancing with his sword drawn high above his head. Jareth had seen that before, as well. He had fought plenty of battles with the legendary naval captain. It was James's stance for beheading.

JARETH HELD ELIZABET UNDER HIS cloak, close to his body as Gabriel and Minh searched for a mode of transportation. He did not want to think too hard about what he was doing or he may release her and yell at her for being so stupid.

James had been about to kill her. Decapitate her—right there before Jareth's eyes.

He was furious. Everything changed in that moment. Using dual swords like a pair of scissors, he lopped off the head of Sir James. His action was swift and executed without mercy. An eye for an eye. No one dared threaten his duchess. He hardly knew where his strength came from—he was weak as a kitten.

At the moment of Sir James's death, the storm winds tapered off. Obviously, Jeremy had discerned his guardian's safety—or Jareth hoped that was the case. The surge would take a while to recede, but the storm had died to a gentle breeze and an occasional drop of rain. Now it was all Jareth could do to sit here with Elizabet in his arms and not cry like a baby. He hurt everywhere. After seeing to exploded knee caps, various sword wounds (some of which he had caused), and five archery wounds, he was exhausted. But this was his life; his portion. He was both physician and knight.

Quill reported that Sir James's family had fled with the monks of the abbey. They were headed for the king's estate. He had found five others who belonged with them. They had been chained to the exterior of the abbey and awaited execution. Only a few monks remained, and were gathering the dead bodies for burial.

"I've never shot a person before," Elizabet said. She spoke into his cloak, her face hidden.

"Hush," Jareth said. "Do not think on such things now. We are not yet safe."

He was well aware that she had never shot a human before. She had been brave to not remain hidden. An idiot, but brave too. He asked her to be brave and she delivered. It was one of the most majestic things he had ever lain eyes on.

She had gone for their knee caps with the intent to slow them, so he and his men could take them down. It was a bold move that took thought and careful execution. It was no surprise that she had hidden a pistol to protect herself. Deep within, he had expected her to join in somehow.

Jareth was quite sure he had lost his heart to her in that moment. He'd observed her in deep concentration as she directed each shot to a precise area. It was the reason he was able to offer her comfort in his arms. He had never held anyone the way he was holding her now. She was a lioness and she belonged to him. She deserved and had earned his comfort. The only thing that got to him about her feat was the torturous sutures and packing he had to perform on her subjects. It was bloody, nasty, and he was sure two of the men would lose partial function in their legs. The bullets had exploded the cartilage to pieces.

Elizabet looked up at him. "Will they come for us?"

"Yes." He would not lie to her as he stared down into the depths of her brown eyes. He moved a stray hair that lay across her cheek. "They will come for me. I have broken a betrothal and killed her father—a nobleman. This will be brought to the king. I will be called to give account. But this is where you come in. You cannot cease to be brave." He wanted to know who taught her marksmanship of the caliber she displayed. Handling a firearm was obviously something she did with ease.

"I'm scared," she said. Her chin rolled to her chest. "And I want to go home. Now. Please."

"You shall. But first, we have things to settle here." He placed his fingers under her chin and lifted her face. It was surreal to be with her and it reminded him of how they came to be this way. She belonged to him. "You married me. Why?"

"It didn't work out the way it was supposed to," Elizabet sounded desperate. "All of this," she flapped her arms and his cloak fanned outward, "was in vain. You're still in trouble."

Jareth's lips curved into a slight smile. "But I am married. I have gained a wife."

"I'm not sure it's official. Minh says—"

"It is official," he said again. Elizabet's mouth closed; her lips pursed as she nodded slightly.

"Figures," she muttered. Her eyes narrowed when she spotted the cuts, scrapes, and bruises on his face.

"This troubles you?" He closed his eyes as her fingertips brushed his cheek and grazed above his swollen eye. "You know I will take care of you. You belong to me and I take that very seriously."

"There is always an annulment," she said, her palm flattened to the side of his face. She tilted his face side to side as if to assess the obvious damage.

He lifted his head and her hand fell away. "No." His eyes went cold and void as he stared at her. "No," he repeated with more force. He gripped her shoulders, his fingers digging into the tender flesh of her neck. There was no way he was letting her go. What was done was done. "It is the way it should be."

"I'm only seventeen," she murmured, and laid her hand on his cheek one last time before it fell to her side. "It's the way of things here, but not where I come from."

"This is where you belong." He added conviction to his voice.

"I don't know where I belong," she said. She sighed and looked away. Gabriel watched from a distance. He averted his eyes when he noticed her attention. "But I did it because I think I do belong here." She faced Jareth abruptly. "Do I still have that time you told me I could have? You won't force me to stay here—against my will?" He shook his head slowly, his right thumb pressed into her clavicle. "Because I need more time. We hardly know each other."

"All right," Jareth agreed. He released her and his hands slid over her shoulders and onto her waist. His body was treacherous. There was not a space on her person that his did not want to know—to touch. "You can have whatever you want." She could have his heart, for starters.

That made her expression turn conniving. "Later," she promised, a smile on her lips. She brought her hands up between them and pushed at his chest with her fingertips. "You're hurt and I've played nurse to you before. I'm sure you've already diagnosed yourself. It's what you do, boss everybody around." He opened his mouth to say something, but she placed her right index finger over his lips. "Just tell me what's wrong with you?"

Jareth's eyes slid to half-mast at the sensations she caused within him. They were possibly caused by a bit of blood loss, but greatly possible this was what life with a wife would be like. "My ribs," he said while he watched her closely. "I will bandage them when we are safe. There is nothing to it. The human body can take much more than we give it credit for."

"Did they beat you?" she asked. Her anger was badly veiled. He barely hid a smile.

"I will be pissing blood for about a week," he replied. Her eyes widened, then she cleared her throat and looked away as if insulted by his choice of words. The little actress. He let out the glee he was holding back with a burst of laughter. It was a short, self-depreciating chortle. A slight indiscreet word had turned the conversation and for that he was grateful. Things were getting too touchy feely and he was not sure about that part. "That is what happens when your kidneys are kicked. Over and over."

"They *kicked* you?"

He shrugged. "I would take a thousand beatings not to marry that hellcat James calls a daughter. She had innocent people killed merely because she is spoiled."

"Gabriel told me," Elizabet said. She pushed him away and wrapped her arms around her body. She was still under his cloak, but put distance between them. She rubbed her arms in an attempt to warm her wet body. "Why didn't you tell me about her when I brought her name up? It would have been nice to know that you're betrothed."

"Prince Edward has difficulty seeing beyond his own desires. He was the one who pressed for the union. It was hoped that when I gained my title, our marriage would unite the coast of Britain. When it became evident that I would not bow to their wishes, Catherine had my men slaughtered to make a statement. If she ever had a chance at becoming my duchess, that chance died when she killed my people. I shall never marry her."

"Marriage to her would be that bad?"

"What do you want to know? Are you politely asking why she bothered having people murdered or are you asking because you want to know where you stand in comparison? Are you jealous?"

Elizabet's mouth dropped open. "No." Jareth allowed his lips to twist into a doubtful expression. She blushed. "Okay. Maybe a little. You did go on and on about me being your duchess."

"That is something Catherine could never attain. She is mean spirited and intolerant. I once saw her have a small child beaten because he soiled her dress. She felt the child was old enough to hold its functions and that he did it apurpose."

"Is she pretty?"

"I tell you she had a child beaten and you want to know if she is pretty?" Jareth lifted his gaze to the gray sky's receding darkness. "God, spare me from the emotional baggage of women." He shook his head and smiled ruefully. "You have me, Elizabet." He unwrapped one of her arms and grasped her hand to lay it over his chest where his heart beat. "If I say that you are mine, then I am yours."

Elizabet's eyes widened. She resembled a sodden doll with her hair hanging in limp ringlets around her face, pressed to her head like glove. "Does that mean I've saved you by marrying you?" Her expression became was mockingly stern. "It is, after all, why I did it. To save your life."

"Consider me saved," Jareth murmured in a lazy tone. His eyes traveled the length of her wet attire. He wanted to say more, but someone approached. He looked over his shoulder to see Minh walking their way. He began talking while still a good way off.

"All we can find is a pair of old oxen and an apple cart." Jareth had her partially hidden by a large tree, and when Minh noticed they were huddled together he stopped short. "I can continue to search if you like. Gabriel said all of the horses are gone from the stables."

"James evacuated his family and most of his staff when the storm began," Jareth said. His smile for Elizabet was lopsided before turned to Minh. Then, his voice became all business. All the while, he kept his eye on Elizabet and took in the details of her face he had missed before. She had a small scar on her left brow. It was white and her hair did not grow over it. "It would be fruitless to search. I am sure there are no horses. The few that remained were taken by the soldiers who fled after their leader fell."

"Should I ride ahead?" Minh asked. "We still have the two horses that we brought down from Kent? I can ride out and track them. Kill them before they make it to their destination."

"That will not be necessary," Jareth replied. He faced Minh, turning Elizabet with him under his cloak. He brought his hands to her shoulders. "We shall use the cart for the wounded and others. Elizabet may ride with me."

"I'm not sharing a mount with Gabriel," Minh felt necessary to point out. He shifted his weight.

"One of you will be needed to man the cart and oxen. I do not care which, but see that you do not behave like little girls while casting the lot," Jareth said.

"Gabriel's manning the cart," Minh grumbled. "And I'm telling him you said so."

"I'll go see if I can help," Elizabet said. She wiggled out of the cloak and away from him.

He caught her arm. "I am yet finished with you, wife."

Elizabet looked at where his hand was wrapped around her arm. She shook her limb, and glanced at Minh with a flush on her face. "Later."

Jareth reeled her body in to his with a simple hinge of his elbow. Her feet skipped until one of her feet rested on one of his. She toppled against him; her head bent back to look up at him. "Do not walk away before we can speak of what happened," Jareth whispered. His expression became somber as he shook her a little. "You shot people. I know this was a first for you. How are you faring?"

"How do I feel?" Her eyes bugged. "You're not about to get all mind quack on me—are you?"

Jareth understood the time was not right to discuss something sensitive. He discerned she was discomfited by the changes he exhibited, but he knew of no other way to carry on. They were married. Things between them had to convert to a relationship with intimacy. "All right, no, but tell me this. Where did you learn to handle a weapon?"

"The farm," she answered without hesitation. "I shoot snakes. There's nothing I hate more than a snake. Except maybe rats now." Her brows rose and her expression turned impatient. Her eye roved in Minh's direction. "Can I go now? Please?"

Jareth glimpsed Minh and let his expression become annoyed. He flicked his wrist to dismiss her, and then turned to Minh. Elizabet marched off with her eyes lowered to her feet. She knocked Minh's shoulder as she passed. Surely it was accidental, but she did not bother to apologize. Minh was grinning too wide to seem to care.

"What?" Jareth demanded when Minh turned his grin on him. "Have a care. I am still angry for having to kill people today. I am obviously unhinged. Do not tempt me."

Minh smile widened. "You called her wife. That's adorable."

"We shall stop at the next abbey and make it official. I know the priest in Portsmouth. He will serve as rector and marry us."

Minh's grin turned lecherous. "And so it begins."

"So it does," Jareth said. He leveled a stare on his friend that dared to be questioned. "I want her." The bald statement hung between them like a gauntlet. There it was. He was now a man entangled in a romantic web and he had no way out. Instead, he was willing to succumb to the natural way of things. Truthfully, he was happy to be buried in it. Elizabet was proving to be a vital asset, despite her sassy mouth.

"What if the priest squeals?" Minh asked. "You know we are being tracked."

"Then I shall run him through with my sword after the registry is signed. We shall keep the certificate of marriage and smite the date. Burn the license you obtained from Ephraim. I want the marriage to be traceable. No one will question the authenticity of the union." His voice lowered an octave, became softer. "There will be children from our union and I want them to be sired legitimately."

Minh saluted. "Yes, your grace. But by all legal means—she is your wife. I made sure of that. Stopping in Portsmouth isn't necessary."

"*I* will know that it is not final. She must consent. I have to hear it from her own lips that she will have me. Only then can I take what is mine. It must be consensual. I think even Elizabet will agree to this. There must be some kind of closure to it. The reality of what has been done must be tangible for her."

"And then you will kill the priest—just in case he talks."

"Precisely," Jareth said. He pushed past Minh and strode to the cart. He was already trailing after Elizabet like a puppy. He scowled at his thoughts, but pressed on. He could see her arguing with Gabriel about how to load an oxen cart. Thirty paces and he would be by her side again.

IT WAS A TIGHT RIDE with Quill and three of Dover's wounded knights in a cart built to haul vegetables to market. Gabriel brooded while Minh smoked and whistled. The tension in the group was palatable. All were on alert. Jareth brought up the rear with Elizabet tucked under his cloak as night fell and their clothes remained damp. It bothered him that he was last when he should be first—a target for anyone they might meet along the path. But Elizabet's protection was paramount to his existence now. It was his responsibility to keep her safe.

Minh sidled up to the oxen pulling the cart. "How long to Portsmouth?" he asked Gabriel.

"Do I look like I have GPS?" Gabriel sniped without glancing at Minh.

"No need to get nasty about—"

Gabriel shushed him by thrusting his finger straight ahead the path. He used sign language to warn everyone an impending guest was about to arrive. He flicked the reigns, but the oxen kept their same lumbering pace. "Who goes there?"

Minh *tsked* at Gabriel. "You sound like a bad movie extra. Where's your French?"

"Put out your cigarette and say that to my face," Gabriel dared. He yanked hard on the reigns, but the stubborn animals merely fought the command and kept at their snail pace. A low growl came from his throat. "I swear we will eat ox flesh before the morning light."

"You shall spook them. Be gentle," Minh scolded. He reached over and patted the great head of one of the creatures. A horn nearly impaled his forearm. He jerked back, scoffed, and flicked his cigarette. "Beast."

"Who goes there?" Gabriel said again, louder.

"Minh, Gabriel? Is that you?" It was a male voice. He flailed his arms over his head. "It's Jeremy. Don't you dare think of throwing that spear, Gabriel."

Minh stood in his stirrups, his eyes narrowing. The moon was half full, so it provided a faint glow to the forest around them.

Gabriel's hand paused on the spear he had been reaching for over his shoulder. He made eye contact with Jareth behind him. Jareth nodded his assent and helped Elizabet off the horse.

"Go into the cart," he said softly to her. She looked up at him with fear in her eyes, but he squeezed her hand before releasing it. "It is only one person. You will be safe. Go."

Elizabet nodded and climbed into the cart. Jareth unsheathed his sword and spurred his horse to side with Minh's. Together, he and Minh framed the cart.

Minh pulled an arrow from his quiver and drew back the bow. "I'm getting chills imagining ten years into the future when host can mimic each other."

"No!" the boy called, and flailed his arms frantically. He was close enough now that they made a visual and recognized him. "It's really me! Don't draw your weapons!"

Gabriel balanced the spear on his shoulder.

Minh frowned and lowered his bow. "He must have dissipated in this area and is waiting for a guardian to fetch him," he said to Jareth. "He'll need assistance. Depending on who has been dispatched to come and get him, it might be a while."

Jareth glanced into the cart. He could see his wife's eyes rounded and terrified staring back at him. He faced Minh and his chin jerked slightly toward the approaching host. "All right," he said. He looked at Gabriel. "Keep the men occupied while we deal with the host."

Gabriel grumbled something about being a glorified babysitter under his breath. Jareth chose to ignore him.

"Who's coming for you?" Minh asked. His voice rose as he swung off his horse. He loosened the frogs of his cloak. The boy was naked, as most host were after they dissipated.

"Gabriel." Jeremy's teeth chattered between syllables. Minh tossed the cloak to him. He grasped it mid-air and donned it. "It's freaking cold! I hate England's dreary weather for this reason. I can't get my heat back up."

"Perhaps you should lower your voice, young master," Minh advised. His teeth flashed in a sardonic smile. He pointedly eyed the cart full of Dover's men who were observing the nudist inquisitively. "Have a care to the information you leak by mere conversation."

Jeremy's gaze flicked to the cart and he nodded. He bowed at the waist when he saw Elizabet. He turned in a circle, saw Jareth and performed a deeper bow. "Your majesties. Forgive me. I did not notice you. You are traveling in an unmarked legion. I see no flag."

"Minh," Jareth said, and tipped his head to the clearing of the forest. "You should be able to find dry wood for a small fire. Let us get him refueled." He glanced at Elizabet. "I do not want to be in forbidden territory with a weak host."

"I'll take this cart apart if I have to," Minh said, and darted into the forest in search of firewood.

Elizabet jumped out of the cart. Gabriel followed suit. He watched her with guarded silence as she passed the cart and stood between Jareth's horse and Jeremy. Her eyes were glued on Jeremy, who grinned at her as she approached on light feet.

She had just left a nine-year-old Jeremiah Cameron back home. This version of Jeremy was all grown up.

"Jeremy?" Elizabet asked. She pressed her fingertips to her lips as if she had just said something false. She went to reach for him, but then pulled her hand away and pressed it to her mouth again.

"Your grace," Jeremy said, his words strained because his smile was so large. His blue lips wobbled as Jareth came to stand next to Elizabet. "*Magister.*" He bowed slightly again. "You look so young. I can't wait to tell—"

"What year do you hail?" Jareth asked. His hand came to rest on Elizabet's shoulder.

"I'm seventeen," Jeremy answered. He lifted his shoulders and let them fall. "I traveled eight years back, I think."

"You were nine yesterday," Elizabet said. She flinched as she shook her shoulder to dislodge Jareth's hand. "And your voice—"

"Is British," Jeremy finished her sentence. "Sort of freaky when you first hear it, eh?"

Elizabet nodded vaguely. Her nose wrinkled as she smelled the air. The faint odors of salt water and tropic humidity hung around them.

"Forgive me, then," Jeremy said. "I've been rude. These things can be nerve-wracking, not knowing whether you're coming or going; who's still alive and on our side. When I saw you both, I should have realized." He shrugged. "It's dark. That's my only excuse."

"You speak so well," Elizabet said. Jareth placed his hand back on her shoulder to stay her as she stepped forward, but she shook him off again. "And you look different. Not just grown up, but . . ." She reached out to touch him, but halted midair and retreated. "The boy I know can barely string a sentence together without looking away, tripping over his words."

"I most certainly can now." Jeremy gazed straight into her eyes to prove his point. "And it feels bloody good." He looked at Jareth over her head. There was a level of anger in his gaze. "I won't hurt her, you know. I can feel it all over you. And I hear you, too. You're scared I'll hurt her." When Jareth balked, Jeremy went on. "You can let her close. I'm in control. I swear it. I'd never hurt Elizabet. Never."

"Perhaps she may be afraid of you," Jareth said.

"I'm not," Elizabet insisted, heat in her voice. She glanced at Jareth. "I'm not afraid of Jeremy even if he is a hurricane."

Jareth narrowed his eyes in warning. "Elizabet."

"Fire's low, but started." Minh appeared from the copse. "I think you can recharge from it, if you want to give it go." He beckoned to Jeremy.

"Excuse me," Jeremy murmured, and bowed again. "I must tend to my nature." He looked at Elizabet. "We should talk later." Jareth stepped between them. "Or maybe not."

When Elizabet stepped to follow behind Jeremy, Jareth stayed her. "Let him go. He needs to refuel. You will see him once he has warmed."

"But I just want to see . . . to ask him how," she said. She watched the retreating form of Jeremy disappear into the forest as he followed Minh. She shook her head as if to clear her mind. "Recharge? How?" she sputtered as she turned to Jareth and pointed to where Jeremy had disappeared. "That's Jeremy Cameron. He's nine years old, Jareth. Nine. Years. Old." She dropped her head into one hand and shook her head again. "I feel as though I can't think straight. I sound like a babbling idiot."

"When Jeremy dissipates, he loses heat, like any storm. Cold air weakens him." Jareth moved his sword over his hip so it rested against his backside. His arms ached to hold her, but she was skittish. "It is a cool English night. I cannot imagine the pain he is in to stay coherent while he waits for his guardian."

Elizabet brought her hand to her brow. "I'm having a nervous breakdown in medieval England." She peeked up at him. "But I'm a glutton for punishment. Tell me more. Make me crazier. I love crazy, obviously."

Jareth smiled and reached out for her. This time, she came willingly, folding herself close to him. He rested his chin atop her head; his arms enfolded her. "He is a category all on his own. He does not register on the Saffir-Simpson Wind Scale."

Elizabet pulled away, her head tipped back to look up at him. "Does that mean he's stronger than any other storm?"

"Yes." He tightened his arms around her, and lifted her slightly off the ground. "What you just witnessed is a lethal weapon that must be protected. The Amalgam was created to protect host such as Jeremy. We must train them to live peacefully amid the world, but go undetected. If they fall into the wrong hands, the world we live in will cease to exist."

"Wow."

"Yes. Wow," Jareth agreed. "Jeremy is physically much like a hurricane. He is stronger on his left side—including his heart chambers. He is impossibly fast and strong. When he dissipates, he literally becomes a storm that can retract and contract to whatever size he desires. He can flood a single city or destroy an entire nation."

"Jareth," Gabriel called. Jareth looked over Elizabet's head. Gabriel motioned to the forest where a large flame flickered upward into the trees. It was winter and dry. No words were necessary.

Jareth thrust Elizabet away. "Wait next to my horse and stay close to Gabriel. I will not be long."

She looked at the roaring fire that could be seen through the trees. "What's happening?"

"It is reverse feeding," he explained. "With young host, one never knows how they will feed under pressure. I assume this is one of his first runs. He is having trouble controlling his urge to consume fuel."

"Won't you be hurt?" Elizabet stepped toward him and put her hand on his arm. He halted. "Can he hurt you?"

Jareth gazed at her small hand resting on his arm and something warm went through his heart. He smiled down at her worried face. "Do not fear, love. You are married to the only person who knows how to kill a host." Elizabet's face fell and she squeezed his arm. Jareth laughed. "It will not come to that—I promise."

Elizabet glanced back at the glowing fire. The voices of Minh and Jeremy could be heard now and it sounded as though they were arguing. The men in the cart were also interested. Their necks were craned as they watched and listened to the eerie display.

"You better come back alive," she stated, head tilted back to peer up at him. She pushed his arm away. "Don't you dare leave me in this place alone."

"Never, duchess," Jareth assured her, and offered his most charming smile. He bowed slightly before he pivoted on his heel and headed toward the forest's edge. "You cannot get rid of me that easily."

Chapter 12

ELIZABET WAS MARRIED TO JARETH by the light of dawn the next morning with no raised eyebrows. Jareth's reputation preceded him, and his ties with John Wycliffe were an asset. The priest was a personal friend of the reformer and had insight into the situation that was arising. Although it was uncommon for his alliance with Wycliffe to be considered a positive trait, Father John Paul had obtained a copy of the scriptures Jareth had translated and developed an opinion of his own. He was currently being investigated by the Archbishop of Canterbury.

This made Elizabet curious, but after the ceremony was concluded, Jareth asked for the sanctuary to be cleared on his behalf. It all happened so quickly she did not have time to ask questions. In a way, she was grateful for a moment to catch her breath. Jareth had gazed at her as though he would devour her while he said his vows. It was unsettling and lovely at the same time.

Before the ceremony began, Jareth had taught her the lines she would be asked to recite in Latin. The meanings were beautiful, but she was forced to either get the unfamiliar words right or focus on the severity of her vows. Her mind only allowed her to get through it without sounding like a total idiot.

There had not been a prompting to 'kiss the bride.' It left her wondering if that tradition had not been made popular yet. Their hands were fastened together with a ribbon, which Jareth removed after saying he did not believe in superstitions. According to Gabriel, the ribbon was to stay tied until after the consummation. Elizabet would rather not think about that. It was not a subject they had discussed. And with everything else going on, she would prefer to enjoy sightseeing and taking in the century it seemed she'd be stuck in. It was comfortable to be a spectator and delusional as long as she stayed at a distance from the reality of her new life.

She sat in the last pew of the church; hands primly in her lap, as she watched Jareth lay prostrate on the wooden floor before the stone altar. Everyone had been removed from the building save for her. He had insisted she stay, but the why of that escaped her; what he was doing seemed too personal for another to witness. Tears clogged his voice, though if he was crying, she could not say. Mournful, woeful lamentations poured from his lips in the language he claimed was his natural one. Latin had a distinguished sound. It was something, she considered, King David might do.

She decided then and there that he was not religious, but something else entirely. Though what that entirety was, she had no clue. As she watched him struggle with a grimace to rise from his prayerful position on the floor, her heart contracted with a different kind of beat. It was the beat that let her know she was in trouble. Jareth Tremaine was an original, and because he was, he would expect all or nothing. If she gave him everything, he may reject her. There was still a great deal he did not know about her.

She got to her feet. "Do you need help?" Her voice echoed in the stillness of the church.

Jareth's face blanched and he reached out to grab hold of the pulpit for support. His breathing was shallow and his face had an odd greenish tinge. He gestured to her. "Reach under my shirt. In my back pocket is a bottle of ibuprofen."

"Isn't that cheating?" she teased as she climbed the steep steps up to the altar. She kept her tone light and approached him as she would a wounded animal. "I wasn't going to say anything, but these are jeans, aren't they?" She tugged up his tunic and tried not to think about what she was doing.

Jareth gripped the wooden podium when he swayed slightly. "Yes," he managed. He rested his head on the podium.

Elizabet dug out the bottle. "Nice rump."

Jareth's head popped up. "We are in church, Elizabet," he said over his shoulder.

She jiggled the bottle. "You plan to swallow these things dry?"

He looked around and saw the baptismal. Standing straight with a grimace, he snatched the bottle from her hand.

"Hey," she harrumphed.

"I should scold you for you making sport in the Lord's house."

She crossed her arms. "Fuss at me, then." She shrugged with one shoulder. "I'm tired and grumpy. That's my excuse and I'm sticking to it. I need a nap."

"You need a spanking," he said as he peered under the baptismal table. He reached for the water pitcher stored there. Elizabet gave her signature snort. Jareth raised a brow. "I see you disagree with me."

"Said by the man who's about to drink holy water," she said. Jareth snapped the bottle open with one hand, then tipped his head back and shook four caplets into his mouth. He swigged directly from the pitcher. "I'd like to see you try to spank me," she muttered under her breath as she glanced over her shoulder. Minh entered the church; the heavy doors creaked as they opened.

Jareth met her gaze over the pitcher, and drank until it was empty. He glanced at Minh and nodded before he turned his gaze back to her. "As much as I would love to accept your challenge, there is something I must do before traveling home, and I intend to do it regardless of whether my life is in danger. So, get *your* rump into gear before I decide to take you to task."

"I'm sorry I fussed at you for drinking the holy water," Elizabet said. She tucked her chin to her chest as the swaying of riding a horse lulled her senses. She had not lied when she said she was tired. Traveling by way of horseback was not something she was accustomed to. Her rump hurt—not that she would bring up rumps again.

"And I apologize, as well," he said. His lips were near her temple and it was a pleasant sensation to feel them move against her as he spoke. It was new, an intimacy she had never experienced before. She felt him smile. "I would only spank you under dire circumstances."

She laughed quietly so not to draw attention. Even though it was only Minh and Gabriel now, she did not want an audience. They were overly curious and it made her uncomfortable to be in the spotlight. "I hope that holy water singes your innards."

"Bloodthirsty wench," he whispered. His arm tightened around her as he pulled the reigns with the other to turn onto an adjacent dirt path. "Lucky for me, it does not work that way. Believing inanimate objects can be labeled holy is unacceptable to me. Incantations and mantras do not belong in the church."

"Excuse me; you might be speaking English, but all I hear is stuff I don't understand."

"All right." His hand traveled up her back and came to rest on the back of her neck. He squeezed slightly. "I do not believe that water was anything but water—so I was free to drink as much of it as I would like."

"Rebel."

"Ah, yes," Jareth said with an exaggerated sigh. "That is what they say." He squeezed her neck again. "But you do realize that it was not blessed water? I would have had to drink from the baptismal urn."

"You're safe from being incinerated from the inside out, then?"

"Perhaps," Jareth allowed with a smile in his voice. "Although most religious fanatics of this day would say different."

They stopped just outside of Portsmouth, at a building that stood alone except for a few rickety cottages. The structure was tall, two stories, and made of brick and dirt mortar. At once, Elizabet knew it was an orphanage. Her mother had a penchant for medieval life and she had never been more grateful. Having a parent obsessed with this time period was proving an advantage.

Elizabet followed behind Jareth, feeling like an obedient little puppy while he spoke with the abbess in sharp Norman French. He sounded angry, and the woman cowered as he stomped around the foyer and barked commands to the few nuns who were present. They all scattered, crossing themselves with their eyes lowered in a prayer pose as they hurried off.

The building seemed too old and damp to house children. The candles were half burned and lent a smell of rancid lard. There was another odor kindred to rotting meat that permeated every room, every corner. The abbess handed her a melting candle nub to light their way. Jareth, who appeared as if he were chewing nails to keep silent, led her up a narrow staircase to a large open landing that had only one door with a circular knob in the middle of it.

"Is this all right with you?" he asked cryptically.

She turned to face him. "You're here for the children." The candle lit his features and she saw again how upset he seemed.

They had traveled all day to get there, and his face was no longer fresh shaven. The weariness and stubble on his face aged him. He wore that look of being both man and boy at the same time and it was disarming, for he killed as easily as he healed.

He blew out a breath in a long exhale. "Do you want to go home? To Dover? We can turn around right now. We do not need to do this."

"Why would you say that?"

Jareth rested his weight against the door. "Because I do not know what is on the other side. I smell death."

Elizabet sucked in her breath. The flame flickered and dimmed before it became stable and bright again. Her eyes widened. "That's the smell?"

He nodded. "It is my best guess. The abbess told me the children have been sick." He lowered his gaze and fisted his hand. "There has been no food or water delivered for two days because they were scared they might become sick as well. But they will have food and care today. Now. Or I will see that they are cut off from any parish or church funding."

She reached out and touched his arm that hung at his side. He lifted his face and she caught his gaze. "We should go in, then, and do what we can."

Jareth reached up and dragged his thumb along the side of her face. Her mouth tipped up on one side as she covered his hand with hers. "You will need a mask."

She nodded. He stared at her for another minute before folding down at her feet. Elizabet braced herself against the doorframe as he ripped the hem of her dress. Just on the other side of the door was something that would change her forever. Being Jareth's duchess would be a menagerie of situations similar to this. This was merely a beginning. She was terrified and excited at once. In her innermost heart, she realized this was what she was created for. This was where she belonged—with him, doing great things that seemed insignificant but affected so many.

Jareth rose slowly, his face contorted. It was still difficult for him to move without accompanying discomfort. "Turn around," he said as he twirled the fabric around his hand. Elizabet put her back to him, her hands flattened against the door. He tied the fabric over her mouth and nose.

"Do not dare to vomit," he whispered. He leaned against her with his chest to her back. She shivered when his warm breath tickled her ear, and tried not to shrug or she would trap his head between her shoulder and cheek. She nodded. His hands came to rest on her sides, his large body caging her. "And I will try not to kill anyone for abetting the demise of these children."

Elizabet was lost for words. He was serious. It would be nothing for him to cut down a group of nuns—she was sure of it. She could hear the anger in his voice and feel the strength of him at her back. He pressed against her, one of his arms snaking down and coming around her waist. She could sense the thinly veiled abeyance of civilization. Seeing him in battle had changed her vision of him. While it did not make her like him any less, she held a greater respect for who he was and what he stood for.

"Give me conscience, Elizabet, for it is failing me."

"You'll do what is right," she said. She licked her lips and felt the roughness of the linen against her tongue. He was sucking the breath from her standing this close, this intimate. She did not know how to respond.

Jareth rested his head against her shoulder. "God help me." He squeezed her against him before he released her.

She quickly forgot how good it felt to be held when the group of children turned and stared at the sound of creaking as the door swung open. Any thought or feeling other than outrage, pity, and mourning would be sacrilegious and mean. The children were of all ages, dirty, under- and inappropriately dressed. The smell, which intensified with the opening of the door, wafted from the room.

Jareth's gaze darted throughout the room. Some children lifted their heads from their pillows as if rising was too burdensome to attempt.

"They are dying," he said flatly. It was not his way to spare the raw truth. "All of them."

Elizabet peered around him and through the open doorway where tiny, hopeful faces awaited. The position required her to stand on tip toes to see over his shoulder. She brought her hand to the makeshift mask to ensure it was secure.

Jareth's mouth turned down in the corners. "We will perform last rites and pray for mercy. It is all that can be done. Make them comfortable, and then we shall go. Can you handle this?" He peered at her over his shoulder.

She nodded. "Is it the plague?"

"Yes," he answered. "But I cannot be sure whether it is bubonic until I assess them." He stepped aside and motioned for her to enter. "Shall we?"

They went straight to the back of the room, passing the many beds that riddled the room. There was a large wardrobe along the far wall; Jareth pushed it aside to reveal a hole in the mud plaster. He crammed his hand down into the opening and retrieved a zippered leather satchel.

Elizabet lifted a brow. "You have medical bags hidden in walls and you carry a bottle of ibuprofen? Anything else you want to tell me?"

"I save lives," Jareth explained. There were seven empty water pitchers laid out on the only table in the room. He shoved them to the side and set the case down. "It is what I do, and I could not care how it is done. Sometimes I choose to cheat fate."

"You love children," she said as he took vials from the bag. "Especially those without families. I so get this about you." She glanced back and noticed he had closed the door. "It's one of the reasons I agreed to help you."

His movement slowed, but he did not stop rummaging deep into the bag. "When you make certain assessments of my character, it sounds as though you romanticize me." He looked up at her. "Do not." His thick, black brows came together. "I am not a hero. Heroes do not cheat."

"Not all heroes have access to the future."

Jareth said nothing in his defense. He said nothing at all of a private nature as they worked. Whatever had passed between them was on hold, and he was all business. He put on a physician's mask and everything else ceased to exist. It was yet another side of him she had never seen.

The room was set up youngest to oldest, although some of the healthier older girls helped with the babies. He commented that it was normal to have males and females together in an orphanage that housed all ages.

Elizabet applied salve to severely blistered bottoms while Jareth listened to lung and heart sounds with a modern stethoscope and assessed each live child. They found twenty dead in their small beds. It broke her heart that no one bothered to remove them for burial. Two of the stronger boys removed the bodies. They resembled walking corpses themselves, but did as they were told and hoisted the bodies over the window sill. Jareth said Gabriel and Minh would know what to do when they saw the collection of dead bodies leaking from the window.

Jareth administered oral pain medicine to the older children and cajoled small infants into sipping from a plastic syringe filled with anti-pyretic medicine. He was a pirate, and she would have smiled at the thought if things had not been so grave. They were using smuggled, modern means to aid these children. She was both proud and in awe that he cared enough for forgotten children. The way he held each baby, each child, was a blow to Elizabet's heart. His voice was soothing and kind as he ministered care to them with tender touches. He was nailing her fate and he did not even know it.

Jareth uncorked a vial of oil and tilted it against his fingertip. He made the sign of the cross on the girl's forehead and bowed over her, then murmured a prayer in Latin.

The girl holding vigil at the bedside looked to be about eleven years old and was ravaged herself. She asked Jareth a question in Norman French. Elizabet paused in what she was doing to listen to their conversation; Jareth would share with her later what was said. It was not hard to imagine, though. The seriousness and fear were heavy as she spoke.

"She is the girl's sister," Jareth confirmed in English. They will both be gone by morning." He asked the girl another question in slow, sympathetic French. Two tears spilled onto her cheeks and her bottom lip sucked into her mouth as she sobbed.

Jareth looked away and wiped the oil from his fingertip and onto the bed. The girl came to kneel where he could reach her. Jareth tipped the bottle against his fingertip. His hand shook, but he made the sign of the cross on the girl's forehead and recited the prayer of the sick—the last prayer said before one died.

THEY TRAVELED HARD FOR SEVERAL hours before they stopped to rest their horse. Jareth kept a punishing pace, as if riding recklessly would change what they had seen. Elizabet rode behind Jareth so he could ride hard, and she clung to him. They wanted to reach Dover by nightfall, because they did not know how many of James's men had escaped. It would be unwise to forget why they were far from home.

Jareth scratched the animal behind her ears as he held a bucket of ravine water for it to drink. It was not the first time she was caught off guard by the way he dressed. It was simple attire; a white shirt, black pants and boots, but all modern. They were custom made to suit his taste, which was a mixture of various time periods. It made him even dearer that he could have a touch of vanity and still be so honorable.

"Do you need the bathroom?" Minh's inquiry shook Elizabet from her thoughts. He grinned slightly and wagged his eyebrows when he caught her gawking at Jareth.

Elizabet leveled a stern expression at Minh. The break in silence captured Jareth's attention and he caught her staring before she could look away. "I can hold it."

"You've been holding it for hours," Gabriel said as he emerged from the forest's edge. Obviously, he had no compulsion against using a tree for a toilet.

"We won't peek," Minh promised.

"I'm fine," she said. In fact, she had been to the bathroom in Portsmouth. It was not something she liked about medieval time and she was rather embarrassed at how the maid remained the entire time she used the chamber pot. She heated and felt a deep blush at the memory. She was planning to learn how long she could hold her pee. "Yep, I'm fine."

Jareth set the bucket on the ground; the horse's nose followed and he continued to drink. "Give us a moment," he said.

Minh and Gabriel exchanged looks. After a beat, Minh shrugged and pulled an arrow from his quiver. "Whatever," he muttered under his breath. He notched the arrow against his bow and walked across the path with it drawn as his eyes swept the perimeter.

"Fifteen minutes," Gabriel said. "There are wolves in the area and we are far from Dover. Another fifty miles." He jerked his head in the direction he just came from. "There's a clearing about twenty paces. I saw a doe about twenty paces northeast—just the head and hooves. Someone's hunting this area. We can't be sure they'll be friendly. We haven't identifying flag or colors."

"I'll go back to the fork in the road and scout. Be sure no one is following us," Minh called over his shoulder.

Jareth motioned for Elizabet to go before him into the line of trees. It was winter and the trees were mostly barren, but the density of proximity gave privacy as they entered the sleeping forest.

"Are you ill?" Jareth asked.

Elizabet jumped. She had not expected his voice to be mere inches from her ear. The heat from his body radiated against her the way it had at the orphanage; he was only inches from her person. She tightened the cloak around her, taking special care to cover her neck and ear lest he make her shiver. His voice alone was lethal. Her entire world was tilting on its axis, yet Jareth went about as though everything was business as usual. He showed no signs of her inner turmoil.

"I'm fine," she stammered. "Just not used to traveling by horse."

"Elizabet, look at me. Something has changed. I can sense it." He was close on her heels. She increased the speed of her steps. Her short legs had nothing on his longer stride, but she did it anyway. She needed space, not a gravely handsome man-boy who played havoc on her feminine senses. It was scrambling her peace of mind.

They had ventured far enough that they were hidden by the dense trees. The sun peeked through the branches, giving a faint glow. It was sundown. The night would be upon them in the hour.

"I don't want to look at you," she bit out and was remorseful at once. He would not understand her irritation.

"Why?"

She could hear the smile in his voice and that made her smile. It killed the anxiety she felt, so she stopped in a clearing. Her hands clenched at her sides as she braced herself. He was close again. The edge of her cloak rustled as he passed, and her eyes went downcast as she shifted to follow him with her gaze. "Because I'm afraid of what I might see."

"Are you afraid, also, of what you might not see?" She sensed that he paused. The wind kicked up and blew a flurry of leaves across her feet. "Because I can assure you that you will not be disappointed."

"What do you think I want to see?" Her breath hitched in her throat, where her heart was racing. Jareth had a way of sucking energy from the air when he was intense, and right now—right here—he was *intense*. It was evident in the way his stride was loped and calculated as if he were either stalking her or trying to calm her. She had seen her grandfather do this with horses that needed to be broken.

That idea caused her to panic. She did not need to be broken, but instead, to stay intact. In her life, she had never been in a relationship. She did not know what a broken heart was and had no compulsion to find out.

He stepped back, the leaves rustling under his boots. Hoby boots again; both the pirate and the rebel in him appealed to her equally, if she was honest with herself. There were so many facets to his personality that she could not pick out the one that did her in—the one that snagged her and engraved his name on her heart. It was impossible to choose when so much of him was perfect and good. He had tarried after Portsmouth to look after orphaned children when his own life was in danger. Who did that?

Someone wonderful, that was who. Elizabet was lost. Even if she only admitted it to herself, she must be honest.

"You are terrified to find yourself married. Married and in a time you do not know. You are frightened because you are no longer considered a child." His voice was deep and soothing. "You are frightened that I may take from you and give nothing in return. You are scared that you will be left with a broken heart."

Elizabet closed her eyes and nodded. There was freedom in admitting that. Freedom and wonder that Jareth could voice the intentions of her heart with assurance. That he could voice exactly what she felt. If he was perfect, she was the opposite side to his coin—the tarnished side that was flawed. While she had come to the conclusion that she was hopelessly enthralled somewhere between Torquay and the orphanage, she was sure he saw how unsuited they were. "How do you know?"

"Consider this—perhaps it is how I feel as well. Perhaps I am fearful that you will find me unacceptable once you see me for who I really am." She opened her eyes and raised her chin. That haughty brow of his winged upward and his lips twisted. "I kill easily. My mind is a tool no one knows quite what to do with. The nature of my birth is questionable. I have a tendency to become obsessed with certain topics, and there is no cure for it."

"I've heard all of this before, but it's you who doesn't know everything about me," Elizabet insisted. "There are things I've learned about myself through Google. Things I've had a hard time believing." The cloak fanned open and let in cold air. She tipped her face to the shrouded sky; the sun's rays bled through the pointed bare limbs of the treetops.

Saying this would make it real. "I am the first Duchess of Dover. I will have six children by you and die when I am ninety-three." She held her breath for a beat, because the air in her lungs had escaped. Jareth's eyes held an intense stare that she could not behold for long, but it was as if he was encouraging her to continue. To get it out; throwing down a gauntlet. While saying the words aloud made it real, it also sounded as absurd as a fairy tale. But it was her life. It was no story. Elizabet forced herself to hold his gaze. "I die after you."

"At least I will never mourn you," he said, his voice soft. It was weird how she thought he was closer but now there was space between them. It was as if he had faded slowly away to give her the room she needed. He was leaning against a tree, watching her with that intense stare that had her nailed to this spot in the woods.

"But I shall mourn you," she said. In for a penny, in for a pound. There was nowhere to hide from what they were barreling toward. There was no time like the present to uncover which direction she needed to go. If she was stuck here with him, she needed ground rules. She wanted to know how he was invested where she was concerned.

"I shall mourn you for only a day and then follow you into death.

It is said that I die of a broken heart." Her shoulders rolled upward and her hands came from under her cloak, her fingers fanned as if she was releasing something. "I say I'm terrified that you will break me, when I already know you will."

Jareth's stepped toward her, his hand extended. Elizabet stared at his outstretched palm, blinking back sudden tears of self-pity she instantly hated. She did not want him to see her cry. He was not a man who understood emotions of a hormonal teenager. She did not know the nature of his care. Sir Jareth Tremaine—his grace—was overwhelming.

Regardless of her efforts, a sob left her throat. "Can it be possible?" The words tumbled from her mouth. "I can't bear it if you go away." She clasped her hands before her as if in prayer. "Please, don't leave or send me away again. I don't know what else to do if I'm not with you. I'm nobody without you. I almost went crazy with depression when you left me before. I don't know if I can take it again."

"Hush," Jareth said. He grabbed her hands and sandwiched them between his, but made no move closer. "I will not leave you. You belong with me now."

"For how long?" she asked. She shook one of her hands free to swipe at her nose. Her composure was returning as quickly as she lost it, because her mind was a sea of ideas. Notions ran through her thought process as if on a conveyer belt. That, and she did not want him to see her runny nose. "You don't know me—not really."

"You are my duchess." He released her hand to lift his to her face. "And I am quite partial to you now. I am sure I will learn of you as we get on. There is no need for histrionics. I promise wherever I go, you will be by my side."

Her nose wrinkled. "I don't think I'm being dramatic, but I do feel as though you're making fun of me."

"Why would I make fun of you?" he asked. "That would not benefit me."

Elizabet reached up to grasp his wrist. Her cheek pressed into his palm gently as she squeezed. "How do you feel about me?" she dared to ask. "I just told you that I'm destined for a broken heart because of you. Surely, you know how I feel about you." It made her skin heat again, and certainly flush a hue that made her face unattractive, but she did not care. She had to know. "Do you like me even a little? Like a girlfriend?"

Jareth's eye's widened a fraction. "You are worried that I do not *like* you?" She nodded. A puff of air left his lips. "Do you listen to me at all?" He curled his fingers into a fist and drew his hand away from her face. "It is as I said a while ago at your home. I thought I made my intentions clear."

She released his wrist and stepped back at the fury that crossed his features. He looked down at her, his blue eyes snapping with an anger she had never seen directed at her before. True, he had said he liked her, but she needed clarification. She wanted to know if that like was platonic.

"We've never been clear on this," she said in a wavering voice. Her nose itched; she wiggled it and sniffed, then motioned between them. "I don't know what I am to you. Your friend? Your nurse? What? How do I act? I mean, you hold me next to you and sometimes I think your touch is something more, but you tell me not to romanticize you. I'm scared I'll miss something and get hurt. It's one thing to pine over you in death, but to go through a life with no affection—I don't know if I can do that. You said we still have free will, so that means I can stop this now before it gets any further."

"You have the power to ruin me," he said, and his voice held a bitter edge. He sliced into the conversation before she was finished saying her piece. His jaw hardened. He stepped further from her as if he now needed the distance. "I know bone aching, soul rending pain that you could not bear, so do not speak to me of broken vows and broken hearts."

He pointed at her. "I made you my wife willingly, because I trust you. You are my friend. My nurse. The keeper of my damaged soul. I stopped in Portsmouth to give validity to our vows. No one will take you from me." His hand curled into a fist before he lowered it to his side. "You ask if I like you as one would a girlfriend?" His voice was mocking, and an acidic laugh followed. "Perhaps you should ask me instead if I shall ever allow you to leave me. As far as it concerns me, you will never go anywhere I am not. Are we clear yet?"

"I would never want to ruin you, Jareth," Elizabet said as a flush of pleasure went through her. He liked her—a great deal. And even though his tone was rough, she knew he was indignant because she just could not keep her mouth shut. She had to ruin things with her incessant questions. She lowered her voice as his expression became less cynical. "Why didn't you kiss me, then? When the priest said we were married? It's what the groom usually does after the vows. Kiss the bride."

His eyes searched her face; she examined their ice blue depths even as their corners crinkled with good humor. Whatever he saw was enough to diffuse the strained situation. Another good thing about Jareth was his ability to switch gears as quickly as she did. It was a fleece that they shared one thing in common, even if it was a deficit in attention. She would take it. "You brought all of this on because I did not kiss you after our vows? You dismissed all that passed between us in the past over a tradition of man?"

She wrinkled her nose again and nodded. Jareth reached out for her with both hands. This time they caught her waist and he pulled her against him. Her neck flexed backward to peer up at him from such a close distance. "Too many people were watching."

It was such a simple answer that Elizabet laughed, the sound misplaced in a dying, darkening forest. "So, this." Her eyes trailed down his face, his neck, and to his chest—at the close proximity they shared. "Is this the *clear* you talk about? I'm afraid you'll need to be brutally explicit with me or I'll mess things up with questions."

"You talk too much," he said as his lips touched hers. His touch was feather light and timid. "Is this what you wanted?" he murmured against her lips.

"Yes," she said. He slanted his head and pulled her body closer. She rose to her toes to give him better leverage. "This makes us clear. We are clear." She was babbling, but did not care.

"I despise traditions," he said. "You have reduced me to following after something I abhor."

A laugh caught in her throat. He was kissing the bride and it was lovely. Who cared if it was tradition? His lips were on hers and it was life changing. "I don't want you to do something you hate."

"Shhh," he hushed, and kissed the corner of her mouth.

"I can't help myself," she breathed, clutching him tighter. She let out a strangled sigh when he dipped to kiss the side of her neck. "My mouth is so inappropriate. It never knows when to shut up."

Their stance was awkward due to their height difference; his body was folded nearly in half. "Now would be an excellent time for a muzzle," he murmured.

Elizabet opened her mouth to deliver the proper parry, but then his mouth was on hers again; silencing her when she could not manage it herself. His arm came around her and he scooped her body to his. He lifted her from the ground, making her his equal height; his hold was firm, as if he wanted to weld them together. When his lips slid over hers with assuredly, she was lost.

This time there were no words. Her brain failed her. It went black—short circuited by a kiss that was whimsical and sensual at the same time. He was everywhere, stealing breath from the air around them. Elizabet was sure that if he was not holding her up, she would melt at his feet.

"Your majesty," Minh called from the forest's edge, "I think we are being followed."

She yanked her lips from his, startled by the intrusion and the intensity of the kiss. Jareth placed his cheek against hers. Their breaths mingled between them in puffs of chilled air. Wherever he held her, it was hot and alive.

"Hush," he whispered into her hair as she fought to put space between them. "Shh, stop. We did nothing wrong." His arms came around her; his hands resting on the small of her back as she slid down his body to the ground. His hand traced her back as he soothed her to still. The beating of his heart was erratic against her cheek.

Elizabet nodded against his shirt. She would do anything he asked if only he promised to kiss her again. And again. For once, she had nothing to say. If she tried to speak, she was afraid it would come out as something unintelligible.

"Jareth," Gabriel called, his voice rough with aggravation. He sounded farther away than Minh. "They're flying your brother's flag."

Jareth growled and then kissed the side of Elizabet's face near her eye. "You may prove to be the worst kind of obsession," he said.

Elizabet leaned into him. "I might need you to do that again. To be sure you did it right."

"I *love* your mouth." His full lips twisted ruefully. "I have wanted to touch it since the first time I saw you." His right hand came between them and he ran his fingertips over her lips. "To be able to touch you like this is . . . sublime."

She smiled. "Sublime? I like that. Will you kiss me again? I'm not sure I like it yet."

Jareth's smile was brilliant. "Me, neither."

Elizabet balled her hand and struck his chest, but his gaze bounced to where Gabriel and Minh approached. The pair had parted the trees to enter their private haven. They were becoming impatient. He turned Elizabet until he sheltered her with his body.

"It's a lookout rider. They are searching for something or someone," Gabriel stated as he came through the copse. He spoke loudly, letting his voice announce him before he came into view.

"Then let us have a look," Jareth said, his breath on Elizabet's face. He gripped her arms, but did not release her. Gabriel and Minh stood a good distance away from them, looking embarrassed that they had interrupted.

Minh cleared his throat. "Yeah . . . I . . . uuuhhhh. . . . .have a pair of binoculars." He fidgeted with the satchel that he wore over his shoulder.

Elizabet pulled away from Jareth. "You said we couldn't take anything modern." Her hand snapped toward Minh as she peered up at Jareth. She let her expression demand he fight for her honor.

"He has his iPhone," Gabriel gibed. "You brought along a pistol." Elizabet whipped her head around. "A weapon, I should point out, that you hid from us. Don't get your panties all twisted over a pair of binoculars."

"There will be no talk of the duchess's panties," Jareth warned, but a smile tugged at the corner of this mouth. He peered down at her as she glanced up at him with eyes narrowed. "We need binoculars," he said. He bent to place a kiss on her forehead before he released her.

"We needed the pistol too," she mumbled. "They fussed at me for having a watch. I didn't tell you about that; I just remembered."

"It is nothing to get your knickers all twisted over," he said in a low voice, and pulled way before she could strike him.

"I'm not done with you yet." She grabbed his arm as he turned away to follow Minh.

Jareth looked back over his shoulder. "I will never be done with you, but duty calls." The corner of his mouth curled. "So be a good girl and say what you must before Gabriel gets *his* knickers twisted."

Elizabet stepped closer. "You either?" She motioned between them. "What did you mean by that: *me either*? I'm just throwing this out there, but that was my first time . . . you know." A strangling noise came from her throat as she struggled for courage.

Thankfully, Jareth put her out of her misery. His stance shifted; his smile was crooked. "I lied. I liked it very much." He leaned down toward her a fraction and murmured, "Too much."

JARETH LOWERED THE BINOCULARS. "IT is Gyula,"

He was sandwiched between Gabriel and Minh, all on their bellies, overlooking the valley where the lone rider allowed his horse a drink in the stream. Gyula was not watchful. He radiated confidence, and this bothered Jareth.

Minh took the binoculars from Jareth and leaned forward for a better look now that the man had been identified. "Do you want me to kill him?"

"God, Minh," Gabriel said. "Do you always want to kill someone?"

"Third commandment," Jareth said, looking at Gabriel with a frown. "Mind it or say nothing at all."

Gabriel nodded and appeared remorseful, but only slightly so. Minh looked smug. "What's the matter? Scared to dirty your Calvin Klein tighty whities?" He spit on the ground, his upper lip curling. "You're bloody lucky I had your back in Torquay. Weren't saying too much about my killing back there."

"That was battle," Gabriel replied. He reached over and snatched the binoculars. "This is a man giving his horse a drink."

"He's armed," Minh pointed out. "He's got a cross bow—a modern one—three blades, and I think I see a rifle under the saddle."

"It's a Smith and Wesson," Gabriel said with a touch of awe in his voice. He adjusted the lenses for better clarity. "Looks old, but in bloody good condition."

"Jareth—" Minh shifted onto one elbow and turned. "He's Hunnish in appearance. Why didn't you tell us this? He has the look of my kin."

Before Jareth could answer, Gyula removed a travel bracelet from his wrist and tossed it the air. The portal flashed open with a sizzling pop as it contracted to receive the traveler.

"He's got travel gems," Gabriel announced.

Jareth quickly lifted the fold of his cloak and pushed back the cloth to reveal his seven travel bracelets. "They are all here." He looked at Gabriel, then Minh. "He must have stolen them."

Gabriel held up his wrist. "Eight. Mine is from the future, so that means his does as well. If you have the original seven, you know what that means."

"Weird alchemy," Minh grumbled. He grabbed the binoculars from the ground where Gabriel had dropped them. "Gideon will not like this." Gideon was the guardian assigned to study the alchemy of the travel stones. He would know how this was possible.

Gyula nudged his horse forward into the portal.

"He's taking his *horse*," Gabriel said. He shook his arm so his sleeve returned into place. He yanked the binoculars from Minh's hands.

"Don't get any ideas," Minh said. He unwillingly released his hold on the glasses. "Your horse has too many bowel issues. Traveling time would never be the same."

Jareth shushed them with a scolding look. Just then, Gyula looked up to where they were hidden and touched his forehead in mock salute.

"That bastard," Minh said, and stood. He yanked back the branches, so he could be seen plainly from below. "Bastard," he yelled.

Gyula smiled and tilted his head slightly before he guided his horse into the circle of light.

"We should have shot him," Gabriel said. He rose to his feet. They were all aware of that, but the circle closed so quickly there had been no time. Gabriel looked at Minh. "I should have let you fire that arrow."

Minh smiled. His mouth opened to speak, but Jareth put his hand up.

"Patience," he advised. He leapt to his feet, repositioning the sword at his side all in one fluid movement. "He wants us to know he has the stones." He looked to where Gyula disappeared. "But I wonder why the drama? Why did he go to this much trouble to meet us here? Now?"

"Jareth," Minh said. "Why didn't you tell us he's a Hun? I can't help but feel if we had known this, we would have more to work with. We have men in the future who see to stuff like this."

"Because I was not sure of it," Jareth said. "He has similar attributes, but his genes are mixed with Scottish, perhaps Viking." He put his hands on his hips and let his shoulders droop. "Also, I do not want to tamper with time." He motioned to Gabriel. "You have said that things are becoming jumbled. The more we access time and jump it, the greater the divide between our thoughts and memories."

"I've got it," Gabriel said. He snapped his fingers twice. "Someone's trying to murder you. The battle with the Huns, remember? They were sent to terminate you."

"Quick thinking, Sparta," Minh said sarcastically. He reached for a cigarette in his cloak and looked up at Jareth. "Why was it you who retrieved him again? I can't seem to remember." He rolled the filter of the cigarette on his tongue before he stuck it in his mouth and lit it. All the while he wore an expression of deep thought. "Oh," he said with no surprise. "He used to be a lethal warrior." He looked at Gabriel. "Key words: *used to be*." He turned back to Jareth, smoke curling from his nostrils. "So, this is why things are getting hazy? Gyula's screwing with us?"

"That's what I said," Gabriel growled. "They're trackers—they'll never stop. It's what they're bred to do."

"We will split up in Dover," Jareth said. "I will handle it from here. I cannot and will not take a chance with your lives."

"You're dismissing us?" Gabriel asked.

"What about the duchess?" Minh asked. He tossed his unfinished cigarette aside. "We can take her back with us until we find the breach. She can stay with Gabriel and Liang."

"Absolutely not," Jareth said, his voice booming. "Elizabet stays with me—always. I know how to protect what is mine."

Minh and Gabriel exchanged glances.

"Of course, *Magister*," Minh said, using the Latin word for teacher as Jeremy would when addressing Jareth. "If that is what you will. But consider the consequences. They will be looking for any weaknesses."

"And obviously," Gabriel said. "Elizabet has become a weakness."

"Even if she's your *only* weakness . . ." Minh added. He jumped to his feet in a smooth jolt. " . . . You must consider that you are married now and things have changed." He looked at Gabriel. "I tease Gabriel, but I know it is the love of my sister that has humanized him."

"All right," Jareth said. "Help me get Elizabet to Dover alive, and then we part. Whatever the future holds must be done fairly. I fear we are tampering with time too often. We are taking for granted that we can fix things. Whatever we do not like, we change. It has to stop."

"And what if that means death?" Minh asked with a growl. "There are people who count on you. Alive. Forget Elizabet. There are host that will not survive unless you train them. Not to mention, the future of the medieval church hinges on your existence. You are the harbinger for the English translation, you fool. Think."

"It's not just training host," Gabriel put in. "It's seeing them gain their humanity first so they can be taught anything. Otherwise, they'll destroy the world with a cocky smile on their juvenile faces all because they had a hormone rush."

"They're a bunch of kids with no guidance," Minh added.

Jareth brought his hands up to silence them. "Just because we can command time, does not give us the right to change the natural course of things. True, someone is attempting to thwart the formation of the Amalgam, but we must let it happen. In our selective silence, we will bring them out." Gabriel and Minh passed a skeptical look between them. "Let us fetch Elizabet," Jareth said, his voice pensive. "She must be impatient by now and wondering where we are. We have left her too long, I fear. I do not want to cause her worry." He regarded both of them. "Say nothing of what we have witnessed. I will not have my wife believing she has anything to fear. Beware the words you choose. We keep what has passed here between us."

Chapter 13

ELIZABET HAD NEVER SEEN THE castle from the outside. The night she was sneaked into it had been dark and foggy, and she had been terrified and unsure of the caliber of people she was in the company of.

As they approached the hill where the castle sat, she had time to take it in and enjoy the view. Its outer walls were squared and plain, and the way it was seated on the hilltop was not beautiful like a fairy tale castle, but majestic and formidable. Breathtaking. She could not fathom that she had recently been held in the dwelling for more than a month.

"The abbey," Jareth announced as they passed the small stone building on the outskirts of the property. He pointed to a dark thatch of greenery near the abbey. "That is one entrance to the underground."

"Tunnels?" she asked. "I thought they were built in the Second World War?"

"You have studied my home," Jareth said in a pleased tone. "They were made use of after years of lying dormant. We use them for secretive purposes. I have most of the tunnels locked, but I will show them all to you."

"I feel special."

He smiled. "You are. I have not shown anyone but necessary staff. They are forbidden."

"What do you have down there?"

"It is a surprise."

They were together, but separate. Atop the tall horse with their bodies pressed close, yet miles apart. Jareth had been broodingly quiet and detached earlier, but with the first sight of the castle, he became talkative.

Elizabet turned her face into his chest as the wind kicked up. Jareth shifted his hold on the reigns to adjust his hold on her. It was inevitable that she would mess things up given the time and chance. It was her way—what she did. She could hardly help it.

"What can I expect here?" she asked. His gaze was fixed ahead, watching the approaching towering castle. "Does anyone know I'm coming? That you're married?"

He nodded, his eyes still gazing at his home, his expression whimsical, forlorn. "Mrs. Wheatley is aware. You will be received cordially."

"What does that mean?" She inhaled deeply against his cloak. He smelled of horse and Jareth. She could smell the sea, as well. It was that singular scent that invoked memories of her time here. "Cordially?"

"You will find that history is distorted here. It is time you see Dover Castle as it truly is. I have improvised my home and it shows. I make allowances for curiosity. I do not make frivolous leaps, but I do enjoy the idea of what progression brings to the world. So, when I say cordially, I mean that you will be properly received as a bride of a duke."

"Can I insert a 'wow' right here?" she asked with a smile. "It's like living a fairy tale."

"This fairy tale has teeth. Do not become overly comfortable." He jerked his chin toward Minh, who was looking over his shoulder as they passed the abbey. "This is far enough. Tie the horses here and I will send for someone to tend them."

Gabriel circled his horse around and sided up with Jareth. "This is it, then?" Jareth nodded, his expression stoic and unreadable. Gabriel's shoulders slumped as he guided the horse to a stop. "I will investigate Gyula. I'm sure you know something in the future. I'll put Gideon on the count of the stones. Maybe he can figure out where the breach occurs."

"Be sure he understands that the count exceeds the tangible number," Jareth directed, then he looked at Minh. "See that Jeremy is tested for possible disturbances. He swallowed a good bit of the English waters when he dissipated. It is different than gulf water. Be sure he is able to transform safely. I cannot have him weak, considering we have an enemy jumping time. We may need him again."

Minh nodded. "What is your plan?"

"Just so we know where we are on the grand scheme of the chess board," Gabriel added.

"I need to secure my bride," Jareth said. "My intuition tells me that Catherine will not let this go, especially now that I have executed her father. There can be no doubt that my marriage is legitimate." Minh smiled, and glanced at Gabriel. Jareth's tone changed and his voice lowered in warning. "I will return to the future in the time that I claim Jeremy. Shortly after the storm."

"Once you've secured your marriage," Gabriel said with a grin.

Jareth scowled. "Are we done?"

"We are," Minh said.

"Good," Jareth said. He spurred his horse forward and passed between them. "Under no circumstances are you to return. Do you understand?"

"Yes, your majesty," Minh said, and bowed even though he was saddled.

Jareth glanced back at Gabriel. Likewise, he bowed. "Of course, your grace. We'll not fail you."

Elizabet craned her head as Minh and Gabriel dismounted and tied their horses to the abbey gate. They were bickering with one another, but they worked in harmony.

"What do you mean?" she asked as she kept one eye on Gabriel. He threw a time band in the air and the portal opened—it never got old seeing that happen. She could not look away until they were gone into thin air. "We're married. Can't get more secure than that."

Jareth's thighs gripped the horse beneath them as he steered up the steep incline to the castle gate. He glanced at her upturned face—just a flicker and then away. "There is the issue of consummation."

She said nothing, but slowly rolled her chin to her chest. Her face was hot and she knew it was red, which made it worse. Try as she might to not think of being embarrassed, her cheeks felt as though they were on fire.

A low rumble came from Jareth's chest, which had her peeking at him. He was laughing—not loudly—barely audibly, really—and lazily watching her through his long, sooty black lashes. And then, one of those blue eyes winked.

THE PEOPLE AT DOVER CASTLE were lovely, Elizabet decided. She also decided that she would not think about what Jareth said or she would panic. He was currently listening to his squire, who was speaking in rapid French, and giving an account of things that had occurred in Jareth's absence.

Jareth should have warned her that he had taken modern to a whole different level. She expected the English to be passable. And she had made provision for things like plumbing and (prayerfully considering) drainage systems. But an infirmary in the tunnels and solar panels on the east wing? There was even an underground hospital of sizable magnitude.

Jareth bit down on the syringe cap, removed it with his teeth, and thrust the needle into Elizabet's arm. After a tour of the infirmary, he gave her a hefty dose of antibiotics. Then he inoculated her with the smallpox vaccine.

She was beginning to see how the Amalgam seeped into every part of his life, and how it would hers as well, now that they were meshed. She only hoped she would not be a disappointment to Jareth. Surely, that would come. Everything she beheld was way out of her league. She had her own secrets, but they paled in comparison to Jareth's. His were grand and had life purposes—hers were just messy and complicated.

"Why didn't you tell him you knew my mother?" Elizabet asked Mrs. Wheatley. Jareth had deposited her quite unceremoniously with the maid, then left her in his chamber and went take of business he said could not wait.

"It is not my story to tell." Mrs. Wheatley smiled at her reflection in the mirror and continued to brush Elizabet's hair in long strokes. Her weathered face was familiar and brought calm to Elizabet's chaos. There was a hollow pit in the bottom of Elizabet's gut. She was doubtful that things would end well; circumstances were barreling out of control. "That is your story, and I trust that you have revealed it in your own time."

Elizabet nodded. It caused the brush to graze her scalp. "I told him when he came back—after I took care of him and he had me sent away. Where did you go? You never came back."

"What could I have done?" Mrs. Wheatley asked. "His grace can be boorish when time is tampered with." Her voice became gruff as she mimicked Jareth. "Things must unfold at a natural pace." She smiled sheepishly and turned a pointed expression on Elizabet. "Besides, you needed the time and space to learn each other. I knew he would make the right decision. I have known you were what he needed since the first time I met you."

"But I was only a child. I was what? Like five?"

"Even then, you were loyal and faithful." Mrs. Wheatley stopped brushing, and gazed at Elizabet through the mirror's reflection. "Look at what a beautiful woman you have become. I was right to choose you." Pride passed over the elder's features and her eyes filled to the brim with tears, but did not spill over. "Your mother would be so happy."

Tears gathered in Elizabet's eyes as well at the mention of her mother. She reached up and covered Mrs. Wheatley's hand that rested on her shoulder. "Don't make me cry. Jareth will think I'm afraid." She lifted her wobbling lips in a smile.

"His grace will never believe that." Mrs. Wheatley squeezed her shoulder. "He would not have married you if he thought you a coward."

They spoke of nothing else as Elizabet was prepared for the next phase of medieval life. She took in the master room after Mrs. Wheatley left her. The chamber had changed little. It was still dark and manly, but now it also held a trunk of women's clothes and the vanity where she was currently seated. It excited her beyond reason that he had thought to make her comfortable—that he had made provision. There were touches of feminine colors and pieces that had been added for her. It made her smile even though she was all alone and there was no one to witness her joy.

Could it be possible that Jareth was planning to do what he said he would? Would he demand a true marriage? Her lips trembled with the burden of maintaining a joyful appearance. Now that ravishment was nigh, all she wanted to do was wretch. She was the worst kind of deceiver and it was time to pay the piper. Jareth was about to discover what an oxymoron she was.

And when he knew the whole truth—would he still want her? All he did to make her feel welcome and comfortable, he may come to resent because of who she was. Or more to the point, what she was not.

Jareth stood outside the doors of his bedchamber long after Mrs. Wheatley left the room. He had given Elizabet time to settle in, but he felt bereft. He was unsure how to proceed, charting unknown waters. Lost, without a compass.

Using his thumbnail, he traced the wood grain of the door and rested his forehead against the polished surface. Faint sounds seeped through the heavy portal. The scrape of furniture moving and then light footsteps. The noises resembled activity from someone trying to distract their mind from troubling thoughts. Elizabet was worried about the upcoming night.

She should join the club. Jareth was a jumble of nerves when he considered what was required of *him* this night. He did not do relationships. He had subjects, tenants, host, and guardians he governed. Gabriel and Minh were friends, but they also were under his employ; it was different. Tonight, he had to cross over into an intimacy he never expected to tread. It was something he could not compromise, and he hoped his bride understood the necessity of having a marriage in truth. He needed everything about their union to be legitimate. Legitimacy was the right of his offspring and he would not leave it to the whim of anyone.

Briskly, with great surety, he knocked and opened the door before he lost his nerve. His eyes scanned the room, searching for her. A moment of panic went through him when she was nowhere to be seen. Not at the dressing table he had Minh find for her, not in bed, nor pacing the floor as he expected to find her.

"I'm here," she said. She motioned to the window she had vacated. He was grateful that she did not witness the way he startled at her voice as she stepped from the shadows. "I thought I'd be able to see the cliffs from here, but I was wrong. It's still beautiful, though."

Jareth's favorite type of night, but he did not say so—he was too relieved that she had not fled or jumped from the castle. He had read of females being self-harming when they were frightened. It was a bonus that she was not given to vapors. At this point, he was not sure he would not expire from some kind of anomaly—possibly due to his rapid heart rate.

He could tell by her tone that she liked his home and the thought warmed him. He could not imagine uniting with someone contrary. It would be inexcusable. Dover was his home, and his duchess needed to form a love for it if they were to get on.

"I like your people," she said. She hugged her arms around herself; the movement made him notice that she was dressed in the white gown Gabriel brought. It was from Paris and he had claimed Elizabet would love it. Jareth did not like to think why Gabriel would know such things. He frowned and looked away. He did not know or understand how, but he did see that the garment morphed her into the most beautiful woman he had ever seen. It grated on him that Gabriel was aware of this, when it was he who needed some inkling into a female's mind—preferably now. Divine inspiration would do.

"But I will have to study French." She shrugged. "I know a bit of the language spoken by my mother's family, but it is different." Her lips twisted. "Very different."

Jareth nodded, feeling awkward. He stared at her lips and looked away, a scowl forming on his face again. Although he had nothing to add, just standing there like a dummy was revolting.

He felt her gaze on his profile. His jaw worked and tensed as his eyes jumped from the bed to the vanity. "Will you teach me?"

"What?" He turned to look back at her.

"Norman French . . . I need to learn."

"Rightly so," he bit out, and followed it with a brisk nod. The words from his mouth seemed to jar him back to reality, gave him gravity where before, he had none. He walked to the vanity table and began removing his weapons because he did not know what else to do. Usually he dispensed of them in the outer sanctuary of his room, but tonight he wanted them close. They were still unsure where the enemy lurked. "I will see that Percival begins in the morning. He is very good at modern English and French."

"I don't want him to teach me," she said. Jareth's fingers paused in untying his gambeson. "I want it to be you."

"Why?" He slowly resumed unknotting the tie.

"I think it will give us more time to adjust to each other," she said. "And to talk. Get to know each other."

"There will be plenty of opportunities to be together," he

responded. The tie came apart. He tugged the tunic hem and with one fluid motion, removed it over his head. "I keep a busy schedule." He frowned when he realized she had looked away; he had forgotten the scars she knew intimately and would remember. He passed his hand over the healed incision, He did not feel the touch because of layers of scar tissue. It was a gesture that may be perceived as an attempt to hide them from view, and perhaps he was. "Percival is most apt—"

"I need to tell you something," Elizabet cut in.

Their words overlapped and Jareth put his hands on his hips. His left eyebrow arched against his will, prompted by impatience. He had things to say and she was interrupting. She should not stop him when he was willing to speak. His new bride had no idea the struggle he was having.

Elizabet glowered and folded her arms before her to squeeze her torso. "Do you have to look at me like that?"

"Like what?"

"Like you want to kill me or something. I have something I need to tell you, before we . . ." She rotated her hand in the air, and cleared her throat when his eyebrows shot up. "It's important to me. I want to be honest. I don't want to learn French from Percival."

"Kill you? No, but perhaps that spanking may be appropriate," Jareth teased. He shrugged. "You keep acting as though you want it. I just might have to give it to you."

An enigmatic smile touched her lips.

Jareth opened his mouth, but thought better and merely growled. "You are beguiling; I will give you that." He passed his fingers through his hair and turned to the vanity where there was a bowl of water for his night ablutions. He plunged his hands into the cold water and searched for the cloth at the bottom of the bowl. "I had a plan—a thought to come to you and reason with you. Tell you that you need not worry of being mistreated. I planned to tell you—"

"I can't read," Elizabet blurted.

Jareth's hands continued to wring the cloth between his hands, even as he watched her in the mirror over the vanity. It was a modern piece—from the regency era that Minh had smuggled in, and the resolution was good. Her throat worked as she nervously swallowed. Her arms uncrossed and fluttered to her mid-section, her fingers playing with the pink ribbon at her waist.

"I have a slew of learning deficits. I didn't even finish high school. It was too embarrassing to have everything read to me." She glanced up and he met her reflected gaze.

He stared at her while his hands mistreated the cloth, practically strangling it and then discarding it on the vanity without using it. Still, he remained silent and schooled his expression to give nothing away.

"My mom read to me," she soldiered on. "I retain what I hear as long as I understand it." She yanked on the already secure ribbon as if she could tie it tighter.

Jareth braced his hands on the vanity and leaned forward. Suddenly the room was swaying and he needed solid ground. His ears must not be working, because he thought he just heard that his duchess was illiterate.

"When she died, I sort of gave up. I didn't like how the teachers treated me—like I was stupid. I could tell they didn't want to read *everything* to me. I put them out. So you see—Percival can't teach me. It would be too embarrassing, and then everyone would know you married a dummy." Her arms flew open, her face wild with emotion as words continued to fail him. "Would you say something? Anything! Tell me to leave, or call me stupid—whatever! But please say *something*."

Jareth tore his eyes from her reflection and lowered his gaze to where his hands gripped the wooden vanity edge. "I think I need to sit down," he said to his hands. He heard Elizabet behind him, scraping a chair toward him. This was the best joke of his life. Thoughts tumbled through his mind. He recalled the times she had avoided reading, times such as when he was wounded and he asked her to read a section of a textbook aloud. She made an excuse every single time—and no wonder.

Fate had him married to a girl who could not read, and who lacked even the basics of an education—even by modern standards, which was minimal. Of all the people in the world, this girl was chosen by time and chance to be his bride? She could not seat a horse while her people bred steeds, and she could not read although her mother had been a teacher. He suddenly had a headache. A massive one.

"Here," Elizabet said. The seat of a chair hit his calves and had no choice but to sit. He folded his body onto the dainty chair. For a moment, he felt he may sway from the narrow seat, but then corrected.

Elizabet stood back, her arms crossed over her chest. A hand fluttered to her mouth where she nibbled at her cuticle, but then stopped and went back to viciously hugging herself.

"You knew things, found information about me." He touched his fingertips to his chest. "And when I was wounded—you knew certain things that I had no hand in teaching."

"YouTube," she interrupted with a shrug. A blush crept up from her throat to her cheeks, but she maintained eye contact. He had to give her that—she was being brave. "It's a website that has videos. No reading required. I used the voice activated app on my phone."

"Resourceful."

"What I couldn't watch, I had Beau read to me."

A rise of jealousy sparked. "Beau?"

"My cousin," Elizabet said. She gestured with her hands to nothing in particular. "She's Jeremy's friend. Best friend—I think. They're inseparable."

Jareth nodded as if he understood, but he did not. He was trying to grasp that she was able to make a life without having the skills of the most basic function. However, he was happy that Beau was a girl. Ladies wore pants in the future and had masculine names. Something he must remember.

"I'm sorry," she said, her voice small. "But I wanted to be honest. I thought you should know before it's too late." Her expression turned petulant. "It's your fault, you know? You didn't let me finish that night you told me I'd be your duchess. I tried to tell you there were things about me you didn't know. Things you'd probably not like. I tried to tell you that I wasn't duchess material, but you shooed me off."

"I remember," he said. He pressed the bridge of his nose with his thumb and forefinger.

"It was wrong. I'm sorry. But . . ." She paused and chewed the inside of her cheek, and looked away when he met her gaze.

"But," he prompted. His hand went to his lap where the other waited. He threaded his fingers together and waited.

Elizabet glanced at him. "Well, we're sort of stuck together now.

You know—till death do we part." Her voice lowered. "You have annulments if you can't get past this. I'd understand. It was wrong not to tell you until now."

Jareth slid his arms down his thighs, his fingers threaded until his elbows rested on his knees. He bowed his head as he released a slow, steady whistle. After several thought-filled moments, he looked up and captured her gaze. "No."

Elizabet nodded, a barely detectable movement. She looked away, but not before he witnessed tears in her eyes. He watched the first tears she could not stop from falling and saw her disgust as she swiped at her cheeks before her face became a mask of indifference. Without a second thought, he reached out and grabbed her hand. She stood close to him, since she had thought to bring him a chair when he nearly swooned like a vapid youth.

She had learning disabilities. He was a progeny with a mind of the highest level of scholars. All of his life he had been pushed aside because people were fearful of his knowledge, of his passion and devotion to translating. How was he different? They were the same in their differences. A match. It would have been better if she was upfront weeks earlier, but there it was, and there was nothing he could do about it. He would accept it as a challenge and overcome it for her. Once his mind processed the information, he saw the possibilities—the exact nature of who she was and how this was to be.

Elizabet gazed through blurry eyes to where his hand curled around hers. Slowly, she tipped her chin up until her eyes met his. She sniffed and he eyed her with a lifted forehead. He tilted his head a fraction.

"You do know that over ninety percent of the population here cannot read?"

Elizabet's eyes blinked rapidly. "You do understand that in my time, not knowing how to read just doesn't happen," she ground out. Her teeth were clenched as though she fought for control over the tone she used. "Don't act like this isn't a big deal. *Everyone reads.*"

"Except you. You cannot read."

Elizabet's head jerked back and an awkward grunt tore from her throat, more animalistic than human. He watched her struggle for words, patience, dignity, or a mixture of all three and his heart contracted with pain.

Finally, she spoke. "Except me."

Jareth had to look away. The agony that infused her features was more than he could bear when he knew exactly how he felt about her admission. Elizabet was a champion for his linage and he would extend her the same grace in an equal measure. She would never suffer shame over this matter again as long as he had breath in his body.

"It is a good thing that I love you, Elizabet Tremaine. Otherwise, we would be stuck indeed. I would very much like to discuss, later, that you have difficulties in learning." She uncoiled her hand from the tie at her waist to grasp his hand in return. "But right now—I would rather discuss what is at hand." He offered her a smile. "We have a marriage that is yet to be consummated and I would like to know, dear wife, if you could trust me enough to give me your innocence? You see, as imperative as this information is, I would like to ensure that no one can take you from me—regardless of whether you are able to read."

"You still want to be married to me?" she asked with wonder in her voice.

"Desperately."

Her lips wobbled as she smiled, her eyes wrinkling in the corners, tears dripping down her cheeks. "I would like very much to be yours, Jareth Tremaine, if you will have me."

Jareth's smile turned wolfish. He yanked her to him, and her body tumbled onto his lap. "I will have you."

Chapter 14

JARETH WATCHED HER SLEEP.

She slept on her stomach with her hands crammed under the pillow, her lips slightly parted. Her hair partially covered her face that was flushed from the day's lingering heat in the room. He had opened the windows, but it would take time to cool the interior.

And time was something he did not have.

Blowing out a slow breath, he buried both hands in his hair and used his palms to massage his scalp as he stared at the floor.

Percival had awakened him in the night with new developments. His brother's men were here to take him to Kent for an audience with Church officials. So it was to be the Church that gave him trouble. Not for the murder of a nobleman, and not for a broken betrothal, but for translating scripture. Whatever the charge, there was a spoiled brat behind the accusation and he would have her head for it. It was ironic that he wore a set of seven time stones around his wrist and could not give his bride another hour to adjust to her new life.

"Hey." Her voice was sleepy and soft.

Jareth smiled at the floor. Once he looked at her it would all be different. He glanced up slowly, taking his time to savor the initial jolt as they made eye contact for the first waking moment of this morning. Everything was new. Last night had been pivotal. He had ventured from being alone in life to united with someone else. He would never be the same.

She smiled lazily, her hair a tangled mess. The sheets were piled over her even though it was warm, and she pushed at them.

He released the hold on his hair. He did not care if he left it sticking up in every direction. He straightened in his chair and returned her silly, lopsided grin. "Good morning."

Elizabet yanked the covers up under her arms. "How long have you been awake?"

"Long enough." He got up and prowled toward the bed.

"You're despicable."

"I am a hopelessly besotted man."

Elizabet tucked the sheets around her. She eyed him with a faint grin. "Really? You expect me to believe that? That one night changes everything?"

"I have already told you that I love you. Last night just sealed the deal." Jareth shrugged with one shoulder. He placed his hands on the bed, his weight causing her to dip and roll toward him slightly. "I have not the time to spar with you, wife." He reached out and grabbed a lock of her wild hair and tugged playfully. "I love you," he mouthed silently. She blushed prettily and looked away.

Jareth sighed. "I say these things abruptly because the Black Prince has sent a small army to collect me." Elizabet's gaze jerked to his. He nodded once, slowly, and released her hair. "I have to go, but I leave you with those I trust."

He stepped back, stood tall, and removed the seven bands from his wrist. It was nonnegotiable to take them along.

He observed her silent turmoil as his hands worked the bands from his wrist. "My brave girl," he said. He placed the bands in his palm and held them out for her inspection. "You need not fear for your life or mine. All will be well."

"You can't promise me that," she grumbled. "I heard what Minh and Gabriel said. Things are changing. Someone is tampering with time."

"Come," he said gently, dismissing the ache in his heart. "Get dressed and see me to the gates of my land. If you send me off to uncertain fate, then I shall go willingly."

She turned her face up, fresh tears held trapped in her eyes. "What do you want me to do? Stay here and pretend that I know what to do? How to act? Do you know how long you will be gone?"

"I expect you to be wonderfully you," he said. "I married you knowing full well what I was getting. Although, I *was* under the assumption that you could read."

She narrowed her eyes. "I would have told you sooner."

"I am only teasing," he said, and motioned to the covers. "Now, get up."

"Turn your head." She clasped the sheets under her armpits when he smiled and shook his head. "I won't parade myself around in broad daylight." Her lips twisted. "Regardless that I've been thoroughly ravished."

Jareth laughed out loud, reached out and pulled her hair again, the same strand as before, because it was sticking out and begging for it. "That's cute. I will remember in the future that ravishing makes you cranky."

"Well, I wouldn't say that," she muttered.

He laughed harder.

Elizabet stuck her tongue out.

"Come," he said. His smile died as a shout rose from below. "I have tarried all that I am able. If we do not hurry, you will have more than a husbandly hand to aid you." Elizabet's expression sobered. Reality was outside, waiting with swords and other assorted weapons. He held his hand out. "Come, I promise not to look at the good parts."

Jareth played the part of lady's maid for his bride. And he tried not to peek at the good parts, which was difficult since neither of them were apt in ladies' wear of the time period. He worked the lacing on the back of the dress, his eyes on her fingers as she piled her hair in a bun atop her head and stuck pins to keep it in place. A bun was most certainly not medieval, but a large, silly headdress had been provided for her and it would look stupid if she left her hair down.

"I'll miss you," she said. Her hands patted the bun she had made and then she smoothed down the sides with the pads of her fingers. Jareth smiled even though she could not see it. "Do I use the time bands?" she asked. His hands paused at her waist where he tied the lacing. "I don't know how or which tunnel to take."

He grasped her wrist that the bands encircled and twirled her to face him. The movement was like a dance step, fluid and practical. A small peep of exclamation came from her at the rapid move. Jareth kissed the tip of her nose to soothe the rough way he had handled her.

"Use them only if necessary. Keep to the paths on the right. Those are the future. Take the widest opening. It is the path we are destined to travel."

"How do they work?" She leaned into him, her cheek resting against his chest. He held her close and relished the notion that she was not a faint girl, one who needed to be coddled through each of life's bumps—or his own shortcomings. She spoke of time travel as if it was merely a trip to a nearby village. There were strengths to contra balance her weaknesses. "I've never gone alone."

"It is strange magic," Jareth said. He realized again how small she was when they stood together. His back was bent as he rubbed his cheek against hers. Something primitive and protective rested in his bosom. No one had ever belonged exclusively to him, and that was what she was: his.

"I cannot explain it with reason. It can be calculated by science, but I do not have the time now. Gabriel claims it will be referred to as the science of alchemy in the future. It is specific, but hidden. Secret. Some things remain unexplained and a mystery. For one reason or another, Dover is the center point of the alchemy of the stones. There are no limits of time travel where Dover is concerned, but there are limitations to travel elsewhere. You will learn these places and times, but for now, stay to the right. You cannot go wrong. There is a marked pathway between medieval Dover and your Louisiana." He squeezed her closer. "I have to go, wife, or they will bust the door down. Remember, it is the widest path. It will be riddled with bright hues of amethyst. Like jewels. That is how you will identify your home."

A loud thumping sounded at the door, followed by a string of harsh French. Elizabet stiffened and grabbed at Jareth with both hands.

"I'm scared," she said.

"Hush," Jareth said into her ear, then kissed her there. "Promise me that you will find Minh or Gabriel. They can be found easily enough. Whenever you reach the destination, find your home and they will come."

"I promise," she whispered. "But only because you're asking me. I don't want to."

Jareth smiled into her flesh, and hoped she felt it sliding along her skin. "Speak as little as possible and only to those who know the language of your custom. Do nothing to draw attention until I return. Trust only Percival and Mrs. Wheatley."

She nodded as the banging grew urgent and the words became insistent on the other side of the door. "I don't want to let you go," she said, but even as she spoke, her hands opened and she released him. She stepped back, as did he.

He leaned forward and kissed her sweetly, as if an army did not await beyond the door and on the castle lawn below. "One last thing," he murmured. The door shook with the insistent pounding of his eager captors' fists. "Take the sheets and burn them."

Elizabet drew back. "Sheets?" Her eyes darted around the room and came to rest on the only possibility. "The bed sheets?"

"Yes," Jareth answered. He stepped closer, his hands coming to her shoulders and let his eyes bore into hers. "If you do not, then the servants will string the sheets for public viewing. They are stained with your blood. It is a custom that the virginity of the bride be proved by the displaying of the marital sheets."

She looked down between them to the tips of his boots.

"Things can be rather barbaric here at times." He squeezed her shoulders. "We can forgo this custom. For all accounts, your blood is mine as well, but I had no blood to shed." Elizabet gaped at him, and he grinned. "What part of my upbringing did you think allowed for the debauching of ladies?"

Elizabet flung herself at him, wrapped her arms around his neck, and seemed to forget her embarrassment. "Please, don't die!"

The door splintered as a meaty fist, joined by a few additional pair, pounded on the door. Jareth glanced back at the door and shouted to them in French. Even so, she clung to him.

Jareth tipped her face upward. "I will not die. I promise." His face was serious, as if he dared death to claim him.

"I won't burn them," she whispered fiercely as she gripped the folds of his shirt to bring him closer. "If I burn them, then they'll have something else to hold against you, and I won't be the reason you're ridiculed in history. Let them all know that your bride was a virgin. If it's your custom, then it's mine now, too."

Jareth's eyes widened and his mouth opened slightly, but words escaped him. A stupefied half grin managed to make its way over his lips. His eyes passed over her messy hair and her face that was creased with sheet lines, as his hands covered hers. The intimacy of the moment was not lost on him. It caused his heart to kick into a gallop even though a mob waited on the other side of the door. "Then let them fly, my lioness. I must admit that Mrs. Wheatley will be relieved. I told her to give you time to dispose of them."

"Are you relieved?"

He shrugged one shoulder. "Customs are not critical. But . . ." he touched the spot wherein her heart beat and then tangled their hands together. ". . . To know that you would do this because of your concern for me makes me love you even more. I will guard your heart with my life, your grace. I belong to you as much as you belong to me."

Elizabet's face flushed at the mention of her new title. "You're breaking my heart—not protecting it. Do I have to go all the way to the gates? I'm afraid I'll cry like a fool."

"If speaking the truth breaks your heart, how can I help that?" He kissed her forehead and stepped away. Their hands parted. The men on the other side of the door were loudly discussing taking down the barrier. "But I can give you this small favor: I will go alone."

JARETH WENT AS PEACEFULLY AS they allowed. His exit was dignified, upon his own mount with a banner of purity taking flight as he passed the keep. He tried not to smile, but it was difficult to appear repentant and glum while his men cheered as the marital bed sheets took the place of his flag on the northern lists. It would not do to leave surrounded as if he were a taken prisoner with a silly grin on his face. A surge of pride filled him when he passed one of his knights who, on bowed knee, gazed up at him with loyal respect. Elizabet had given that to him—the respect of his men. She had tossed aside her own embarrassment to validate him. She was priceless.

It was ironic that the men who escorted him and were sworn to protect him until he reached his destiny despised him. They hated that he was a bastard, yet titled. It did not sit well with them that they were sworn to see him safely delivered to the archbishop by order of the prince. They were, no doubt, the prince's best men, which meant they could best him if he were to rebel. He would not attempt escape. To escape meant they would send word back to Dover, where others waited. One word and they would kill Elizabet for any of his transgressions.

Jareth was in turmoil as he thought of the many possible horrors that could befall his young bride while he was incarcerated. He had taken Percival aside and instructed him to watch out for her, but the squire had two broken legs and was hobbling around on crutches. There was only so much a lame man could handle, but he was the most trusted of his men.

Mrs. Wheatley was never good in dire straits. He had learned that the less she knew, the better. The woman had no filter. She would give away the coordinates of an entire regiment and think she had done something great.

His main consolation was that Elizabet was in possession of the travel stones and using them was simple. The path she needed to take was the brightest and easy to identify.

The location of the inquisition had changed. The small village of Kent was being honored with a visit by a traveling bishop, the Archbishop of Canterbury, no less. Jareth knew him as Walter Reynolds, the son of a baker from Windsor. He'd learned the bishop was behind the house arrest of John Wycliffe, not that it was a bad thing. The privacy afforded the scholar the opportunity to translate in gross amounts. Time was all he had and he used it wisely. The bishop would never understand that. Church officials believed that if Wycliffe was out of the public, he would be rendered unfruitful. There had never been such a vast misunderstanding of a scholar bent on exposing truth.

"Sir Jareth," the archbishop addressed him as Jareth was led through the doors of the solar in the small church. The church was in the center of the village, surrounded by tall gates. "What an honor to have your presence." He spoke in cultured French.

"The honor is yours," Jareth answered in Latin simply to aggravate the man. He refused to bow or kiss his outstretched hand. Instead, he stepped back and turned his gaze to the priest cowering in the darkened corner. It was Ephraim.

Ephraim had been allowed to read some of the transcribed documents and had his doubts regarding the church's beliefs. Jareth would not regret enlightening the priest, though it had been a risk. He would take the gamble again if it meant spreading the truth and freeing men from the bondage of the church.

The bishop snatched his hand away and sneered. "You forget yourself, Jareth." He shook his head and clasped his hands together, and took a step back. "But come, tell me of this treason I hear. Explain why you would aid John Wycliffe when you know he is not recommended by the Church. This cannot be true. The prince will be most upset if this rumor is not proven false. Give me your testimony that I may set you free."

Jareth opened his mouth, but was cut off by the door flying open.

"Make way for the Prince of England!" At the loud proclamation, he turned in annoyance that his demise was being put aside. Indeed, the prince was present and coming down the aisle trailed by a dozen of his men, all of whom were dressed for battle. "Speak of the devil and he appears," Jareth muttered. Everyone but him and the archbishop fell to their knees.

Prince Edward stalked into the solar with his helmet beneath his arm, his drawn sword swinging at his side. His eyes traveled the length of the room, appearing to take in all who were present. He looked at Jareth and inclined his head in greeting before turning his attention to the bishop.

"Your majesty," the archbishop said.

"Godfather," Prince Edward responded smoothly. He turned to face Jareth. "What is the meaning of this?" He waved between the two of them, and then held out his hand, open palm suspended in air. "The king had me summoned as one would a child." A young servant placed a scroll into the prince's awaiting hand.

"I would think it is obvious," Jareth said in Latin. He grinned when Edward cut him a look of murder.

"I am inclined to believe you deserve this," Edward drawled in perfect French. "But it seems that by royal proclamation . . ." He untied the document and allowed the red cord to fall to the floor, " . . . the man standing trial is innocent."

"Nay!" the bishop blurted. Edward leveled him a stare over the scroll. His expression indicated he not accustomed to being interrupted. "Pardon me, your majesty, but it is said he is aiding a scholar who has been placed on house arrest by the Church."

"I know this," Edward said while frowning down at the scroll he held. "My father knows this." He looked around. "I dare say everyone present knows this." He jiggled the scroll. "May I continue? Royal proclamation and all—no small matter here, and I am very busy."

"Go right ahead," Jareth said in plain English.

"Must you do that?" Edward asked in a weary tone. His eyes cut to Jareth. "It is very disturbing. Speak the king's language or hold your tongue."

Jareth smiled and faced the bishop. "Shall he continue?" he asked in Latin. The bishop frowned and waved his hand. "Do go on," Jareth said to Edward in French.

Edward cleared his throat, his expression thunderous. "As I was saying, the king knows Jareth is . . . er . . ." He looked at the bishop, but he merely shrugged, so he turned to Jareth, who let his lips lift in a smirk. "Well, then, I shall just read this." He held the scroll before him and read the fine print. "By proclamation, King Edward II, His Royal Highness, does hereby pardon, for life, the Duke of Dover from any Church skirmishes—" "Skirmishes," the bishop echoed.

Still holding the scroll, Edward cut his hand through the air. "Do you dare interrupt a royal decree?" He scrutinized the document, then drew it back a fraction to focus to his eyesight and reread the word. Vaguely he nodded. "Skirmishes."

The bishop opened his mouth, but Edward waved the scroll in the air. "You may well be my godfather, but I dare say that my brother's life is more important to me than your favor. The Duke of Lancaster is in route as well. We both speak on behalf of the Duke of Dover. I would highly advise you to proceed with caution."

"But this is possible treason," the bishop said, confusion on his face. His voice ricocheted off the high ceiling. "He can never be recognized by the Church. He is a bastard."

"He is a son of England, not of your Church," Edward said. He lowered the scroll and turned to Jareth. "Understand my dilemma, brother, and spare me a word of the wise. You have always had a silver tongue, although it knows not what language is best."

Jareth made himself step forward. His feet were heavy with the adrenaline coursing through him. *A son. A prince. His brother.* He had waited his whole life for acceptance, but it happened at time when it no longer mattered. What mattered was that Elizabet was safe and she would be honored. This would secure his future as nothing else could. Of course, the proclamation had not deemed him legitimate, but to be recognized as protected by the king himself was practically a confession. And Edward was here—now—calling him brother before witnesses. Twice. He had gathered his courage and come here expecting nothing short of an inquisition, and instead the prince rode in and offered him redemption? It was more than he could understand.

Jareth bowed. "I only want to go in peace and live my life in service to the crown of England," he stated in eloquent Norman French. He straightened, and caught the pleased expression on his brother's face. He owed it to Edward to speak in his father's tongue—the language of the king, who was indeed his father. The prince was handing him his freedom. "And to be provided access to the scholar, John Wycliffe."

"Treason!" the bishop repeated. He stepped boldly forward as well, waving his ringed finger. "This will not do. Wycliffe has begun an uprising. I will not have it!"

"You shall stand down," Edward roared. Jareth fought an urge not to cower along with everyone else as his brother's commanding baritone boomed into the open space. As a young squire, he had often been on the receiving end of that bellow that could scare a grown man to tears. It was ironic that the sound of it today was joyful music; it made him want to smile.

"Edward," the bishop entreated, and then took a step away. "What has become of you? I cannot recommend you if you proceed thusly."

"The man who stands before you is a prince of England, not a vessel of your Church," Edward retorted. He lowered the scroll. "I have orders to see that Jareth is unharmed and that he is returned to his position of honor at the seat of Dover Castle. I know no other way to keep the peace. It is either please you or my father." He tilted his head. "As my father has the authority over my body and soul, I shall choose him."

His eyes rolled heavenward and he muttered under his breath, "May God have mercy on me."

"I see," the bishop said. He eyed Jareth. "Will you indeed continue—"

"Aye," Jareth said, stepping forward. "I shall. And I am prepared to accept whatever consequences the Church sees fit to bestow on me." He inclined his head. "May God have mercy on me, as well. I can do no other but be faithful to God and the land of my father."

"The Church may not touch you," Edward said, his voice deceptively soft. He began rolling the scroll. "It is written as law." He pointed the scroll toward the bishop, offering it. "If the Church dares to touch a hair on your head, I shall know of it and act according to the law of the land."

The bishop cast a glance between the prince and Jareth. He stepped further away, making it clear he would accept neither the scroll nor the law.

His stubbornness rankled Jareth. "I cannot stand before God with a clear conscience if I ignore what I have read in scripture," Jareth said. "To do so would sentence me to a thousand fiery deaths, and I would rather have one death of honor if the Church is so inclined."

"They will not," Edward said, his gaze on the bishop.

The bishop stared at his prince who was his godchild. A minute passed before he looked away, and blinked oddly at the people crowding the room. He seemed to realize they were surrounded by witnesses; anything he happened to say would be remembered for ages.

"I shall send well wishes to Mother in your name," Edward said, and bowed to the bishop. He arched a brow and looked toward the exit. The hint was unmistakable.

"Quite," the bishop said, and took his leave. When a prince prompted—you did as you were told; archbishop or not.

Jareth approached his brother as the room cleared. "How?"

Edward was busy handing off the scroll to a squire. "You vex me, brother. Did you not see how I challenged my godfather publically and called you my own before all present?"

Jareth nodded, and because Edward deserved it, he gave voice as well, in eloquent Norman French. "I am grateful."

Edward shook his head and widened his stance. "It is not me who deserves your loyal thanks. You had another person speak in your favor. Your lady wife visited the king two days prior. She implored him that it was to his advantage to extend the crown's protection."

"Elizabet?"

Edward gave a single nod. "Aye. She is the reason I was sent. The king trusted no one else. It was rumored you would be beheaded without a trial."

"My wife said this?"

"She did." Edward reached into his cloak and took out a letter. "This is for you. This missive will ensure that wherever you go, you do so under the protection of the King of England."

Jareth lowered his brow, but he reached out to take it. He noticed the letter had the king's personal mark. "I do not know how she was able to get word so quickly."

"And just in time, too," Edward said. He clasped his hands and made a motion over his stomach as if it were rounder. "She is great with child." He made a fist and knocked Jareth's shoulder. "Provided the king with proof of marriage and made a mess of your betrothal to Catherine of Torquay. I should be furious with you for not being honest with me concerning your choice of bride. You went and found an Irish girl. Noble. Not well done, though, as it was I who promised your betrothal."

Jareth only heard 'great with child' and knew what had happened. It had been the right decision to have Gabriel and Minh limit interventions. Things were becoming a jumbled mess. No one was sticking to priorities, and the privilege was being abused. People were leaping time and mucking things up.

But Elizabet had saved his life.

The bishop had planned for a private execution—that had to be it. The only way she could have known was because she had seen the future and it had already happened. He had been killed and she mourned him. So she reversed time and set it right the only way she knew. As benign as things had played out, he wondered what had been said to provoke such a drastic outcome.

"The king has pardoned you for the murder of Sir James as well."

He thumbed over his shoulder to the squire who held the scroll. "It will be read publically so no one will seek vengeance. You have the support of crown and country. What a mess you made." He shook his head. "I shall miss him. Best captain on the sea there ever was."

"I have the crown's protection," Jareth said out loud as if he were testing the truth to see how it sounded.

"Aye," Edward said. He turned and motioned for Jareth to follow. "But you will never take the throne. If you try, I will kill you myself."

"Of course," Jareth responded in plain English, but when Edward looked back at him with a scowl, he switched easily back to French. "I am honored to be acknowledged by the king."

"Perhaps you can request a new coat of arms," Edward suggested. They had come to the outer courtyard where the horses were tied. He motioned to where his own flag flew. "One without a small dog and wheel."

Jareth smirked, but said nothing. His brother wore a mocking grin that he had witnessed before, but his flag was of no concern to him; he would keep it. They could mock him all they wanted but his flag suited him. "I am free to go, then?"

The corners of Edward's lips turned downward. "Aye. You are free to return to Dover. I, on the other hand, must intercept John. The Duke of Lancaster will be quite angry if he travels all this way and does not get to thrash a man of the Church." He offered Jareth a grim countenance as he used their brother's title with an edge to his voice. "You know how he is when it comes to being harsh with Church issues."

Edward had no idea—not really. The Duke of Lancaster was a larger problem that the Church would deal with eventually. He would let history tell that story. Instead, he found where his horse was tied. He had time to make it home if he hurried.

He rode fast and hard, but when he came to the halfway point; the path was blocked by a band of riders. He did not recognize them, but they flew his flag. Their colors were bolder, brighter—and wrong.

Not again.

"Stand and deliver," one of the brigands cried out when he neared. He slowed his horse and came close.

Jareth drew the sword that his brother loaned him for safe travels.

"Shut up," a female voice demanded. "You'll be bloody lucky if he doesn't kill you where you stand." She lowered her voice. "Stand and deliver—are you barking mad?"

Jareth paused at the sound of a woman's voice amid the cloaked band, but he could not tell which she was, so he kept his sword at attention. They had a strange inflection to their voices, but it was familiar. He had heard it on a tape Harrow had him listen to on heart valve replacement. The surgeon speaking was British.

"I've always wanted to say that," the boy said. He turned to the rider next him. "And you shut up or I'll tell Mum you kissed Christian." Jareth presumed that was the girl he spoke to.

"Quiet!" the tallest rider ordered. He spurred his horse forward, and approached Jareth slowly. "Before you get us all killed by our own father."

Jareth gripped his sword. They would not dare.

The rider uncovered his head as he approached.

They *did* dare.

Staring back at Jareth was his mirror image, but finer—more handsome. He had his mother's cute nose, thank God. This day was becoming most bizarre. The four riders who stayed behind followed his suit and removed their hoods. One was a girl with hair the shade of Elizabet's. Jareth's sword fell from his hand as he opened his fist in utter surrender. The breath was kicked from his lungs and gushed from his mouth in a noisy exhalation.

"You're frightened," the boy said. He tilted his head and halted his horse a foot from Jareth, then stared as Jareth felt the color drain from his face.

"No," Jareth said, but his heart was in his throat. He glanced to the others who had also begun to come closer when he threw his sword. They mistook his action for fear, but he cast aside his weapon as he would never bear arms against his own flesh and blood. "I am confused. Overwhelmed."

The girl had hair like her mother, but she was the only one. Three of the boys, including the eldest, had dark brown hair. One boy had black hair, like Jareth himself. He was the one who had spontaneously shouted something peculiar.

The one with the black hair smiled. He was clearly the most handsome of the bunch. "You look so young, Dad."

"He's in shock," the eldest said. He motioned to the girl. "Perhaps we should introduce ourselves."

"Please," Jareth managed to say.

"I am Abigail," the girl said. When she smiled, she had a dimple in her right cheek. She looked like Elizabet, but she appeared to be tall even though she was seated on a horse. Her feet were secure in the stirrups, even though it was a large stallion. "Solomon and I are twins. We are the oldest." She motioned to the rider nearest him, the one who had approached first.

Solomon inclined his head.

"Peter is the stupid one," Abigail said with a tone of annoyance.

"Hey," the black-haired Peter protested. "Don't listen to her," he advised, looking at Jareth. "She's a spoiled brat, that one. Can't have any fun when she's around."

"Peter," Solomon warned, and shook his head.

"I'm Gideon," one of the boys in the back said. He seemed young, but not as young as the remaining boy, who gave the impression of shyness. "This is Benjamin. He only came because Mrs. Wheatley is cooking gruel."

"I don't like gruel," Benjamin, the shy one, said, but then he leaned forward in the saddle. He smiled revealing a set of dimples instead of only one like his sister. "I say, Dad, you are a handsome devil. Mum doesn't exaggerate."

"Of course she doesn't exaggerate," Peter said with a sniff. "They say he looks just like me."

"Boys," Jareth said, overwhelmed with them all. Abigail frowned, to which Jareth offered a faint smile. He felt a bit queasy, and was afraid the tilt of his lips came off as more of a grimace. He was only married yesterday and not yet in tune with the dealings of females. "And lady. Please, there must be a reason that you are about in a time not your own, obviously.

"I just left your uncle back in Kent. By proclamation of the king, I have been given amnesty." He half expected his children to cheer at the news, but his words did not have any excitable effect on them. It was new to him though, and reason to rejoice. "My day has exceeded the exhaustible mark and is bordering into 'I may go mad' territory. Do you care to enlighten me as to why either I or your mother would send you?"

"It's Mum," Solomon announced, and tilted his head. It seemed a habit of his. "If you continue on your way to the castle, she will drown and we will never exist."

"What?" Jareth exclaimed. He yanked on the reigns so tightly his horse balked. The stallion pranced as Jareth felt the last of his sanity slip away.

"Things are complicated," Solomon said. He adjusted his mount as his horse danced along with the sudden movement of Jareth's steed. "There was a breach in time, but we singled it out to today. Mum saved your life by going to Grandfather and pleading your worth, but there was yet another breach."

So the children were accustomed to having a king as a grandfather. There was some relief in that. It meant the proclamation had held and the Church had either not tried or not been allowed to tamper with it. Something was finally going right.

"Of the bands you left with Mum, two were stolen," Abigail reported, "By the same person who gave them to you."

"Gyula," Jareth said, and gripped the reigns. "Where is your mother now?"

"Gyula's taken her to the cave where he resides, but he left her at the lower end that becomes engulfed when the tide comes in," Solomon answered. "We know where it is, but we must hurry. Mum made us promise that we would not go into the cave. By the time we get there, it will be partially submerged. She can't swim."

Jareth yanked on the reigns he held. This was Elizabet, the walking oxymoron they were dealing with. She was the duchess to an area known for its shore—of course she could not swim. That would be expected, and Elizabet was never what he expected.

"She is forever a mother," Abigail said. She rolled her eyes, but somehow on her it was a charming gesture. "We promised not to risk *our* lives. We are to fetch you and bring you to the location."

"She trusts only you to save her," Gideon said.

Jareth looked over his children, imprinting each of their precious faces onto his memory. They were so fierce and serious. He loved them already, if only because they loved their mother.

"Then let us not keep her waiting," Jareth said. She would be alone and scared. The thought caused his heart to stutter.

"Dad," Solomon said, but spurred his horse to follow at a canter. "There's something else you must know."

"Something you need to know so you can make a wise decision and not a hasty one," Abigail added.

Jareth was ahead of them already; he wanted a bruising pace. The thought of Elizabet in a dark cave, afraid, was enough to make him panic. What if they were too late? Would the children vanish and cease to exist? He could not think of such things.

He glanced back and caught a glimpse of the worried gaze the twins shared. "Out with it."

Solomon met his eye. "Catherine of Torquay sold Mum to Gyula. She tricked her and lured her out of the castle. The reason only two of the bands were stolen is because that was all she was wearing. She buried the rest."

"Mum didn't know who she was. She thought she was someone from the village."

"Catherine of Torquay will die," Jareth growled.

Peter let out a whoop and spurred his horse, matching the pace Jareth set. Jareth was amazed at how well his children rode for being stuck between ancient and modern times. Horseback was no longer the preferred mode of transportation. They rode much like him; as though they were born equestrians. It would seem they were able to live within both fluidly.

"Peter," Solomon warned.

"Who are we to stop a man in love?" Peter yelled back at his brother. Their horses were all in full gallop now. Peter sidled next to Jareth and gave another loud war-like call into the night air. His cloak billowed out like a victory flag.

Chapter 15

THE CLIFFS WERE IMPOSING IN the early moonlight as Jareth's children crowded around him at the precipice. "It's a small tank, but all you'll need." Solomon showed Jareth how to use the oxygen tank they had brought. "Remember to breathe only through your mouth. It's a bit tricky. There's a light attached to the mouthpiece. It will illuminate the way as you swim and help keep your hands free."

Jareth nodded while he yanked off his boots. "I shall go under, three feet to the right, and then straight up?"

"Yes," Peter said. He passed a coiled pair of ropes from one hand to the other as if weighing them and peered over the ledge. "We will guide the descent. Once you come to the craggy opening, tie the rope around your waist and we will give it slack."

"But remember," Abigail instructed as she came up behind her twin, "You must tie the rope around Mum once you get to her. She doesn't know how to swim yet."

"She cannot read nor swim," Jareth muttered. What else was she keeping from him? It was not anger, per se, that had him babbling, but fear that she would not make it. Fear that the brutality of life would crush her and he would be forced to watch it happen. How could he possibly protect her when she was laden with weaknesses?

Abigail placed her hand gently on his arm. The gesture halted his brisk motions of taking off his heavy gambeson. He wanted to be as light as possible, but Abigail's touch gave him a heavy, pitted sensation in his gut. He almost brutally pushed her off, so unaccustomed was he to gentle persuasion.

"She reads well," Abigail said. "And swims. You teach her both and she teaches us in turn. She's a wonderful mother."

Jareth cast his gaze to where the soft white of his daughter's small hand rested against his darker forearm. He could get used to this—gentleness given by someone who held love in their eyes while they did the persuading. He accepted it because of the one extending it. He would love his daughter fiercely.

"Forgive me," he said. "I am overcome by many emotions." She met his gaze and he saw that she had his eyes. Elizabet's hair and his light eyes was a lovely combination. "I am not a man given to them." He stopped there, unable to go on. It was inappropriate to tell one's daughter that he had only recently found himself capable of love. That he loved her mother so much he would switch places with her and go to death willingly. It was gut-wrenching to discover how something as simple as love could reduce one to such moments of weakness. He could not seem to think other than in riddles.

It embarrassed him.

Abigail smiled. "I love you, Daddy." She rose on her tip toes and kissed his cheek. "Be safe. You must live long enough to experience a rainbow of feelings with me. And believe me, you shall. I'm extremely vexing."

A grin tickled at half of his mouth. He peered at his daughter and did not know what to say. Something unfamiliar burned in his chest, but Solomon intervened before he could make a fool of himself.

"Give one of the ropes to Abigail," Solomon told Peter.

Abigail stepped back and reached into the rear of her cloak to produce a bow and arrow.

"There is a branch about halfway down," Peter said, and peeked over the ledge again. "It's looks to be sturdy."

Benjamin flew at Jareth, throwing his thin arms around his middle. "I love you, Papa."

Jareth's arms remained weighted at his sides; he was stunned. He looked up at the three expectant pair of eyes of his other sons and lightly patted Benjamin on the back. None of them moved to help him, as if this was a normal family occurrence.

Abigail tied the rope to the arrow, using a precise knot. "I've tethered horses and now my expertise is needed to land this arrow at a far-off mark . . ." She shook her head. " . . . While you boys have a Hallmark moment. I can't wait to tell Mum."

"Hush, Abigail," Solomon chided. He put his hand on Benjamin's shoulder. "Come, runt. You can't keep Dad. He has to save Mum."

Abigail took aim, her strong arms holding the bow taunt. She blew a breath out slowly and let the arrow fly.

"Dad," Gideon said, his voice sounding scratchy. Jareth looked at him over Benjamin, who was still attached to him like an octopus. Gideon swallowed down an unmanly sob. "God be with you."

"Aye, Papa," Peter said, his handsome face serious. He blinked twice, rapidly, and looked away when Jareth met his gaze.

"Alright, alright," Solomon said. He tugged Benjamin away; the boy gave Jareth one final squeeze before he went willingly. "When we get home, we can all pile up on him and tell him how much we love him."

Jareth looked at his eldest son and realized that he was seeing his heir—the second Duke of Dover. The boy had taken control of every situation and guided his siblings. It was not lost on him that the future Jareth trusted Solomon with the lives of his family.

"How grateful we are to have him as our father and how very precious his life is to each of us," Solomon said. He became choked up on the last words, but while his eyes filled with tears, none dared fall. He tipped his chin toward Abigail, who was holding out the rope.

Benjamin buried his face in Solomon's chest as if to hide from what was happening.

"Come," Abigail said.

Jareth considered his sons before turning to his daughter.

She smiled. "Remember to breathe through your mouth." She pointed to the tank near his feet.

He reached down and picked it up. It was light, as Solomon said. He glanced at the odd apparatus and frowned. "I shall remember," Jareth said, and took the rope from her. He looked over his shoulder. "I shall remember all you have told me."

Solomon and Peter raised their hands to solemnly wave. Gideon turned away, his shoulders slack, his head down.

"We'll stay until we're sure you have Mum," Solomon said. "Give the rope a firm tug twice when you have cleared the crevice. Peter shall watch and once he makes a visual, we shall depart."

Jareth nodded and turned back. Abigail was face to face with him. She kissed him again and threw her arms around his neck. "Bring her back to us."

"I will," he said, and put his arms around her. She was taller than her mother. He smiled into her hair, thinking how much he would enjoy spoiling her. "I am so happy to have met you, daughter." He kept his voice low, as if it were their secret.

Abigail pulled back; a tear coursed down her cheek. She smiled through her sorrow, and the tear landed in the dimple of her cheek. "Be safe," she mouthed and stepped back. She placed her palms together in a prayer pose.

Solomon handed Benjamin off to Peter and stood next to his twin. He took the rope from Jareth. "I will hold you until we make a visual and then we will secure the rope to an anchor we have. The other rope Abigail secured is the dummy rope in case this one fails. We won't leave your safety to chance. We are not leaving here without being sure both you and Mum are safe."

"I understand," Jareth said. He let one foot step behind him off the edge of the cliff, and tested his footing. The white chalk gave way until he dug a place for his foot to rest. He leveled himself and climbed down another step. This would be the last glimpse he had of his children until they were born. "Son," he said abruptly, and locked gazes with Solomon.

Solomon shook his head, his jaw becoming rigid. "Don't say it," he said. "You don't have to. I know."

Jareth gave a jerky nod and continued his descent. His heart beat frantically in his chest with worry over Elizabet and the pack of children he left on the cliff. What if Gyula returned and hurt them? What if things were botched again and this was not the final thread that must be fixed to ensure they had life in the future? He was not accustomed to worry; it was something he did not do. It seemed having a family changed him, and in ways that were not always positive.

He glanced up and saw that the twins were still watching, and that the girl's lips silently moved as if in prayer. Using all of his strength, he descended at faster rate. They depended on him. He would save Elizabet so he could see all of their dear faces again. He would be worthy of the love he saw mirrored when he gazed into their eyes.

ELIZABET HELD HER HEAD ABOVE water as another wave came through and made her gasp. Her nose scraped against the cavern ceiling; her cheek was bloodied and bruised from the repeated impact as each wave brought her higher.

She was about to die and she had not even lived yet. She had not told Jareth that she loved him and would never get the chance now.

For the past hour she had prayed, bartered with God, and then cried until her sinuses wanted to collapse. She was at the point of acceptance now, although she did not understand how things ended so badly. Had no one seen this coming?

Another wave pulsed through, and caused her to stretch to her tippy toes on the rock she waded above. It made her wonder why she did not just give up and take a big swig of water and go down.

The thought nearly made her hyperventilate. She did not want to die.

Tears formed in her eyes and she blinked up at the roof of the cavern. It was a horrid view to die looking at. She wished she had been sent out to sea so she could have seen what the white cliffs looked like. She had only ever looked down on them, and she had seen them in pictures. She would never be allowed to witness the landscape that her husband loved.

A sob echoed around her; her bottom lip puffed out in an ugly cry. She gripped the firm narrow walls, and dug her fingers into the rocky crevices to stabilize her body and prepare for the next wave. Soon when the wave hit, it would not recede.

She began to breathe in short pants, sucking in air and bawling at the same time. "Please, God," she cried as the water level rose to her chin. She slipped on the rock and bobbed in the water, but came up coughing.

The fear in her belly was acute. She was terrified of water and had been since she was kid. Everyone else could swim and they made fun that she could not learn something so simple. It was like reading. But she could not do that either.

Beau understood because she could also not swim, no matter how hard she tried. Elizabet promised herself that if she made it through this, she would learn to swim and be sure that Beau did the same. It was the worst way to die for someone who feared water. The cavern walls were narrow and she was sandwiched into a three foot rectangular cell that appropriately resembled a tomb.

She glanced down into the water to eye her footing. There had been light coming from the coastline, but it had dimmed. It was nearly black out now. She wiggled her toes and tried to force her vision.

A beam of light flickered beyond the rock. Elizabet blinked rapidly; maybe she imagined it. But it came again, even brighter, and then something grasped her toe. She gasped and jerked her foot away. Something grabbed her other foot and held on this time.

Elizabet frantically grabbed at the walls and ceiling around her, searching for leverage to pull herself higher. It was fruitless; there was no place to go. She knew that, had tried it before, but could not help the frenzy that her fear was building in her.

The pressure released from her foot and was replaced by a solid mass filling the space next to her. The wavery light traveled upward through the water, and she suddenly realized that it was not a sea monster or a deadly fish, but a person.

Jareth surfaced next to her, yanked his mouthpiece out, and let it bob away at the end of the air hose. He grabbed her face and tilted it down. "You're alive," he gasped. Before she could answer, he was kissing her.

Elizabet closed her eyes and gave up a silent prayer. She did not care why or how he was here, just that he was.

He found her.

Jareth's lips were warm, his body pressed to hers in the small space they shared. She released her hold on the rock and grasped his shoulders.

"Thank you," she said against his lips.

He drew back; his hand ran the length of her neck and over her shoulder. "Are you hurt?"

She shook her head. Her teeth chattered, whether from the cold or shock, she did not know. "I can't swim," she said. "I got stuck and couldn't get out. A man came and grabbed me . . ."

"I know," he murmured. He scanned the tight space and then used the light to look down into the water. He peered back up at her. "You have to trust me, my love. We don't have much time."

The water level rose and engulfed them. Elizabet clung to Jareth, her eyes on him, even underwater. He met her searching gaze with an expression that was not hard to interpret.

When the water receded this time, it left even less air space. They had to tilt their heads back to remain above the water line.

He guided the mouthpiece into her mouth. Her arms were clumsy and slow in the resistance of the water but she fought him. The next wave would be their last. He shoved the oxygen at her as the rush of seawater hit.

"Trust me," he said. His words became garbled as saltwater filled his mouth.

His next actions did not feel infused with love, but were quick and brutal. Grabbing her waist to halt her panicked wiggling, he steadied her while he worked the rope he carried around her middle. He labored quickly, using the dim glow from his light to guide him under the murky water.

At last he was able to secure the rope. He looked into her fearful eyes, jerked a nod, placed his palms atop her head, and pressed her down.

She thrashed.

Why was he pushing her under the water? She kicked, screamed, lost the breathing piece, and he shoved it back into her mouth. He shoved her until he had her head down and was forcing her through the narrow way that led out to the English Channel. She wiggled, panicked, and bucked until something gave and she floated upward. Jareth reached up past her and jerked on the rope—twice.

Suddenly, water was rushing past her as she was propelled upward. She squeezed her eyes closed and held on to the mouthpiece, breathing deep the life-giving oxygen. When she broke the surface, she was surrounded by darkness illuminated only by the moon.

"Mum!" someone hollered from above.

Elizabet looked up, the mouthpiece still in her mouth, lighting the way. A group of people peered over the ledge of a cliff a good distance above her.

Mom?

She spit out the mouthpiece and grabbed at the rope with both hands. It was the good grace of those overhead that was keeping her from drowning.

She searched for Jareth on the water's surface while she held the tank under her arm in case he needed it. She used leverage to light the way around her as she searched.

"Dad!" someone yelled, then "Mum! Over there!"

Elizabet thrashed, using the rope to turn in the water. She grabbed the light and pointed it into the darkness while she held the rope with one hand.

"Jareth!" she called when she saw him treading water only a few feet away. She put the piece in her mouth and reached out for him.

He was bleeding. There was a gash on his temple and a scrape down his cheek.

"Get him to the ledge," a girl's voice called from above. "Use the spare rope tied to the arrow there."

Jareth clasped her hand in his and Elizabet scanned the area for a ledge against the cliffs. He was heavy and brought them down a bit; they bobbed in the water.

"Get on my back," Jareth directed her. He treaded water and shifting their positions until he had control of the rope and she was under his care. She locked her legs around him and encircled his chest with her arms while he grabbed the rope with both hands. He took the light from her and flashed it upward. The blurry faces of what was apparently their children were still above.

Jareth began the ascent while the boys formed a line and pulled. The girl watched with her hands on her knees as she peered over the edge of the cliff.

"Almost here," she encouraged.

Jareth's biceps bulged as he climbed the rope with her on his back. It would not be his way to passively allow his children to haul them to safety. The sooner her feet were on firm ground, the better. She had become so very cold. Stripping down to her underclothes had been smart at the time, but she was paying the price now.

"I've got her," the black-haired boy called. He released the rope and reached for her, then grasped her arms and hauled her over Jareth's head. Her body slid stomach down onto the soft soil. He stood over her, grinning. "I'm Peter."

The older boy reached out and grabbed his dad's thin shirt from the back and pulled until he lay safely next to Elizabet beside the precipice.

Jareth rolled his head to face her. "This is Solomon, the oldest and Abigail's twin."

"We did it," another boy said, his voice shaky. He eyed the youngest of the bunch and ruffled his hair with a smile. "We did it," he repeated.

"Mum, I'm Abigail. That's Gideon and Benjamin." The girl dropped to her knees and stroked Elizabet's hair from her eyes. "You're safe now."

Elizabet gazed into the face of her daughter and knew who she was immediately. The hair, her eyes, the resemblance between her and Jareth—she was a perfect mixture. She reached out and touched Abigail's cheek with her fingertips.

"My love." Jareth rolled until they were side by side, and drew Elizabet into his arms. Her hand left Abigail's face but remained suspended as if she did not want to lose contact with her daughter. "You are so cold."

Solomon jumped to attention. "We have blankets.'

Elizabet gazed at the tribe surrounding her, peeling her eyes from her daughter and took them all in. *Her children.* Her mind could hardly wrap around the concept and yet, they were here, all of them brave, adorable, and loyal. Something in her heart tugged as she realized that they were the proof of her love for Jareth. She could not stop absorbing them with her eyes. Their features, their voices, and the way they moved as a unit and in tune. Her precious family. Her eyes watered with an emotion she had never felt before.

"You are still here," Jareth said with wonder in his voice.

Peter shrugged. "We did say that we would see you both to safety."

"We wanted to leave nothing to chance," Abigail said fiercely. "Someone is trying to stop the Amalgam from forming. It's not just a family issue at stake, but everything we have worked for."

"The Amalgam?" Jareth asked. He narrowed his eyes. "What do you know of it?"

"Don't look so suspicious, Dad," Peter said. He pulled a face. "We're your kids. We know everything."

"We are guardians," Gideon said. "We each have a part."

Jareth's lips parted and his eyes widened. "You are Gideon."

The boy smiled. "You remembered. See that I'm in charge of the physics department. It's my forte."

"We watch over time and host," Solomon commented from behind a pair of blankets. He fanned one out and placed it around Elizabet's shoulders. He threw the other and hit Jareth in the face with it. He gave him a devilish smile. "I am stationed in medieval Dover, because I am heir, but the others are free to belong to other times."

"I know Napoleon," Peter said, but when his sister scowled at him he grimaced. "Well, I live in his time. I am a rifleman in the British Army."

"But you are so young," Elizabet said, and felt her forehead crease as she drew her brows together. She dabbed tears from her cheeks using the blanket.

"I'm eighteen, Mum." His chest puffed out a bit.

Abigail rolled her eyes. Solomon hid a grin by biting on his bottom lip.

"I've been in His Majesty's Army for a year now," Peter said with great pride.

"And he's titled," Benjamin tossed in. He shouldered his way until he was next to her, and went down on his knees. "Dad says he has the luck of Saint Peter himself."

"Did he say that?" Elizabet asked as the boy nestled beside her, half burrowed in the covers with her. She placed her arms around him and peered at Jareth over his head. It was evident this one had an overabundant tendency for snuggling.

"I cannot imagine why I would say such a thing," Jareth said, and Peter grinned like a fool.

"Our title is almost lost," Peter said. "Seems the dukes in that century could only produce girls." His nose crinkled. "But I saved the title. I swoop in as the last distant male relative when ol' Benedict curls his toes heavenly." He blew a raspberry. "Girls! Can you believe he had eight girls? No luck, that one. It was easy to get me in as Duke. A couple of forged documents and yours truly was no longer the spare, but the heir."

"Yes, because you are so very randy and virile—the ducal lineage can always count on you. Hardly something to brag about," Abigail said. She waved him off. "The only reason he has a title is because he almost got killed in medieval times and he had to be hidden, so we sent him to a different time." She smirked and shook her head. "He's practically a criminal." She turned to Elizabet and Jareth. "Now, we must stop talking about how stupid Peter is—you'll find out all about that in due time. Papa needs to get Mum back to the castle or she will become hypothermic."

Benjamin tossed his arms around Elizabet's neck and hugged her tight. "Please, don't die, Mummy. If you die, no one will read to me at bedtime. Mrs. Wheatley is ghastly at reading Dickens. She doesn't even change her voice between characters."

Elizabet blinked back the tears that sprang to her eyes at the mention of reading and her in the same breath. Dickens, no less. She looked owlishly at Jareth.

"It seems this one is the baby," Jareth said fondly, and reached out to pull Benjamin from her. Benjamin gave one final squeeze before he let go. The children all shared curious glances. Jareth's jaw tightened as he hauled Benjamin to his feet, only to have the boy turn on him with a wild embrace as well.

"Ahh, I'm afraid that although Benjamin has a vast wealth of affection, as one does as a younger child," Abigail said. "He is not the caboose."

"He's not?" Jareth asked as he hugged the child, and then patted his thin back.

"Mum's pregnant," Solomon announced.

Gideon pulled a face. "It's another girl."

"Hey!" Abigail scolded. She turned to her mother. "Her name will be Honor. You said that 'on your honor, this is the last one' and you've run out of biblical names."

"How about Sara or Esther," Jareth suggested.

Abigail's face puckered. "Really, Dad? Leave the naming to us. We have a greater understanding of these delicate matters." She passed Elizabet a look that baited conspiracy.

"Please, let the girls have their way," Solomon said as he hunched down to disengage Benjamin from his strangling hug. He transferred the boy to his arms and lifted him as he stood. "They get crazy when we make suggestions."

"Yes," Peter said, touching the area over his heart with his fingertips. "When I suggested Arabella, everyone was appalled."

"Arabella is a dairy maid on our property," Abigail explained. When neither Elizabet nor Jareth understood the connection and silence stretched, she mimed humps over her chest. "He's a bit infatuated."

"Oh," Elizabet said. She turned a scolding eye on Peter, while Jareth appeared truly shocked. Then, *"Oh,"* as reality dawned.

"Well, you must be on your way," Solomon said. He shifted Benjamin in his arms and embraced his father as though it was the most natural thing in the world. "Get Mum back to the castle. I'm sure they have formed a search party by now."

Solomon moved to Elizabet and hugged her while the other children followed suit. Benjamin began to cry.

Elizabet grabbed Jareth's arm. Her bottom lip trembled as Solomon consoled the child and Abigail twisted a time band from her wrist and tossed it in the air. The light was brilliant as the portal opened.

"Mummy," Benjamin wailed, and extended his arms to her.

Elizabet went to rise, but Jareth held her back, his arms folded around her shoulders and pressing her to him. He nodded to Solomon, who was having a time controlling the wriggling child in his arms, while the others took turns stepping into the portal. Each glanced at them before disappearing.

Solomon shook his head. "What a silly head he will be when he sees Mum waiting on the other end."

Elizabet lunged forward as Solomon stepped in and the circle closed.

Chapter 16

JARETH GRIPPED HER TIGHTER. "LET them go," he murmured into her hair. He placed a kiss there. "It is not good-bye. We will see them again." She dipped her head and began to cry. "Do not cry." he rested his cheek on her head, and rubbed her arms to warm her. "You are alive and I am here. You are safe."

"That's not it. Did you not hear?" she cried out. "They said I can read." She spread her hands. "I can *read*, Jareth."

"You shall read," Jareth promised. His arm tightened around her. "I will teach you myself, and until then I will take you to every play, every opera, and every theatre in your nation to see that you enjoy the things your mother taught you to love."

Elizabet pulled away and stared up at him. "How . . ."

He placed the tip of his finger over her mouth. "You said your mother read everything to you; this way you shall see everything you have learned."

"That's the nicest thing anyone has ever done for me."

"It is just the beginning. You will want for nothing. I will see to it." Jareth swiped the tears from her cheeks.

"Well, you might want to hold off on making any promises to me," Elizabet said. She winced as her memory jarred. "I've lost two of your stones."

"You did not lose them," he responded mildly as if she would shatter if he raised his voice. "They were stolen from you."

"How'd you know that?"

"The children," he said. "They were sent to me. By you. It seems things went badly once we parted ways this morning. You were watched and taken advantage of. I blame myself for leaving you with such a burden."

She shook her head. "Percival helped me bury the others. That's the only reason they didn't get them all. When we were leaving the abbey, he called out for me to watch for Catherine, but I didn't know who she was. By then it was too late. She turned me over to that ugly little man."

"Clever girl that you hid them, but kept one close in case you must flee."

"No. *Stupid* girl. That's why they tried to kill me." She sniffed and swiped at her nose with the back of her hand.

"They would kill you because Catherine wants you out of the way." Jareth said. "Gyula has no need of seven stones. One is enough. Greed had him steal two from you." He grabbed her cold hands in his. "I shall kill him for this."

"Don't." She shook her head but then thought better and nodded. "Please do."

"Bloodthirsty wench," Jareth murmured, his lips kicked up in the corners.

"Seriously," Elizabet said. "I'm learning that this time requires desperate measures. They'll never stop until I'm dead or you're dead, or *someone* is dead. It might as well be them."

"You shall be dead of cold if I do not get you home." Jareth helped her stand. Keeping the blanket swaddled around her, he encircled her with his arm. "Can you walk to the castle? We are a good bit away. I can carry you."

Elizabet shook her head. "Don't be silly." But her lips trembled.

Jareth shook off the blanket from his shoulders and doubled it over hers. Although she protested, he did not listen. Instead, he led her slowly and steadily up the hill to the castle.

He ended up carrying her when her strength failed. Her dignity, though, was another story. She hid her face in the crook of his shoulder when he toted her through the castle hall where dinner was being served.

He stood her upright once he closed the door to their chamber. The massive stone fireplace covered a good portion of the west wall; he hunched down to build the fire higher.

"How are you so hot?" Elizabet shivered. She frowned and huddled deeper into the blankets. "You don't even look cold and you're as wet as I am."

Jareth shrugged. "My anger, perhaps." He smiled ruefully. "My thought of vengeance is exceedingly warming. You gave me the go ahead to execute those who have betrayed my family. I do this best, Elizabet—exacting revenge on those who deserve no mercy."

"I didn't mean it to sound so cruel." With damp blankets sagging around her, she walked to the privacy partition.

"I can be cruel when necessary . . ." He poked the wood and stirred the embers with an iron. " . . . If it means protecting those I love."

She tossed the blankets over the wide partition and wondered if the screen was medieval. She decided it was not. She looked it up and down and frowned at it before she ducked behind it and yanked at her ruined shift. "We speak of killing and murder while I dress. It should bother me, but I find myself falling into character the more time I spend with you. I even sound like a gothic novel. I hardly recognize my speaking."

"Good!" There was a rustle of movement; Jareth rising to his feet. "That is not apathy, but empathy." His footsteps neared. "Do you need help?"

Elizabet's hands stilled on the waistband of her thin undergarment. He came to stand at the partition's fold, his arms crossed. She peeped and jumped.

"I am here to keep you warm." He smiled. "To offer you the use of my hot body."

She scowled and reached for a folded towel that lay on the small chair—which was probably Chippendale. The furniture was becoming scandalous. It was not just her attitude that was adjusting to her new life, but she was seeing clearer and recognizing objects that did not belong. They were everywhere, and it vexed her that she had failed to notice before.

"It puts me off how you get slang." She hurriedly wrapped the towel around the remains of her wet clothing. "You understand play with words." She crossed her arms too. "And you shouldn't. I say I'm playing my part, but sometimes you just get me."

He waved his hand, then turned on his heel and aimed himself toward a solid wall. "Have it your way. Be prudish. Go on and finish your ablutions. My hot body and I are going to shower."

Elizabet reached up and grabbed him by the collar. "What did you say?"

Jareth righted his lower body to match the stationary upper half she held hostage. He pointed straight ahead without looking back at her. "Behind that wall is a modern bath and I am prepared to make use of it."

She twisted his damp shirt in her hand. Jareth shrugged to disengage her, but she only tightened her grasp. "You mean to tell me, that while I was here nursing you back from the dead, I could have had running water?" she asked incredulously.

Jareth peered at her over his shoulder. "You stand there like a wet mouse in dire need of a warm bath, and you are unearthing an insignificant piece of the past? Or could I be hopeful that you have decided to use my hotness?"

Elizabet released her hold of him and pushed him away. Belatedly, she reached out and slapped his cold, sodden back before he was too far off. "I'm going first."

She felt her hands along the wall as a blind man would, and searched for the way to open it. Jareth was no help; he bit his lip as though trying not to laugh.

JARETH AND ELIZABET LAY NOSE to nose in the dark and under a canopy of covers. He decided they would leave at daybreak, travel through the wormhole, and face whatever giants awaited them. It was selfish not to return home tonight—they were free to go, and it was time—but he was greedy and wanted one more night with her before she knew everything. Tomorrow her world would change forever. Their lives would be spent running from disaster to disaster.

"I didn't think," Elizabet said. She spoke of the circumstances that led to her losing the travel stones. "I couldn't think. Gyula threatened that he had men who would kill you on his command if I didn't give up the stones."

Jareth traced the bruise on her back with his fingertips. The imprint of it was on his brain, and he touched it without having to look. Anger erupted in his chest as he envisioned how it got there. His fingertips walked the edge of it along her spine, almost a foot in length. He did it to soothe her as she spoke. At first, she did not want to tell him what happened. She was ashamed, but he persuaded her. "But you gave them to him anyway." He let his mouth curve into a crooked smile. "That means you trust me."

Elizabet grimaced. He was not sure if it was due to the pressure against her bruised back or that she was confused. "I was scared. I didn't know whether he telling the truth."

She was confused, then. "You knew that no matter what, I would protect you, and that I would be all right. You were brave not to give him all of them. It was a risk, but you took it. You trust me."

"I wish all of that didn't have to happen for you to come to that conclusion."

"Catherine will pay for this," Jareth said. He pushed up onto his elbow, his body leaning over hers. He kept his hand on her back, bracing her close to him. "I will not stop until I have erased her memory from history. She will never harm you or any of my family again."

"That is sweet of you," Elizabet said. She reached up to touch his face. "But not necessary. It's too much for me. This isn't how I'm used to living. Just turn her in to the authorities and let them deal with her." Elizabet's palm pressed to his face.

"I am the authority."

"Oh!" Her eyes widened a fraction. "I forget that part." Her fingers curled into a ball before she withdrew them, and her voice lowered. "What will you do?"

"Have her executed."

"Jareth! You can't do that."

"I can and I will."

"Isn't there anything I can say that will change your mind?"

"Probably not."

Elizabet struck his chest with her fist. "Not even I love you? That you don't need to murder someone for me? That it doesn't sit well with me that killing people—"

"You love me?" Jareth asked. He lowered his face toward her; their noses almost touched. He wanted to relish what she was saying, but the anger in her tone made it impossible.

"Of course, I do." She hit him again and shoved him back. She was not happy yet, even though she smiled. "Why wouldn't I? You're my husband . . ."

"You may stop at I love you." Jareth grinned. He ran his nose along hers, and let his lips graze her cheek in a feather light kiss. He wanted to distract her so he would not be forced to make promises he had no intention of keeping. "Do not ruin it by giving me excuses. Stop talking before you spoil it for me."

"Okay." She giggled as though what he was doing tickled. He pulled back and allowed his smile to grow. One of his favorite sounds was her laughter. "I'll shut up if you promise you won't kill anyone for me."

Jareth's smile faltered. His distraction had not worked. "You cannot ask me to turn a blind eye to what was done. As lord, I must make an example of her for what she has done or my title will lose respect. I have to show justice or my people will not trust me. It is the way of things, Elizabet. I cannot allow Catherine to get away with what she did." He touched her back again. "She marked you." His voice went rough. "Kicked you, had you flogged."

"She didn't hit me very hard," she admitted. "I must bruise easily."

"She is the one who flogged you?" Jareth nearly roared.

She nodded. "Isn't there another way other than killing her?"

She was persistent, and that irritated Jareth. "She is the one who held you down for a flogging and you want her to go free? You would have her hurt your family next time? Our children? She is in allegiance with Gyula, which means she has access to the alchemy of time jumping."

Elizabet frowned. "I didn't think of that. And besides, he held me while she beat me." Jareth gave way to his rage and screwed his face into a thunderous expression. "Do you think she would really go after the children?"

"She flogged you," he snarled. He did not care about the mechanics of the situation. "What *lady* would lower to that?"

"You have a point."

"I do."

"Can't you just send her away?"

"Really?" Jareth asked, fury giving way to exasperation. She had ruined his perfectly good feeling. Her declaration of love had made him exuberant, but he could not enjoy it as long as she badgered him about things she could not comprehend. "You would have her alive? Where she could be found by our enemies and used to hurt us again?"

"You're not listening to me." Elizabet's voice held a touch of annoyance.

"I hear what you say, but fail to see the reason. You do not understand this life, but I do. Here, I am lord and master. There are no democracies. It is the law of the land, and I make that law." Jareth pulled away and rolled to his back. He folded his arms behind his head and peered up at the canopy above them. "If you insist I banish her, however, it is an option."

He offered this reluctantly. His wife scrambled his thoughts; that was the reason he could not touch her while he spoke of important things. He would gladly give her whatever she wanted, and that bothered him.

Catherine of Torquay needed to die. The safety of his family was at risk as long as she walked the earth. He stole a peek at his wife and was further aggravated by how fetching she looked when she was upset. "I can send her to France. Gabriel can oversee it. He will get a kick out it; they cannot stand the sight of one another."

"I love you." Elizabet said, and then leaned into him, her arm across his waist. She hugged him, her nose buried in his chest.

Jareth studied the top of her head and curved his mouth into a smile—even though he wanted to thrash her for being manipulative. She would be the death of him. He would give her whatever she wanted and the consequences be damned. He would have to employ more assassins and henchmen to keep them all safe. "So you have said."

She peered up at him with her hair framing her face and spilling down onto his chest. She was so beautiful to him that it nearly robbed his breath. For all of his days he would remember this moment as the instant he lost his heart for good. It was gone—into the keeping of his wife. "And I'll say it again and again."

"Hhhhmmm," Jareth hummed and allowed his mouth to kick up in the corner.

Her eyes widened. "You don't believe me?"

"Oh, I believe you," he said. "I just do not know how much it will cost me."

"Let's play a game," she said.

"You and your games," Jareth murmured. He reached out and pushed her hair from her face. "Are you trying to make me forget that I want Catherine's head on a platter?" He let her hair slide between fingers; the silky strands gleamed in the moonlight cast through the open window. "I want you safe. I want the children safe, yet I find myself agreeing to banish the vile creature who parades as a lady instead of killing her." He narrowed his eyes as he regarded her face that was flushed with anticipation. "You leave me little choice, wife. I am at your bidding."

"I like that," she said with a cheeky grin. She folded her hands under her chin, resting on his sternum. "I'll go first."

"Of course you will," he muttered.

"It's just that I'm very curious."

"Curiosity kills more than just cats." He grasped a strand of her hair and twirled it between his fingertips.

She smiled broadly. "Which leads me to the first question. Cat or dog?"

Jareth's eyes tapered, but he answered. He had an idea of how far she could take her games and he was leery. "Cat."

A laugh popped out of Elizabet's mouth. "You've got to be kidding me?"

"I assure you I am not," Jareth said flatly and gave her a scowl. He brought his arm back behind his head to use as a pillow and then crossed his ankles. "Canines lick their bits. Nasty creatures."

Elizabet giggled. "Cats lick themselves, too."

"But they do it with flair of refined style," Jareth said. "Next question. Or would you prefer to see the litter of cats I have on site? I can prove to you that I am partial to the feline persuasion."

"You're serious," Elizabet said with a touch of awe. Jareth glowered mockingly. She smiled. "I can't believe you like cats. It just doesn't fit with the knight thing you've got going on."

He smirked. "Next question, your grace. You emasculate me with your lack of discernment. I will have you know that my tolerance of cats has never hindered me in battle."

"Dancing or singing."

"Neither," he replied with great conviction.

"But Jareth . . ."

A burly hand sliced through the air, just grazing the top of her head. "No. Never. Next question."

"Did you ever love someone before me?"

His jaw dropped; he was dumbfounded that she had the gall to ask. "No," he answered quickly, and seemed to surprise her. "Never."

Elizabet's facial features morphed to mimic his humorless one. "Never? You never felt anything for Catherine. I've seen her, and she's beautiful, Jareth."

Jareth's searched her face: her mouth, her eyes, and the charming way her cheeks glowed pink when she was nervous or shy. He took his time, gauging the answer he wanted to give so she would understand. "You want to know if I have ever wanted to spend time with another? If I have ever waited in anticipation for the next moment I would see someone whose presence I missed no matter if it were only mere seconds that separated us? Did I ever have the feeling that I would expire if that person did not accept me and return my affection?"

Elizabet nodded when he was finished. She swallowed visibly as he let his eyes circle her face again.

Jareth shook head; so slight was the movement that he wasn't sure she noticed. "Elizabet, what is it you want from me?" he whispered. "Would you have me write it in the heavens? Are you so insecure that you must goad me with silly questions?" His arms came out and around her, scooping her closer to him; their faces inches apart. "You foolish girl—what am I to do with you?" He ran his nose along the side of her face, closed his eyes and silently prayed for patience. "I came to you untouched. My heart has never belonged to another and it never will. It is exclusively yours." He smiled against her cheek, and ran his nose up her face again.

"You're just so . . . massively handsome."

He drew back. "Massively handsome?"

"I'm trying to talk fancy like you," she said with a shy smile. "You speak in poetry."

"I have the largest, ugliest nose ever beheld, and I have scars all over my body. I would say that cancels massively handsome from my list of personal attributes. There is poetic justice. I am the Duke of Dover with the nose of pelican."

She ran her finger down the imperfect bridge of his nose. It had been broken in the past, more than once. "I like your nose."

"And I like everything about you." He shifted so he could kiss the finger she was tracing him with. "You must be sure with me, Elizabet. I love you. Only you. There was never another, nor will there be one after you."

"I can't believe you're mine."

"*Dubium*"

Her eyes smiled and then her mouth followed. "Next question, husband."

"That is your grace to you."

Elizabet levered up and slapped her hands against his chest. He tensed in preparation for her assault, then tipped his head back as he laughed. "Fine! Your grace. Your majesty," she drawled. "Where will we live?"

Jareth grabbed her hands so she could not strike him again, his face still alight with laughter. "Here, and in modern Kent." His hands tightened over hers. "The Cayman Islands when I am between sessions and as often as I need to be there."

"Kent, I expected," she said. "This island place, not so much. How did this pop up? You've never mentioned it."

"There is a commune of host known as the Brac there on the main island. Most host thrive in the environment. It was privately owned by a Presbyterian minister until I purchased it recently."

Elizabet clicked her tongue. "So, we're rich too."

Jareth laughed again. "No. Not yet, at any rate. I had to sell a few artifacts I collected over the years to purchase the reserve and a home in Kent." His lips twisted grimly. "My castle is a travesty in modern day. A tourist trap. Admission is charged and fellows stay overnight in hopes of seeing my ghost." He looked upward. "Ghastly thought. Here I thought I made a difference in vague superstitions and people are chasing my ghost. Reformers worldwide are turning over in their graves—perish the thought."

Elizabet smoothed her index finger between his eyes where creases lived, and he relaxed. "Sounds like we will have a good life, besides you pining for your home. At least we'll have time here. Now. With Percival and Mrs. Wheatley." She smiled. "I still get to be a real duchess."

"I am not pining for my home," Jareth insisted, but when Elizabet narrowed her eyes, he relented. "Perhaps a bit." He looked away. "You do not know what it is like to see your home and know that it is no longer yours."

"You saw Dover in modern day?"

He faced her and nodded. "Gabriel took me there once. He showed me the future and all of the possibilities. I think he did it to entice me." He shrugged one shoulder. "I would have done this anyway. It is right. Being the first guardian is an honor I do not take lightly, but it is hard to see the things I love fall out of my grasp. I cannot just walk into modern Dover and claim it—it is not done that way. I have no rights to it. It belongs to the people. My rights to it were lost long ago."

"I'm sorry."

"It is not yours to be sorrowful," he said. He brought his arms around her and let one hand trail lightly along her spine again. "You are the brightest of my future. Wherever you are, I shall find contentment. We will make a grand go of it."

"Where do we start?"

Jareth grinned. "I have it on strict confidence that the twins are conceived on this night . . ."

Elizabet playfully smacked him, open palmed against his cheek. "I meant, where do we go from here?"

"We fetch Jeremy," Jareth said. He grabbed her wrist easily and pulled her hand from his face, then pressed a kiss in her palm. "He will be lost after the storm, but we will find him and bring him to the Brac."

Elizabet's eyes widened, fright unfeigned in her expression. "You'll meet my dad."

Jareth beamed. "There is that—yes. Where should I start? With the fact we are married or that you have been thoroughly ravished?"

She made an attempt to hit him again, but failed. He grasped both of her wrists. "He'll kill you."

"Highly unlikely," Jareth responded. His head left the pillow and he kissed her on the mouth. "I shall give him the best regard and he will gladly welcome me to the family."

"You plan on paying him off?"

"It will not come to that," he said. "Gabriel told me this will be an easy transition. I will meet with your grandmother first and then approach your father." Elizabet's face ashened. "No, no," he crooned. "Do not be troubled." He twisted their bodies until she lay partially beneath him and he was leaning over her. "I cannot bear it when you are distressed." He smoothed her hair from her face, and nuzzled her with his cheek and then his mouth in small kisses across her lips. "You must trust that I will take care of you. I will not allow harm to come to you. You are safe with me. I will take care of everything. I promise."

"I didn't think about the repercussions of what I've done." She turned her face into the pillow. "I'm seventeen. This just isn't done, Jareth."

"It is done every day in my world. You are older than most. Marriageable age varies in different time periods, but it does not change the fact you are of age." She glanced at him, her eyes imploring him for an explanation. He took the opportunity to kiss her. "I have done my research concerning your laws. I am known for my lawful compliance where the deflowering of virgins is concerned. I only deflower those of age and who have been given my last name."

Elizabet's smile was quick, as if she could not help it. "You're smart; I'll give you that, but he'll still kill you. I'm his little girl regardless how he treats me."

Jareth smirked. "He may try, but in the end, I am sure he will see reason." His face heated with emotion. "And I see no evidence of a little girl lying in my bed."

"And if he doesn't see reason?" she asked. She did a poor job of hiding the fact she was thrilled at his possessive tone. His confidence in what he could do was bolstered. He would have her father eating out his hand before it was all over. She may be married young, but she married well.

"I am taking you anyway," he rumbled. "You belong to me, with me. He cannot stop me, nor can your laws, Mrs. Tremaine. You. Are. Mine."

Elizabet smiled cheekily at his insolent tone and added her own as well to her words. "That is your grace, to you. Don't you forget it. My title supersedes simple salutations."

Chapter 17

BEAU WATCHED HER TWIN BROTHER Rixby shovel ice into plastic bags from the machine behind their parents' store. Their mother was a twin also—to Elizabet's mother. Twins ran in their family, and the women had shared a bond that was broken only when her aunt died. It had devastated her mom.

The wonderful kinship of being twins was lost, however, on Beau and Rixby. She was quite sure that he hated her, even though they were only nine, and it did not seem things would change. Beau felt more of a bond with her cousin, Elizabet. They should have been twins, or at least sisters. She was glad Elizabet was back from wherever she had disappeared to. One person being lost was enough to worry over. Her best friend, Jeremy, had been missing since the hurricane ripped through. And Elizabet had gone missing too, but turned up married and fine as ever.

Married.

Beau narrowed her eyes as said husband turned the corner into the alley that housed the ice machine. He was talking to the Sheriff's deputy. She could see why Elizabet had been cajoled into marrying the guy. He was extremely good looking—to the point that his physical appearance was distracting—even to a child such as herself.

Beau did not trust him. He talked funny, and he did not smile. Which made him the total opposite of Elizabet. Her cousin had worn a stupid, full on grin since she was resurrected yesterday. It was disgusting.

He looked uncomfortable in his skin, too—as if what he wore chafed him or something. His lack of self-confidence did not match up with her demeanor. Either something was off or he was a fake.

"Great!" Rixby stopped shoveling and spit on the ground beside the ice machine. A clump of tobacco fell from his lip.

Beau narrowed her eyes until they were barely slits. "You're not supposed to chew."

"You don't matter, so shut your face," Rixby snarled. He jerked his chin to the approaching cop and cousin stealer. "Get off your rump and go help them. I don't need you crying around me and telling me what to do. Go find your precious Jeremy, and keep them away from me, too."

Beau felt her lip wobble. She would not cry—again. It was giving her a headache, but when Jeremy's name was mentioned, she cried.

"Beau," Deputy Mike said. He nodded to her and she offered a shaky smile. "This here is Dr. Jareth Tremaine. He's helping us look for Jeremy. He'd like to ask you a few questions."

Beau tipped her face up to look at them. From her seat on the upside down five gallon bucket he was tall. She had spied on him, hidden from view behind Grandma's barn yesterday, but she had not officially met him. He was larger up close, like the items in a rear view mirror. And he was a doctor.

That was . . . unexpected.

She squinted against the sun that was behind the men. "What you want to know? I told everybody I haven't seen him since before the storm. He went to the shelter and I stayed here—at home."

Everyone knew her dad refused to evacuate. He wanted to be home to open the store as soon as the storm allowed. People would need ice and beer. They had a generator that had kept everything going. Their home was attached to the store, so it was easy.

Or not.

Beau would have nightmares for years having stayed through the mega storm that destroyed everything around them. By grace of God, they survived, and so had the store and their home. It was providence. There was no other explanation as to why she was still alive and sitting on bucket speaking with a man who looked too young to be a doctor.

And married to her teenage cousin.

Bleh.

"I have a few questions," Jareth said. He smiled at her, proving he was able. She noticed that his teeth were nice, too. It proved her theory that he was perfect. Not even his teeth refused to be anything but pearly white and straight. "And I wanted to meet you. Elizabet is very fond of you."

Fond? Did he mean that she was liked? Beau smirked. "Where is Lizabet? She hasn't come around since you brought her back. As your *wife*." She looked away and managed not to gag. Rixby was leaning on the shovel with his hand on his hip, taking in the interrogation with feigned disinterest. He inspected his dirty hand for splinters. "I only saw her from far away. She didn't even come talk to me."

His smile positively blinded her, more so than the sun at his back. "Lizabet," he repeated as if testing the sound. "I like that." His head tilted slightly and his lips twisted. "Do not be angry with her." He touched his chest with his fingertips. "It is my fault. The marriage, that is. I insisted on it. I am to leave in a few days for England. I have to complete university. She has been busy packing and making provision for your grandmother. I assure you that she wants to see you soon, but we must find Jeremy first. It's important."

"You talk funny," Beau mumbled. She did not understand why Jeremy was so important to Elizabet's new husband. He did not know Jeremy. It bothered her that he was here to discuss the search. He should be with Elizabet—his new wife—not worried about a boy he never met.

She eyed Mr. Mike, who looked like he wanted out, too. The deputy frowned at Rixby. "Where's your daddy?"

Rixby frowned back. "In the store." He spit, but the tobacco was long gone.

"Dr. Tremaine," Mr. Mike said without removing his eyes from Rixby's face. "Do you mind if I leave you here to handle business? I have to discuss underage selling. I don't want to seem sloppy in the aftermath of the storm."

Jareth nodded. "Of course. I will stay and speak with Miss Beau." He smiled at her again, but this time Beau was sure to bristle outwardly. "We will be famous friends."

Rixby laughed, a curt, barking sound. Beau stuck her tongue out at her twin. The idiot. People were capable of liking her, too. She was not popular the way he was, but she was likable. The doctor said so.

Deputy Mike motioned for Rixby to lead the way, which he did—reluctantly. It was not his first offense with tobacco. The laws were strict, more stringent than Church regulations. The government guided what was eaten in the home, what was watched, what was taught. They were everywhere. Tobacco was a controlled item; Rixby knew that. It served him right for getting busted.

Beau focused her attention on Jareth. She waited until she heard the back door of the store close before she spoke. "What do you want to know?"

Jareth motioned to the bucket beside her. "May I?"

"Sure." She shrugged. "You might get your jeans dirty, though."

He glanced down at his radiant white T-shirt and light denim pants. He reminded her of Jeremy, who never had a hair out of place. Jeremy was the most conscientious dresser she knew—and this guy was his equal. That said a lot. Nobody was cleaner than Jeremy. They even sort of looked alike, but Jeremy was a younger, puny version.

Her heart clenched painfully in her chest. First Jeremy, then Elizabet.

She was relieved that Elizabet was home now, but what of Jeremy? He had been missing for over forty-eight hours, and each hour that went by made the prospect of him being found dead more likely. She was already thinking of him in past terms, which made her ashamed of her lack of faith. Jeremy would be full of faith if it were she who was missing.

"I welcome it." Jareth tugged at the neck of his shirt. "They say cotton is the choice if one wants comfort." He shook his head. "My opinion differs."

"Hmm," Beau hummed and narrowed her eyes. She watched him flip the bucket and push it back a few feet. He sat and leaned forward with his elbows resting on his knees. He had the lightest eyes she had ever seen. They were blue, but almost gray they were so pale. The contrast with his black brows and hair was startling. So much like Jeremy.

Her lips slid to one side. "You're very cute."

"Thank you," he said, and he smirked as well. "Your cousin says the same."

"I'm sure she does."

"For one so young, you are perceptive and bold."

"I read a lot."

"I should thank you for that," he said.

Beau pulled a face. "What?"

"You read to Elizabet. She told me you read to her. You helped her study. About wound care."

"That was you?" She tried not to seem surprised, but she realized at once it was he who had been hurt. She should have known it was not merely the curious project Elizabet claimed. Her cousin had been too nervous. She had rambled on and on about how she was interested in wound therapies when she was about as interested in medical procedures as Beau was about taxidermy. Not one bit.

"It was," he admitted.

"I thought it was an animal." She shook her head. It had to be an animal, because who would have a wound like the one she described? "She's always doctoring some creature. I guess the *human* medical books should have tipped me off. How did you get injured? She said it was like a knife slash."

"I will explain later," he said. He steepled his fingers. "I have other things on my mind."

"Like Jeremy?" she asked. "You want me to forget that somewhere under your sparkly clean clothes you have a nasty scar that my cousin helped with."

"You speak well for your age."

"I read," she repeated. "Does it bother you that she can't read?" She shrugged. "I mean, she must have told you, 'cause you know I read to her."

"I love your cousin, Beau, and she is safe with me. I will take care of her, I promise. And no; it does not trouble me that she cannot read." He smiled. "I recognize that you are concerned for her. I understand, but you will have to trust me. I want what is best for her and I am best able to take care of her." He shook his head. "You are more difficult than her father."

"Yeah, well, he was probably drunk." She looked away at nothing in particular. "He's always happy with a few beers in him. You had him at 'I'm a doctor.'" She shook her head when he said nothing. There was a stray cat climbing a nearby trash heap. She tossed a rock at it and it ran off. "So, what do you want? If you won't tell me about how you got a knife wound, then tell me why you're here. I've got things to do. My dad will have a heart attack if he comes out here and I'm sitting here talking to you and not doing nothing."

"I want you show me the spot where you and Jeremy fish. It's a bridge—"

"I know what you're talking about," she interrupted. She fixed her gaze on him. "Do you think that's where he is?"

Jareth considered her as if he were sizing her up. Those light eyes assessed her, peering into her soul, it seemed, before he nodded slowly. "Yes. I know that is where he is."

If he was assessing her, she had already done the same, and for some crazy reason she believed him. He did not strike her as a liar.

Beau stood, and the backs of her knees knocked the bucket. "What are you waiting for, then? Screw my chores. Let's go get him."

ELIZABET WAS TORN BETWEEN WATCHING Jareth drive and watching Beau, who was watching her watch Jareth. Both of them were exasperating. Jareth, because he had never driven a vehicle before and had only read about it and observed. Once. It was uncanny how quickly he picked up a skill. And Beau, because she was silent and had a controlled malice about her. Jareth might drive like a natural, but Beau was creeping her out.

"Where was it you said y'all are moving to?" Beau asked.

"She speaks," Elizabet said out of the corner of her mouth. She twisted to face her friend in the back seat. "England and the Cayman Islands. Have you heard of that?"

Beau shook her head.

"Me, neither." Elizabet smiled. Beau did not return it, but Elizabet pressed on in a joyful tone anyway. "It's in the Caribbean. Exciting. I've never been outside of Louisiana and now I'm going to live in two places. Of course, I'm talking about Cayman Islands and not England, because England is in . . . England. And the Cayman Islands are in the Caribbean." She made a face, stuck her tongue out and rolled her eyes heavenward. It was something Beau thrived on for comic relief once upon a time.

"You've been to Holly Beach," Beau grumbled. She eyed Jareth as though she wanted to murder him. "If you've seen one beach, you've seen them all."

Elizabet laughed, but it was forced. She hid the hurt she felt. "That's *in* Louisiana." The truth of it was that Elizabet felt misplaced since returning. Being married to Jareth and living in another time had changed her. She felt disconnected to her life in modern times, and the place she once called home was far away and foreign. She was a stranger among her family.

"I know that," Beau said. "But you're talking like all these fancy places will be better."

"I didn't say that," Elizabet said. She turned back and reached over to pinch Jareth's shirt at his side. If she could touch even a part of him, she would feel strong. In such a short time she had come draw security from him. She gathered that intimacy did that to you. She felt connected to him no matter where he was, as though they were tethered by a string. "You must know how hard it will be to leave you."

Jareth glanced down to where her fingers twisted his shirt. He took his right hand off the wheel, grabbed her hand and entangled their fingers together. She instantly felt stronger.

"But that's what you're doing," Beau said.

"I would take you with me if I could, and you know it," Elizabet said. Her jaw stiffened and she looked out the window as tears threatened. The roads were covered with muddy sludge that the storm surge had left behind. Pieces of grass were stuck in the fencing, marking where the water had risen.

Beau had to know she was telling her the truth; Elizabet was aware of her home life. It was a good thing she had Jeremy. Once Elizabet was off into the world, she would need a friend she could trust—one who would hide her and protect her when necessary. Jeremy's parents knew of her situation, too. There was comfort in knowing she would not be alone once Elizabet moved away.

It was why Elizabet was crying, because she knew how bad things could get in the Benoit household. And she should cry—Beau would never leave here. She had protected Elizabet's secret until Jareth came along. It was not her fault he found out. The fact Elizabet could not read was not her secret to tell, and in turn, she should get the same care. Her cousin should protect her. It was what families did—at least it was what they had done since forever.

"There!" Beau sprang up and leaned over the front seat of Elizabet's grandma's dual cab truck. She pointed toward the approaching bridge. "That's the one. There's a driveway near that pump shed. You can pull in there."

Beau barely waited until the truck was parked before she swung the door open and hit the ground running, hollering for Jeremy.

"Beau!" Jareth called. He came from the truck, slamming the door behind him.

Beau cupped her hands around her mouth to throw her voice further. "Jeremy!" she yelled. She seemed unaware of how desperate she sounded. If he was there, she was determined to find him.

Something was making the air hum around them. A low, yet high-pitched drone penetrated the air. Beau glanced up at the electric poles. Some were snapped from the recent storm, and the power had not yet been restored. It would take a week or more before they had electricity again in this area, but the sound vibrated like an electrical current.

"Listen to me," Jareth commanded as he caught up to her. He grabbed her arm and spun her to face him. "Do not call to him. Do you understand?"

Beau jerked her arm, but could not shake him off. She swallowed as she looked up at Jareth. Elizabet knew he could be scary to behold when he was angry, but Beau would not expect him to appear so fierce and strong. Someone with his beauty was not supposed to look as though he could kill her where she stood if she disobeyed.

"You can't tell me what to do," she shouted. Beau had never been overly smart, or one to follow rules. Jareth stood over her and surrounded her with his presence. Elizabet sensed the lethal grace he held back not to truly hurt her into submission.

"Beau," Elizabet said, and took a step closer. She held her hands up as if to calm her. "Listen to Jareth. Jeremy is sick, and it's important that we don't force him to do something that could hurt us." She stopped talking to bring her hands to cover her ears. She looked up at the electric lines, searching for the source of the noise.

Beau twisted her arm until Jareth reluctantly released her.

"Do not call out again or I will tape your mouth shut," Jareth warned, pointing at her.

Beau's mouth fell open to speak, but the humming grew louder. It hurt her ears.

"What is that noise?" Elizabet asked.

Jareth maintained eye contact with Beau, his eyes narrow and threatening. "He is close and he is afraid." He motioned to Beau. "She is giving off vibes of fear, and he can sense that." Beau tensed to run, but Jareth sprang on her like a jungle cat. He was quick and precise, and pinned her in his arms before she could gasp a startled breath. "Easy," he murmured. His arms were like a vice around her.

Beau met Elizabet's gaze, and mutely implored her for help. Being restrained would bring up terrible memories for Beau.

"Be still and stay quiet," Elizabet said—not what Beau would want to hear. "You'll scare him away." Beau answered her by throwing her head back, effectively head butting Jareth. She pierced the air with her best rendition of a scream worthy of the Bates Hotel.

"Bloody hell," Jareth cursed. Beau fought against him. He looked at Elizabet, his face enraged, his lip curling with anger. A smear of blood seeped from the corner of his mouth. "Get the tape from the glove box. The heavy, nasty silver tape."

Elizabet frowned and did not make a move. "She'll behave. She just doesn't understand." She leveled a look at Beau. "Stop it. Stop or you'll hurt yourself. You'll get us all hurt. Jareth is not your dad; he won't hurt you like that. You're making a ninny out of yourself."

"He wants to tape my mouth and you're okay with that?" Beau asked. The noise got louder and she threw up her hands to cover her ears. "You're *my* family."

"Jareth is my family now, too," Elizabet said. "I don't have to choose. I love you both, and he wants to help you. You don't understand what's going on and you could be hurt. Trust me." Beau lips wobbled as she held back tears. She twisted in Jareth's arms and spit in his face. Elizabet looked at Jareth's shocked, disgusted expression. "I'll get the tape."

Beau screamed and the humming got louder. So loud that Jareth instinctively released one arm to cover his ear. He pressed the other ear to the top of Beau's head, while she used the advantage to cover both of hers instead of escaping.

"He hears us," Jareth said over the humming. "And he thinks we are going to hurt Beau." He released Beau and reached for his wife instead. Elizabet was hunched down, clasping her ears. She reached out to Jareth and he jerked her into his arms. The volume of the drone was so profound that it was difficult to hear.

"We won't hurt her, Jeremy," Elizabet called. Someone had to try to calm the force that was either angry or scared. And Elizabet knew Jeremy. He was a reasonable kid, but he was crazy about Beau. "I've never lied to you!" she threw in for good measure. "I swear that we are only here to help you. We won't tape her mouth shut. I promise!"

The noise reduced as if a stereo dial had been turned down, but there remained a deep, pulsating throbbing. Elizabet uncovered her ears and slowly stood, as did Jareth. Her plea worked, which met he was close and could hear them. Jareth's arms curved around her as he surveyed the area.

Beau circled, searching for Jeremy. Her features perked, as though she sensed he was near. She started up the narrow dirt pathway that led to the canal bank and small shed that housed a water pump the area farmers used to flood fields.

"Let her go," Jareth said when Elizabet started to run after her. He grabbed her arm and slid his hand down her arm until they were holding hands. "I think he heard us and he is angry." He peered down at her. "You were right to reason with him."

"What if hurts her?" Elizabet asked.

"He cares for her." His hand squeezed hers. "He will not hurt her, but we will follow at a short distance and keep watch."

Elizabet looked ahead at her cousin who was not hurrying, but wary and watchful. They began up the trail in Beau's wake. "I heard you talking to Gabriel." She peered over her shoulder at Jareth, then tugged on his hand for him to keep up. "You said host are unstable when they first turn."

"I have a dagger in my boot. If he even breathes wrong where Beau is concerned—he is dead."

Elizabet halted. Was this why Jareth was so calm? Because he could kill Jeremy if he had to? "You can't use her as bait," she hissed. "And I don't want you to kill him. It would be all my fault." She thrust her arm in the direction Beau had gone. "You heard me tell him we were here to help. I practically threw my cousin at him."

"Have a little faith in me, love," Jareth said, his lips turning down. "Of course, I know how to kill my host, but it should not come to that. I think you underestimate the pull of the heart. Jeremy is tied to Beau somehow. We will use it to get him to safety. That is what is important right now. We must remove him before he really gets angry or frightened." His expression turned grave. "That would be nasty for all mankind in the general vicinity of say . . . a hundred miles or so."

"You always know what to do. How do you do that?" Elizabet asked as they started walking again. She kicked a clump of clay that was in the way. "Is there anything you can't do or reason through?"

"I cannot, for the life of me, learn to speak German."

Elizabet was shocked. Partially because it was the last thing she expected to come out of his mouth, and partially because it was such a random confession at a strange time. "You're a natural translator." She narrowed her eyes as she stared at him. If only it was the time to dig into the subject of his learning deficit—obviously, his *only* learning deficit. "I thought you could speak whatever language you tried."

Jareth shrugged. "Who am I to understand the depths of my own gray matter?" He tapped his temple. "There's a kink in there that blocks German receptors. And probably mathematics to a certain degree, although perhaps I simply have a keen dislike—or laziness—for numbers." He rolled one shoulder to dismiss the topic. "But I digress. You digress." He tipped his chin to the shed they were approaching. "Jeremy felt that Beau was near. One of his abilities is that he can sense what someone feels—specifically if it is someone he cares about. That is how I know he will not hurt her. I can sense his emotions. She is safe with him, as are we. As long as we play nice with Beau, all should end right as rain."

"He can feel . . . things?" Elizabet asked.

"Under the best of circumstances, he must be touching someone to communicate through his senses, but in cases where he is connected emotionally—it is different." He glanced down into her face and must have noted the combination of wonder and annoyance that he had not already told her this.

"You do know that I do not deliberately keep things from you?" he asked. "The issues of the Amalgam are so vast it would take a library to fill its theories. I am addressing them as they present. The fact Jeremy can siphon emotions never presented itself earlier, but it has now."

"I hate surprises," she said. "Especially those that involve people I love. Jeremy means a lot to Beau. I don't know how she will handle all of this." Her gaze followed a line of ants in the dirt. The trail was long and looped up toward the levy and the pump shed. There must have been a million ants marching in single file. Beau was nowhere in immediate sight. "What in the world?" Elizabet muttered as she hunkered down to study the trail.

"Hey!" Beau called. "He's here! I found him!" They could hear her, but not see her.

Elizabet stood and bumped into Jareth as she turned toward the shed where Beau's voice came from. They made their way up the slope of the levy, following alongside the army of ants that seemed to be leading the way.

"Stay close," Jareth said. He took the lead with her tucked behind him, one hand on her so she would not dart ahead.

Rounding the shed, they saw Beau on her knees before Jeremy. He was sitting, knees bent and head bowed, with his back to the shed exterior. The ant trail did not end there, however. They merely circled around Jeremy and came back to form their line like an endless form, an infinity sign. It was the strangest thing. The tiny creatures were scurrying and frantic, but remained in formation.

"He can't talk," Beau said. She leaned forward to peer into Jeremy's face. "And he doesn't want us to touch him, either." Jeremy nodded.

Elizabet took in the battered form of the boy she had known for many years. His clothing was ripped, dirty, and hung from him as if he had taken it off and tied the pieces back on. Jeremy, the neat freak, was a mess. But being a mess was not the clincher—it was him not seeming to care.

Beau cast his gaze at Jareth. "I can hear him talking in my head."

Jareth passed Elizabet a concerned glance before he crouched next to Beau. "I am Dr. Jareth Tremaine, Jeremy, and I am here to help you. I know that you are scared, but you have to trust me." He motioned for Elizabet to come forward. "I know what has happened to you. Everything will be all right." Jeremy flexed his fingers in a claw-like fashion. "Are you hurting?"

Jeremy glowered.

"He doesn't like you," Beau stated. She sounded pleased, as if Jeremy had impeccable taste. "Thinks you're too young to be doctor."

"You can trust him, Jeremy," Elizabet said. She put her hand on Jareth's shoulder. Beau looked away, her chin jutting out. "He's my husband and he really is a doctor. A good one."

Jeremy's filthy face screwed up in a scowl.

"He says he can kill you like he killed the rest of them," Beau sneered, then her face fell, as though what she said registered with her brain. She gaped at Jeremy, who still glared daggers at the doctor. The smugness was gone from her tone. "*Huh?* What are you talking about, Jeremy?"

"That's enough! Harness your anger," Jareth demanded in a voice filled with authority. His countenance changed from guarded friendliness to such a level of sternness that even Beau flinched. "If you do not, then you risk the safety of these ladies. Is that what you want? For Beau or Elizabet to be hurt?"

Jeremy's chin came up a fraction and he stared at Beau. His gaze held a child-like worship as it wandered over her as if checking for damage to her person. His intentions were heard by all of them, the intensity of his emotions so raw.

"It's okay," Beau assured him. She offered Jeremy a fractured smile. "You won't hurt me." She addressed Jareth with tapered eyes. "He thinks you will hurt us, not the other way around."

Elizabet's jaw hung open after being mind-raped for the first time. They did not need Beau's commentary. They had heard it directly from Jeremy's mind.

A grunting noise came from Jeremy, calling them to his attention. He thrust his arm out and pointed to the adjacent field.

"He wants to show you something," Jareth said. He turned his eyes to Beau and inclined his head in the direction of the field.

Elizabet nudged Beau and followed her in that direction. Beau halted and drew her breath in sharply. Elizabet put her hand to her mouth so she would not scream. In the field lay hundreds of dead animals. A multitude of them—raccoons, neutras, minx, armadillos, possums—too numerous to count. Their bodies were twisted in piles, each carcass disfigured in a violent throe of death.

Jareth came up behind them. "He did not mean to kill them," he murmured. He put his hand on Elizabet's shoulder. She reached up and squeezed his fingers. "He does not know how to control what is happening to him. He hid rather than return home and hurt a human being."

Beau peered up at Jareth, blinking tears from her eyes. "You can hear him too?"

Jareth nodded. He and Beau shared a kind glance for the first time since meeting. "Yes, Beau, I can hear him too."

Epilogue

THEY WERE FLYING COACH. NOT first class, as a duke should, but they had managed to rake together enough funds for the lowest priced tickets available. Three one way tickets to the Cayman Islands toting a wild force of nature. It was a bargain, considering what could have happened if they had stayed in Louisiana.

Jeremy had nearly killed his father.

Elizabet peered down at the boy who had a violent storm churning inside his small body even as he slept peacefully. His black hair was a mess, but his face was serene as he rested against Jareth's arm.

They were going to a safe haven located on the Brac of the Cayman Islands where Jeremy's uncle, Eddie Cameron, had a mission for the Presbyterian Church. Eddie was a scientist as well as a pastor, and had been one of the leading explorers who studied the eruption of Mount St. Helen's back in the 80's. And he had never been the same, Pastor Jed told them. Jed did not have to embellish that statement. His look, his sneer, and the way his body went rigid—all was enough to give them the information they needed.

It had been easy to take away a child when his parents were eager to give him up; that fact was not lost to either Elizabet or her husband. Even if the child was stricken with the same mutation that plagued his Uncle Eddie, it was not reason enough to abandon him with such zeal.

Elizabet was brokenhearted. Not only for Jeremy, but for herself, too. Her own father released her easily enough, and her grandmother took the money Jareth offered for her to hire help on the farm. He gave it to silence her whining demands that they were leaving her to go broke and die. It disgusted Elizabet to discover she was only a means to an end to people she had cared for. Even if the relationship between her and her father had deteriorated, he was still her dad. For a brief moment, she understood why Jeremy attacked his father. It was the worst feeling in the world—considering herself unwanted and easily dispensable. The life of one's child should be the most precious commodity, not something to be bartered and sold.

Leaving Beau behind had been the most difficult for Jeremy. It took a healthy dose of reason for him to understand that his presence was not protection enough for her problems. Those kinds of worries did not belong in the mind of a nine-year-old. Beau would have to watch out for herself while Jeremy learned about his new life.

They promised him that they would eventually allow him to move home, but his training was not something they could compromise, and it was not a place for Beau. At all cost, they had to keep Jeremy's nature a secret, and Beau had already seen too much. They prayed that in time she would forget what she had seen. Time had a way of making memories hazy.

Brac Island was not that different from Dover. Instead of white chalk cliffs, it had black lime cliffs. It was a smaller island in comparison to Grand Cayman. It was as it should be—private and sequestered from populated areas. The compound, or mission, where Eddie lived was situated on the eastern bluff.

They took a smaller plane from the main island to the Brac. Eddie met them at the airport.

He was not what Elizabet expected. His thick, brown wavy hair was long and unkempt. He wore khaki Bermuda shorts, a rock band T-shirt, and ratty Crocs. His expression, however, was a picture of peace. When he smiled, his cheeks became rounded and his face resembled a half moon. She imagined his countenance was similar to the one books described as cheeks of sugarplums and bright expressions. No one would ever guess he had a raging volcano living inside him. He was a walking oxymoron, just like her. She liked him immediately.

"Dr. Tremaine," Eddie greeted, extending his hand.

Jareth's arm left Elizabet's shoulders and he shook Eddie's hand. "Call me Jareth, please."

They stepped back and examined one another. Jeremy hid behind Elizabet, gripping the tail of her denim shirt, seemingly aware that the two men destined to protect him were having a proverbial spitting contest. He peeked around her, acting bashful and unsure of how he would be received. Elizabet smoothed her hand over Jeremy's cheek and smiled down at him. The only thing missing from the absurd pair of men was growling and howling. Spare her the dominant males in her life. There was a child watching and *learning* the way of things. Last thing they needed was Hurricane Boy seeking to be alpha.

"Jeremy," Eddie said, and his voice held a hint of surprise. "I didn't see you there—hiding." He gestured with a sweep of his arm. "Come out here so I can get a look at you."

Jeremy's hand pressed further into Elizabet's side. He gazed at his uncle with uncertainty.

Eddie crouched. Even though Jeremy was tall for his age, the stance was made to be non-threatening. "You remember?" Eddie asked, his voice soft in that peaceful aura he radiated.

Jeremy looked to Jareth, who gave him a slight nod. Not that Jareth or Elizabet knew what Eddie was speaking of, but it seemed significant, and a memory possibly shared between nephew and uncle.

Jeremy stepped partially into view, but kept his hand tangled in Elizabet's shirt. He nodded.

"He can't talk." Elizabet felt the need to explain. "Since the storm. Jareth thinks he will recover. The trauma and all. But you can hear him if he'll let you."

"Oh, I hear him," Eddie said, his eyes on his nephew. He smiled, none of his teeth showing in that half-moon smile. "If anyone understands—it's me. I couldn't walk for months after. Had the hardest time learning how to toddle about like a newborn babe. Deuced embarrassing. Being awesome like us sucks sometimes."

Jeremy smiled at that. Eddie held out his arms and Jeremy ran into them.

AFTER SETTLING INTO THEIR TEMPORARY quarters, they met in the church. It was a white wooden building, complete with steeple, black slate roof, and stained glass windows.

The conservative building looked odd amid the tropical backdrop, and it was surrounded by military fencing that encamped the entire perimeter of the compound. The rectory was a large, plantation-style house. There was also a warehouse on the property. That building was the largest and the topic of conversation.

"Who?" Jareth asked, his jaw ridged. He leaned forward and gripped the pulpit he stood behind. He had been drawn to the Bible that lay there, curious to see what translation it was and if it was accurate.

Jeremy looked up from the piano; his fingers stilled over the keys he had been lightly plucking.

Eddie knew all about them. He had expected them, had been warned to watch for them. But they knew nothing of what they were walking into. Jareth had been led by Gabriel and Minh to seek this destination and make it the hub of the Amalgam. He had even been told of Eddie, but not given details. Classic Amalgam secret style.

"Gabriel. Minh," Eddie said. He crossed his arms and leaned against the partition of the first pew.

"How many?" Jareth asked. He was not surprised that Gabriel and Minh had ventured this far. They were meddlers of the worst kind, and he was grateful, in a way. It made things smoother—easier.

Eddie glanced at Jeremy. "Fifty-two."

"Fifty-two," Elizabet repeated. She looked wide eyed at Jareth. "Fifty-two kids. What the heck will we do with all of them?"

"They are perfectly safe here," Eddie said. "And not all of them are kids. The oldest is a little over ninety." Jareth pinched the bridge of his nose and closed his eyes. "I've collected them over the past thirty years," Eddie continued. "Followed leads like strange articles bearing news about aliens or superpowers. Where there is smoke, there is fire."

"Jareth," Elizabet said. She did not like the way he seemed to shut himself off.

Jareth took a deep breath and brought both hands to the pulpit. He smoothed his palms over the shiny wood. "Can you control them?"

Eddie's eyebrows raised a fraction. "I was told that's what you're here for."

"I do not have the time to tarry here forever," Jareth said. "I am expected in London in a fortnight." Not to mention there was the task of fetching Gabriel and Minh from their respective time periods. He had no idea how extensive grooming them to be guardians would be. He suppressed the urge to curse; he was in church after all.

"I will continue to man this station," Eddie said. "I've managed for this long without a league. I can certainly do so long after you leave."

"I did not mean to insult," Jareth assured him. "There is no need for puffed up pride." He turned to watch Jeremy, who was still absorbing everything being said. "Jeremy will come with me, of course, and I will send two of the best guardians." He smiled ruefully. "Names are Gabriel and Minh—fancy meeting them again?"

"Jeremy is my nephew," Eddie replied. "He should stay with me. I know how to handle people like us."

"You just admitted that you have no control over your charges. With all due respect, your nephew will stay with me and my wife. We are his family now. Your brother gave me full custody."

"Jed is weak," Eddie scoffed. He pushed off and stood tall. "He's scared of my kind. He would do anything to eradicate us from the planet. He may be an unregulated pastor, but that doesn't make him right in the head. He's trouble for us. Mark my words."

"All the more reason for Jeremy to be far away. London. Kent. Dover. The king's good country. An ocean between him and his sire should suffice. He is different from the others. Stronger. His abilities surpass anything you can imagine. I must be sure he is trained to harness his abilities. I plan on integrating him back into a normal life. We must prove that host can live among us safely."

"So, you plan to take him to England where he can be discovered? What if he turns in front of someone?"

"He has not made that mistake, and I would say that shows great restraint," Jareth answered. "When we found him, he had hidden away to protect people. He was smart enough to realize he was a danger and he removed himself from that situation." He looked fondly at Jeremy who sat taller as a plant preening under a watering. "We will take our chances. Jeremy is coming with us. For all that matters, he is my son now."

"What if I decide I don't like that plan?" Eddie asked. A flash of yellow heat flared in his eyes. The serenity he exuded was gone.

Elizabet gauged the distance between her and Jeremy, silently giving him strength to be calm and stay still. Jareth's eyes flickered to her, his eyes filled with concern. Jeremy could take care of himself, but Elizabet would be toast before he could take a step forward to save her. Eddie, on the other hand, would be cut down before it came to that.

"You do not want to cross me. I can kill you where you stand and not move an inch," Jareth said. "Come, let us reason together. We are to be allies. We both want what is best for Jeremy and the Amalgam."

Eddie bowed his head and closed his eyes as if willing his body to stand down. When a host began to dissipate, it took a great deal of self-control to reel it back. "I was told that you had the knowledge to kill us." He shook his head, but did not look up. "How is it that I'm the one everyone is scared of, when you are an assassin of our kind?"

"Chance—really," Jareth replied. "It sucks to be awesome like me sometimes."

Eddie lifted his gaze, the foreboding look disappearing instantly and replaced with that perpetually deceptive serene expression he owned. He smiled ruefully at the joke meant to break the ice

Jareth's lips kicked up to one side. "See. I have a sense of humor. And you are still alive and standing, so that means I am merciful as well."

"You will have to fight some," Eddie said. "Kill a few, possibly."

"I understand that," Jareth said. "If I must terminate those who are rebellious for the greater peace of my league, then I shall."

"We aren't animals," Eddie said, his anger instantly flaring. He closed his eyes and turned his gaze downward.

"You shall never be treated as animals as long as you maintain your humanity," Jareth said, his voice deceptively soft.

"Some have lost their way. I've done the best I could with what I had." He blinked against the blur of tears, and turned back to face Jareth. "A few died by my hands."

"You have done well," Jareth said. "But you do not have to do this alone any longer."

"Would you like to meet them, then?" Eddie asked.   Elizabet's heart burst with pride . . . and concern. There was no longer use in grappling with the inevitable. They were staring at the guardian of the Amalgam, the man who would tame the rage so prevalent in the host who were turned by nature. Her husband was a living, breathing legend.

"Yes, I think it is time." Jareth met her gaze. "I will need my wife to help me suit up and I shall go alone. I think it is best that way."

"Suit up?" Eddie asked.

Jareth turned his attention back to him. "I battle best in my customary raiments, and that would be a suit of armor. I am a knight. Google me. It will save time." He bowed at his waist. "Sir Jareth Tremaine, the Duke of Dover, at your humble service." Gesturing Elizabet forward, he removed a time band from his wrist. Traveling with a suit of armor by way of coach was never an option. They would have to make a quick visit to medieval Dover to suit up. "Let us get on with this. Somewhere in time, a Spartan warrior and an Asian Minister of War awaits me." His smile was charming. "May I be the first to welcome you to the age of Dover's Amalgam."

THE END

About the Author

ELIZABETTA HOLCOMB IS A WRITER trapped in a nurse's body. Mother to 5. Marmee to 1. She lives in South Louisiana with her husband, children, and 2 cats.

www.facebook.com/ElizabettaHolcomb/
www.instagram.com/elizabettaholcomb/
https://twitter.com/DuchessofDover

Made in the USA
Charleston, SC
19 March 2016